Three Golden Rivers

A John D. S. and Aida C. Truxall Book

Three Golden Rivers

Olive Price

Foreword and Afterword by
Margaret Mary Kimmel

Golden Triangle Books
University of Pittsburgh Press

Published 1999 by the University of Pittsburgh Press, Pittsburgh, Pa. 15261
Copyright © 1948 by Olive Price
Foreward and afterword copyright © 1999, University of Pittsburgh Press
All rights reserved
Originally published by The Bobbs-Merrill Company
Manufactured in the United States of America
Printed on acid-free paper
10 9 8 7 6 5 4 3 2 1

Library of Congress Cataloging-in-Publication Data
Price, Olive M.
    Three golden rivers / Olive Price.
    p. cm.
    "Golden triangle books."
    SUMMARY: When recently orphaned sixteen-year-old Jenny and her younger
brother and sisters move to Pittsburgh, their resourcefulness makes possible a career in
glassmaking for Stephen.
    ISBN 0-8229-5707-8 (pbk.)
    [1. Orphans Fiction.   2. Brothers and sister Fiction.   3. Resourcefulness Fiction.   4.
Glass craft Fiction.   5. Pittsburgh (Pa.) Fiction.]   I. Title.
    PZ7.P9316 Th 1999
    [Fic]–dc21   99-6495
                                                      CIP

A CIP catalog record for this book is available from the British Library.

*To lovely memories of my father
who gave me many happy years
on the
Three Golden Rivers*

Contents

Foreword

Pittsburgh is a city of rivers and bridges, of museums and libraries and schools, of music and dance and sports. But most of all, it is the people of the city and the region who have worked hard and dreamed dreams that have made it the place that it is. For a long time, people have come to Pittsburgh hoping to find adventure and a better life for themselves and their children. Their stories have been told and retold to many different audiences and in many different ways. Sometimes these tales have been used by writers to weave new stories with old ways of living; sometimes the stories are old ones in new settings.

Three Golden Rivers is a book for young people, but should appeal to a reader of any age interested in the development of Pittsburgh and its people. It is the story of four brothers and sisters who have been orphaned and who come to Pittsburgh to seek a future. Pittsburgh of the 1850s is vividly depicted as the place where sixteen-year-old Stephen dreams of working with the glass craftsmen on barges in the Monongahela River. His sister Jenny takes care of the family and works in the Monongahela House, an early Pittsburgh hotel. Carlotta and

Mady are younger sisters who complete the "brood" that Jenny cares for. Their lively personalities involve the reader in the life of the city and friends and Pittsburgh personalities they meet along the way. A young Andrew Carnegie and Stephen Foster are just two of the many people who touch their lives.

The author of *Three Golden Rivers,* Olive Price, was born and raised in Pittsburgh. She grew up on Mount Washington and attended the University of Pittsburgh for a year. She worked in the advertising departments of several downtown department stores before she began her writing career. Price is the author of a number of plays, collections of short stories, and other books for young people, but *Three Golden Rivers* survives as one of her most readable novels.

Readers will be intrigued by the many glimpses of early Pittsburgh and by the adventures of this plucky family. Their story is but one example of how people have come here to build a better life, to find friends and a future full of hope in a city by three rivers. Here is the first glimpse of the rivers as the children come into town:

"A turn of the road had brought before their eyes a broad view of the rivers. From above the wooded wall that formed the south hills, the lowering sun sent down shafts of golden light to illuminate the waters. . . . This sunset hour was making three flowing rivers of gold. Nothing else in the town seemed so bright. Buildings were etched in shadowy outlines compared to the tawny brilliance; bridges hung darkly, suspended as in golden mist across the three rivers."

And so it begins.

Margaret Mary Kimmel

Three Golden Rivers

 *One*

The Dream

*J*enny stood in the doorway of the ramshackle farmhouse looking down the lane. She was waiting for her "brood," as she affectionately called her brother and two little sisters, to come home from Enon Valley. They had gone into the little town to buy a few last-minute supplies for the trip they would all start on tomorrow. She should have gone with them, she was thinking now, but there had been so much to do. Last-minute packing took time.

Fifteen-year-old Stephen wouldn't loiter in Enon, she knew, because he wouldn't want to tire King the day before they began their long journey. The horse had been such a patient creature all through these days they had imposed double tasks on him. They had hired him out to help neighboring farmers with their spring plowing and had used him for home chores as well. Their "spring plowing fund," as they called it, was the only way they had had to raise money to embark on their great adventure, and King had come through nobly. Yes, Stephen would be considerate of him and eight-year-old Mady would be too. Of thirteen-year-old Carlotta, however, Jenny was not so sure. That impetuous little sister was just as apt as not to persuade the others to skip the little town of Enon Valley and go on across the state-line road into East Palestine. She said it always gave her the feeling of "having been somewhere" to cross a state line. East Palestine, Ohio, had a much more faraway sound than Enon Valley, Pennsylvania, although there was actually only about six miles' difference.

Jenny shaded her eyes from the sunset, and strained to see farther down the road. Still no sign of a horse and buggy. There was only the sound of crows, *caw, caw, cawing,* in the wheat field, winging darkly above the golden grain. Then the mooing of a lonely cow came up from the pasture in back of the barn. There was the sleepy twittering of birds nesting in the beech woods. All this made Jenny suddenly sad. These were dear and familiar things. They spoke to her as the farmhouse had always seemed to speak, saying, "This is home." And tomorrow they would leave all this for new and unknown things. Tomorrow. What would really happen tomorrow when she and the brood and Sandy, their goat, climbed into the farm wagon and set out for Pittsburgh, more than fifty miles away?

She looked at the calendar that hung above the wash basin on the porch. Tomorrow would be June seventh. June 7, 1850. She hoped the date would bring them luck. They had sold almost everything they had, given up this farm, which their parents had rented for years. Jenny wondered if she, at sixteen, was not taking on too much. She remembered that her mother had often told her to "plunge into things with courage," but not to "plunge beyond your depth." Would Pittsburgh be beyond her depth? she wondered, now that she alone was left on earth to look after the little brood?

But her mother, too, had wanted to go there just a few

months before she died. She had once been employed by the wealthy Blakewell family and had hoped that she might be again. Jenny was only carrying out what their mother had planned for them. They *had* to go to Pittsburgh because of Stephen and *glass*. His interest in glass making must be encouraged if he was ever to become a great master craftsman and artist. His mother had believed in his talent for creating designs. She had thought he inherited originality from his grandfather, who had been known throughout Europe as a designer. As many fine artists had worked in paint and in marble, he had worked in crystal and glass. Many of the exquisite things he had created adorned the palaces of kings. Jenny's mother had dreamed of such a creative life for Stephen, and Jenny had promised to make this dream a reality. Once they had arrived at the Blakewell mansion in Pittsburgh where her mother had been a young seamstress, surely all would go well.

"Yoo hoo, Jenny! Yoo hoo!" Carlotta's gay voice called through the rosy haze of the sunset.

Jenny sighed with relief as she saw the horse and buggy turning into the lane. It was still light enough to have supper out here on the porch. She was glad she had spread a table cloth on top of a packing barrel so they could sit here and watch the sun lowering over the wheat field as they ate their evening meal.

Stephen drew King to a stop in the lane below the porch steps. Mady climbed out of the buggy first, her arms filled with packages. Carlotta followed her quickly, while Stephen picked up the reins again and drove King on to the barn.

"Look, Jenny," cried Mady, her hazel eyes dancing, "we got everything you wanted. Everything!"

"Looks as though you got more." Jenny laughed.

Mady laid her packages, one by one, on the red-and-white-checked tablecloth.

"Needles and pins," she enumerated. "Thread, black and white. A brand-new lantern to hang on the farm wagon so we can travel by night." She held up the lantern for Jenny's inspection. "Look, it's got a new kind of wick."

Jenny was examining the lantern as Carlotta came blithely up behind her. She, too, was carrying packages.

"Look what I brought!" she said. "It's much gayer than that old lantern!"

Jenny turned to her pretty sister with the wide blue-green eyes and red-gold mop of curls, instantly suspicious. "You— you didn't!" she exclaimed.

Carlotta laughed as she unwrapped her package. "I couldn't help it, Jenny. The colors were so—so right."

"I told her not to," put in Mady; "that we needed the money for other things."

"We'll always need 'the money for other things,'" Carlotta mimicked as she unrolled several yards of calico. "Just look at this bright sunny yellow." She went to Jenny impulsively and draped it over her sister's shoulder. "I knew it would make you look like a flower. Go look at yourself in the mirror."

"But, Carlotta!" Jenny reproved as she walked to the mirror hanging over the washstand.

The yellow calico actually did give her a flowerlike loveliness. It enhanced the light in her soft curls which were the warm brown of autumn leaves. It did something flattering to her eyes which were a deep shade of blue, almost violet, fringed with extraordinarily long lashes. Jenny's eyes were compelling. They were large and sometimes seemed alight with dreams. Someone had once said, "Her eyes are unforgettable."

"This is a pretty color," she said softly.

"I told you! I told you!" Carlotta cried triumphantly. "And, look, I got this blue for me."

The periwinkle blue gave the lovely little Carlotta a suddenly luminous quality. She looked ready to dance with the lightness of a summer cloud.

"That's made just for you," Jenny said, and added reluctantly, "I guess you couldn't help buying it." Suddenly she turned back to silent little Mady. "But what about Mady? What did you buy for her?"

Carlotta unwrapped a third piece of calico, the jewel-like color of a ruby.

"This," she said dramatically. "It certainly ought to bring her out."

Mady cried with delight, "Oh, Carlotta, Carlotta! I get so awfully mad at you—then you do something nice!"

She draped the calico on herself and rushed to look into the mirror. It made her straight brown hair glow with warmth and brought out the color in her eyes until one scarcely noticed that Mady had a little snub nose. Jenny smiled at her affectionately.

"You see how pretty you can look!" She turned back to Carlotta. "But when am I going to make these dresses——"

"When we get to the Blakewells', of course," Carlotta answered calmly. "Aren't you going to sew for them as Mamma planned to do?"

"If they'll let me," said Jenny. "But for them, not for us. And, remember, they don't even know yet that we exist." She greeted Stephen as he came up on the porch. "Hello, Stevie. Got King tucked away for the night?"

"Unharnessed and fed. He was as hungry as an ox—and so am I."

"Go down to the pump and wash up, all of you. Supper will be ready in no time."

As they raced down to the pump, she turned and went into the kitchen. She was glad she had planned to eat outdoors. Everything looked so bare inside. The few possessions they hadn't sold were already packed in the farm wagon that would take them to Pittsburgh. The buggy would be left here in the barn because it, too, had been sold. As she poured a pitcher of milk, she wished that this night were over, that it were already sunrise and they were on their way. Farewell to this farm where they had all been born would not be easy.

When supper was over they sat for a time on the porch, watching the gathering twilight. Sunset had vanished. A vagrant wind, like a gypsy, frolicked in the wheat field. Now and then there came the cry of a mourning dove, the raucous call of a wandering crow. Beyond the wheat fields the countryside looked quiet and peaceful and charming in the soft half-light of evening. Here and there, curling smoke rose skyward from a chimney in a neighbor's house. And beyond an old rail fence a gnarled apple tree in blossom spilled its delicate pink and white beauty. All this tugged at Jenny's heart.

"We shall always remember this farm," she said softly. "Always think of it as a place apart."

Little Mady cupped her diminutive chin in the palm of her hand.

"I'll remember the apple tree, and the swing that Papa made

me. I used to sit there for hours looking up at the sky through the leaves."

"I'll remember the barn and the wheat field," said Stephen. "Before Papa went to California, we'd sit in the haymow and watch for crows that came to steal the grain. Papa used to shoot them from there. One day he bagged nine."

"I like to hear the crows call," Carlotta said half-defiantly. "And what are a few shocks of grain?"

Jenny laid a hand on her sister's shoulder. "What will you miss most, Carlotta?"

Carlotta spoke without even thinking. "Little Beaver Creek, I think. It's dancing all the time and you can hide a boat in the willows that hang over it."

"And what will you miss, Jenny?" asked Stephen.

Jenny mused for a moment before she answered, "Spring-time in the beechwoods, where we used to wait for Papa. We'd go through the woods to the crossroads and sit on the fence until he came along whistling. Under the trees it was like a garden. Tall white lilies grew in the shadowy places. There were May-apple blossoms, too, and pink trailing arbu-tus." She mused again for a moment before she went on: "Papa was always so merry. He called us his turtledoves, don't you remember?"

"Yes, I remember," said Stephen. "He always had a story to tell. Wherever he was, folks were always gay and laughing."

Carlotta rose restlessly and walked to the steps of the porch.

"I'm like Papa, I hope," she said. "I'll never waste any time in tears. He was always adventuring—following something to somewhere. That's why he went to California. If the Indians hadn't attacked his wagon, he would have found the gold at the end of the rainbow for us." Suddenly Carlotta looked at the sky with the eagerness of a child. "And that's what I shall do too. I'm glad we're going to Pittsburgh. It will be gay and exciting in the city. Stevie will make a fortune in glass—and——"

Jenny laughed merrily, too, as she got up from the porch steps. "You're perfectly right, Carlotta. We mustn't mope about anything. As Papa used to say, 'Everything lies ahead.' And now we'd better get to bed if we're to be on our way at daybreak."

"I'm sleepy." Little Mady yawned.

"So am I," said Stephen. He looked at Jenny and grinned. "Mind if I sleep in the haymow tonight?"

"Maybe you'd better. I don't suppose there'll be many haymows in Pittsburgh, especially at the Blakewells."

Exactly at sunrise the next morning, Jenny locked the door of the old farmhouse. She had resolved through the night to keep looking ahead—to make herself believe that success would come to them in the city. Someday, she dreamed recklessly, they would come back and buy this place and live here the rest of their lives. Then they would make a great house of it, like Stoneybrook Farm a few miles away.

As Carlotta put it fantastically: "We'll build white fences and have sunken gardens and all ride pedigreed horses!"

Stephen cracked the whip as they turned out of the lane. "We're off!" he cried.

"We're ready to make our fortunes!" Carlotta chimed in.

Mady put on her old straw hat to shade her eyes from the sun.

"Sandy looks as though she'll like it!" she said, smiling at the milk goat who peered at them comically from the back end of the wagon.

"Let King set the pace," said Jenny as they drove down the hill to the crossroads. "He has a long way to go."

"We should hit the Steubenville Pike tonight," Stephen estimated. "That brings us in through the south hills of Pittsburgh."

"And the storekeeper said we'd cross a big river somewhere," Mady said in delight.

"That will be the Ohio," Carlotta told her loftily.

All that day they drove through a countryside incredibly green.

"I've heard of the emerald hills of Ireland," said Jenny. "But surely they couldn't be more beautiful than these."

"Papa saw a lot of states in his travels," Stephen commented. "But he always said that Pennsylvania is prettier than all the rest."

Sometimes the hills had slopes where orchards were in bloom. Pink clouds of peach blossoms blowing delighted the children with their beauty. Apple and pear trees in flower were exquisite to see, but Jenny liked the fragrant quince blossoms best. Clad in the ethereal pink of a cloud at sunset, they seemed to dance on the boughs like petal-skirted dancers she had once seen at a country fair.

The names of the towns they went through also charmed the children. Enon Valley, meaning "Valley of Peaceful Waters," and lovely it was indeed, with Little Beaver Creek winding around the little town. The name "New Galilee" made them think of Bible times. Mady said she fancied she could hear the sound of camel bells. Darlington nestled in the hills like a tiny English Village. Brighton was a busy place where they stopped at a blacksmith's shop because King needed his shoes mended. There, also, Jenny weakened and spent a few pennies for candy. She allowed Mady to buy chocolate drops in a general store which smelled of peppermint and rubber boots.

When evening came, they drove into a woodland clearing. Stephen gave King a bag of oats and took him and Sandy to drink from a clear-flowing stream in a pasture nearby. Jenny spread a tablecloth on the grass. They had a picnic supper from the basket of food she had brought. Cows were munching pink clover in a meadow across the road. Mady heard a whippoorwill.

"I told you we'd get to the Steubenville Pike," Stephen said with satisfaction.

"We're right on schedule." Jenny smiled.

They lighted the new lantern and hung it on the farm wagon. Darkness had already fallen when all four tumbled exhausted into the wagon and went to sleep. Jenny awakened once in the night. A new moon hung low in the sky. The Milky Way was ablaze with stars. Sleepily she wondered just where she was; then she smelled clover, and knew. She had the practical thought that she was glad it hadn't rained. Muddy roads would have hampered their progress. They might even have had to dig themselves out of ruts.

It was late the next afternoon when they arrived at the Blakewells'.

"We're here!" Jenny's voice was joyous as she climbed down from the wagon.

The children watched their sister eagerly as she walked to the ornate iron gates that guarded the beautiful house, perched high on a wooded cliff. It commanded a panoramic view of Pittsburgh at the forks of three great rivers in the valley far below.

Jenny thought that it must be a house of magic windows. One would show a flower garden, reflected in a lily pool. Another a gabled carriage house. A third, cliff that fell away to the dense green foliage of trees and huge boulders. But the largest window of all would give a breath-taking view. As if through panes of enchanted glass, it would show a busy city lying on a triangular point of land in the very arms of the rivers. Always, too, this picture would be variable, Jenny was thinking. Sometimes alight with the gold of the sun. Sometimes dark with an oncoming storm. Often at night it would be majestic, lighted by great fiery arcs of furnace lights that would send up multicolored clouds of smoke like rockets to the sky. Yes, this window would look down on so many things it would take days to discern them all. Crooked streets. Office buildings, shops and houses. Mills and factories under the bluffs. Graceful white packet boats on the rivers, gliding like swans beside grimy coal barges and keelboats. Eternal rivers flowing between eternal hills. And on this highest hill, Mount Washington, this house, looking down. Jenny looked again at the magic windows.

She turned to her brother and sisters who still sat fascinated in the farm wagon. "Well, aren't you coming?"

For once they were stricken with silence, but only for the flash of an instant.

"Look at the roses on the gates!" cried admiring Carlotta.

"And there's the white pavilion where Mamma used to sew!" said Mady.

"Dare we go in?" asked Stephen gravely, wide-eyed at the beauty of this place.

"Dare we go in, Stevie?" Jenny laughed. "Didn't Mamma tell us—well, come on!"

Sandy wore a quizzical look as the children got out of the wagon. She watched them as they rushed to the gate.

"Wait!" Jenny took a broken comb from her pocket. "Here, Stevie, let me. Mady, you too. Mamma would want our hair presentable even if our clothes are mussed."

All four were thinking of what Mamma would have wanted as Jenny opened the gate. They walked up the winding gravel path to a big white door with a shining brass knocker. So they were here at last. Jenny's endurance and courage had brought them. She would see them through now, even against all this grandeur.

Jenny smiled, but not so confidently as they had expected. It was "a smile that had a hard swallow to it," as Carlotta sometimes described such things. Now that she was actually here it was suddenly occurring to Jenny that the unheralded arrival of an old battered wagon containing household belongings, Sandy the goat, and four nondescript children might be something of a shock to anyone, certainly the Blakewells. If only Mamma——

Jenny smothered the wishful thought and knocked on the big white door.

Two

The House on the Hill

*I*t seemed an interminable time until that door was opened. Mady's eyes popped wide as the most enormous houseman she had ever seen stood before them. He had a big smile and he wore livery. His short red vest was brocaded with silver threads; his wide black tie was a flowing bow. His eyes widened as he discovered the children standing at their best attention.

"Well, I declare! What do you youngsters want knocking on this front door?"

Jenny drew herself up to her full height. "We are Marie Bayard's children and we have come to see Mrs. Marsha Blakewell."

The houseman shook his head. "Never heard of Marie Bayard. And old Madam Marsha's gone to live in New Orleans."

"New Orleans!"

"Been there two years, young lady."

"But—but the Blakewells?" continued Jenny faintly. "Are none of them here now?"

The enormous servant hesitated to answer. From some-where inside the Bayards heard a girl's voice calling. "Samson! Samson! Where are you?"

He took a step backward and called over his shoulder. "I'm here, Miss Rosalie, at the front door."

Beyond him now the children could see a wide, white-paneled hall with a beautiful winding stairway. The hall went from the front of the house to the back and opened onto a terrace bordered by a rose garden. What a great house this really was, thought Jenny.

Then suddenly she saw the look on Stephen's face. He had discovered the crystal chandelier hanging in sparkling splen-dor from the ceiling. It was big enough to hold fifty candles and the prisms were so intricately cut that surely a great artist must have fashioned them. Only a great artist could have made it, an artist in glass much as Stephen hoped to become someday. The look on his face was rapt. He was studying that chandelier. In his mind, Jenny knew, he was following its pattern, making his first glimpse of it a lesson in design.

Jenny squared her pretty shoulders. This was as it should be, this intense interest of Stephen's in that crystal chande-lier. Hadn't they come here only to foster his ambition to make glass? Wasn't that their only reason for invading the glassmaking center of Pittsburgh? She must get beyond this houseman somehow. He turned back to her as suddenly she smiled. Jenny's smile was a heart-warming thing.

"So your name is Samson. I like that. It suits you."

The servant felt a quick glow of pride. "Yes, young lady," he drawled, "I'm Samson."

"Been with the Blakewells long?" asked Jenny slyly.

"Almost ten years."

"Some of the Blakewells are here, then?"

"I guess you got me." He chuckled. "Yes, the younger Mrs. Blakewell, Madam Victoria, is here. She's Mr. John's wife. Mr. John is old Madam Marsha's son. They live here with their daughter, Miss Rosalie."

"Please let me see Mrs. Blakewell."

"She's mighty particular who she sees," he said at last, his eyes glued to Jenny's cheap cotton dress, Carlotta's frayed out sandals, and Mady's old straw hat with a ring of forlorn forget-me-nots around the crown.

Jenny's voice held a note of pride. "Tell her, Samson, that Marie Colbert Bayard was my mother. She was a seamstress for Mrs. Marsha Blakewell and lived in this house with her nine years."

Samson considered all this a moment. Again he studied Jenny. Something about her was compelling. At last he stepped aside and admitted her and the brood to the hall.

"Now, you children be very quiet and I'll tell Mrs. Blakewell you are here."

The brood watched him turn and go down the corridor. He disappeared through an archway at the back of the house. Solemnity was on their faces. Little Mady stood very still, her hands clasped tightly behind her. Carlotta stood very still also, seeing rooms such as she had never seen before. While Stephen's dark eyes took in nothing but the crystal chandelier, Carlotta's roved about the luxurious parlor on one side of the hall, and the dining room with its gleaming silverware on the other. Everywhere there were vases filled with flowers! Everywhere there was spaciousness, sunlight, perfumed air! Carlotta felt instinctive pleasure. Someday, she, too, would live like this!

Jenny saw Rosalie Blakewell first. She was coming down the winding stairs. She reminded Jenny of the lovely girls who were pictured in Carlotta's *Godey's Lady's Book*. Carlotta always saved such sketches. She had a whole collection of them put away for Mady to cut out and play with.

"Well!"

The girl paused halfway down the staircase and stood staring at the brood with ill-concealed astonishment. She had hair the color of yellow gold. It was brushed back in small golden wings from her temples and arranged in a cluster of curls on her forehead. There were curls, too at the nape of her neck, caught with a bright blue ribbon. Her dress was powder blue. Made of sheer batiste, it was trimmed with tiny ribbon bows from the neckline to the hem, which was a froth of cream-colored lace swirling about her ankles.

"Well!" Again she spoke the single word of surprise.

Jenny took a step forward. The girl on the staircase measured her with her eyes. Suddenly she smiled. It was a captivating smile, companionable and gay. Jenny's heart filled with warmth as the girl came down the remaining steps and stood facing her in the hall.

"So you were the one talking to Samson!"

"Yes—you see——" Jenny hesitated.

"Please go on."

Jenny was about to continue when a woman's voice called imperiously : "Rosalie! Is that you, Rosalie?"

"Yes, Mother." The girl half-turned and looked into the parlor.

"Come here at once and close the door after you."

Rosalie looked at Jenny again, then at the brood. She smiled at them all as she walked across the threshold of the parlor.

"Rosalie! Must you keep dawdling?" The impatient voice called again from within.

Rosalie smiled at the children again as she softly closed the door. They looked after her, fascinated.

"Wasn't she pretty!" exclaimed Mady.

"And such a beautiful dress!" Carlotta sighed.

Stephen looked at her, teasing. "All you ever notice is clothes."

Jenny silenced him with a gesture. "You must admit she was pretty, Stephen. And, yes, Carlotta, the dress was beautiful. But——"

"But–but what?" asked Carlotta as Jenny stood looking at the closed door.

"She had something else," Jenny began.

"Well, what was it?" prodded Mady.

Jenny was about to answer when suddenly the door was opened. A woman the children knew must be the younger Mrs. Blakewell stood looking at them, aghast. She had had some warning from Samson but had not really expected such a tattered little group. Her long face plainly showed annoyance. She wore a pale-green afternoon dress, and what meant most to Carlotta, a pair of emerald earrings.

"Well!" Strangely enough she uttered the same astonished word Rosalie had used a few moments before, but Mrs. Blakewell's "Well!" struck like a blow, while Rosalie's had been full-throated and warm, rather fun to listen to.

"Good afternoon, Mrs. Blakewell," said Jenny.

"Good afternoon." She looked beyond Jenny to little Mady, who was timidly shifting her feet on the rose-red oval rug that lay at the foot of the stairs. "Stop that child from squirming, will you?"

Jenny held out her hand to Mady. "Stand here beside me, Mady. There, that's better."

Again Jenny looked at Mrs. Blakewell, hoping that she would begin any conversation that was to be held between them, but Mrs. Blakewell waited for Jenny to speak. She began a bit nervously, trying to keep her voice steady. "I've already told Samson——"

Mrs. Blakewell interrupted. "Never mind what you told Samson. I am the one to hear your story."

Jenny began again. "I want to apologize for the fact that we must startle you. We wouldn't have come if we had been strangers. Real strangers, I mean." She flashed Mrs. Blakewell a smile. "But you see, my mother's name was Marie Colbert before she was married, and she lived in this house nine years. She—she did Mrs. Marsha Blakewell's sewing."

Mrs. Blakewell was unimpressed. "I never knew Marie Bayard," she said slowly, with emphasis on the *I.* "And what you children might want here, I cannot imagine."

"We had really planned to come before my mother died," Jenny said softly. "You see, she felt that Stephen—" she reached out and laid a caressing hand on the silent boy's shoulder— "this is Stephen," she explained. "My mother had faith in his talent for glassmaking."

"Glassmaking!"

Jenny nodded. "Someday he's going to be a great artist in glass like the—well, like the one who must have made that chandelier. Mother knew he had talent the first day he saw the glass blowers in Zanesville. You should see his pattern books!"

Mrs. Blakewell looked at Stephen coldly. He was a goodlooking lad, she was thinking, and probably had some intelligence, but all this nonsense about making glass!

"I'm not interested in pattern books," she said to Jenny, who was right in thinking that Mrs. Blakewell had never seen a glass-pattern book in her life.

"Let's go, Jenny," Stephen said bluntly.

Jenny kept a detaining hand on his shoulder. She smiled valiantly at Mrs. Blakewell.

"If my mother had lived," she explained, "she was going to come with us. You see, we lived on a farm, but my father went to the gold fields." Her eyes were glowing with the pride she always felt in her parents. "He died in Kansas where Indians attacked his wagon along with thirty others. Word was brought back that he saved many lives—that he fought with great courage."

Mrs. Blakewell shrugged her aristocratic shoulders but made no comment.

"The work on the farm was too much for Mamma," Jenny went on, "even though we all tried to help. That is why she was glad for Stephen's interest in glass. She felt that if we came to Pittsburgh she could sew again for Mrs. Blakewell, and maybe I, too, could work for her. Then Stephen could be apprenticed to the glassmakers, and——"

"As I said before," Mrs. Blakewell interrupted, "I never knew your mother. And if Marsha Blakewell were here I'm sure she wouldn't want to be bothered." She turned with a sweep of her long skirts. "I employ freed slaves and have no need of any help whatever. And, now, good afternoon."

Jenny looked at her steadily. "Good afternoon, Mrs. Blakewell. I'm sorry we came. We have no wish to be beholden to anyone."

Even Victoria Blakewell was not unobservant of Jenny's young dignity as she gathered her brood around her and prepared to leave the house. They followed her silently out through the big white door through which they had entered.

Out in the afternoon sunlight Jenny blinked her eyes, then suddenly stood taut and still.

"Stevie!" she murmured, horrified.

Stephen looked in the direction she indicated. Across the clipped green lawn stood Sandy, blissfully up to her neck in flowers. She was munching pink phlox with such a look of nanny-goat ecstasy that Carlotta exclaimed: "Look at Sandy! She's having dessert!"

"Hush!" warned Jenny. "You and Mady open the gate. Stevie and I will chase her through."

"You stand right here," Stephen told Jenny. "And when she comes along, just grab her."

"We'd all better stay," said Mady. "Sandy's in one of her playful moods."

"She's playful all right," said Jenny grimly. "But you and Carlotta stand at the entrance in case she tries shenanigans. And don't say a word—not even one word—or Mrs. Blakewell will hear you!"

As the brood prepared to obey her, Jenny stood under a window ledge, waiting. While Stephen tiptoed slowly toward Sandy, she was conscious of voices just above her in the parlor. Victoria Blakewell was saying: "The very idea! You look sorry I sent them away— the ragged little impostors!"

"I wish you hadn't been so cross," Jenny heard Rosalie answer.

"Cross!" echoed Mrs. Blakewell. "Would you have me take four young savages into this house?"

"They didn't seem like savages to me."

Jenny was glad to hear Rosalie defend herself and them,

but it didn't lessen the sting of her mother's implications. Jenny's cheeks burned with anger as she stood there listening.

"They wouldn't," Mrs. Blakewell was going on. "You're so much a part of this uncivilized manufacturing town that you no longer recognize culture. Now don't tell me I'm wrong. It isn't you fault I didn't oppose your father in the very beginning. You should never have been reared in Pittsburgh. If you had been brought up in Boston as I was—if your father had been a part of its intellectual world instead of a so-called captain of industry, you would be a different girl from what you are today."

"But I like Pittsburgh, Mother," Rosalie protested, "and I like our life here. Father's building marvelous steamboats and carrying out Grand'mère Marsha's plans for the whole Blakewell Line."

"Grand'mère Marsha!" Jenny heard freezing disdain in Mrs. Blakewell's voice. "She's really the one to blame for all this. If it hadn't been for her I might have persuaded your father to change his business to Boston where you would have known a different world."

"I wonder," Rosalie murmured. "From what I've seen on our visits to Boston, I don't think it's so much better than this."

Jenny could almost see Mrs. Blakewell blaze with indignation.

"Rosalie, I'm ashamed of you! Have you no awareness at all of music and books and art? Are you so glued to these surroundings you do not realize that Pittsburgh is an uncouth, Pioneer town where we seldom hear a concert or see an outstanding play? Why do you suppose I take you to hear Mozart played in the Boston Athenaeum? Why do you suppose?"

Her mother's voice was raised higher now. "Has Pittsburgh ever produced an Emerson or a Thoreau, a Lowell or a Longfellow? Do you——"

At a signal from Stephen, Jenny started moving slowly across the lawn toward Sandy, but not before she heard Rosalie say: "Don't become so excited, Mother. You'll talk yourself into one of your headaches. I promise to behave as though I were 'civilized.' I'll even try to like Boston!"

And Jenny also heard Mrs. Blakewell's haughty answer: "I ask you only not to be taken in by riffraff like those children— to realize that formal manners and formal living are the essence of the world you belong to."

While Jenny had been forced to learn about the invisible lines that divide society, she also felt the injustice of them and for the first time in her life rebelled. She didn't attribute the injustice to any accident of birth, but nevertheless she realized what formidable walls were there. She would climb those walls, she vowed angrily now, she would show a person like Victoria Blakewell what uncouth Pittsburgh and America as her own father had known it could produce. But while Jenny rebelled, she had really no way of knowing what had gone into the making of Victoria as a social belle in Boston.

Victoria's father, like Rosalie's father, had been a wealthy builder of ships. His father before him had built a line of stately clippers which unfurled their white sails to the sea and traveled with the wind to every known port in the world. Victoria had been taught all the social graces from her cradle days on through her girlhood. Her mother's drawing room had been as formal as a Grecian urn. Etiquette, from the carrying of her fan to the way she sat down in a chair, had been a matter of paramount importance.

One evening her father had brought young John Blakewell home to dinner. Their mutual interest in shipbuilding had made them friends as well as business associates. John Blakewell was different from anyone she had ever known. He was pioneering steamboats in "the West." He had "ideas," Victoria's father used to say; he was building a fortune as well as boats in Pittsburgh.

And Victoria had captivated John Blakewell that very first evening. She was to him a fragile, butterfly beauty reigning over Boston from a red plush pedestal. John Blakewell courted her, even though he realized that she was reputed to be a young and gay coquette. His rugged charm won her heart. She had never met any young man in the Boston drawing rooms who was so vital and natural.

But she rebelled at the fact that he wanted her to live in Pittsburgh. He could build boats in Boston, she pouted. He could become a part of her own family's concern. In this one thing, and one thing only, he had held out against her. He belonged in Pittsburgh, he explained. The West was a challenge to him. He had promised his own family to carry out their plans for building steamboats on the inland waters.

So Victoria had had no choice. She could live in Pittsburgh or give up John—and that she could not do. From the very day she was married, her helplessness in this matter of choosing her own place to live had been a thing of constant rancor. She was too much of an individualist not to make her surroundings subordinate to herself. Her life became a compromise. She brought her Boston drawing room to industrial Pittsburgh. She vowed to make Grand'mére Marsha's house on the hill a formal kind of fortress, since live in it, at least a part of every year, she must.

As Stephen cautiously shadowed Sandy, the goat looked up with a loud and startled "Baa!"

A servant girl, coming out the side door of the house with a message for one of the gardeners, flew across the lawn. "That old devil goat!" she shrieked. "Help me, someone! Help me! The goat's at Mrs. Blakewell's phlox!"

Both Victoria and Rosalie appeared at the parlor window.

"Oh, the savages! The savages!" Mrs. Blakewell cried. "Chase that goat, Azalea, chase her!"

"Sandy! Sandy!" Jenny was wailing as Stephen ran around in circles. "Oh, Sandy!"

Sometimes Sandy's face seemed to wear a superior kind of grin. It was so in this moment. Light-hearted Carlotta sensed it immediately.

"She's glad she ate them! She's glad!" she said in delighted undertones.

"Hush!" scolded Jenny.

Azalea, the servant girl, was shaking a savage fist at Sandy.

"You old devil goat!" she repeated. Then she ran toward the gate. "Get out o' here, all o' you! Get out! Get out!"

Sandy followed the children docilely enough, as she seemed to have had her fill of fresh pink blossoms. She grinned at Azalea once again when she was back in the farm wagon.

Stephen turned troubled eyes to Jenny. "It wasn't as Mamma said it would be. They weren't glad to see us."

Anxiously Jenny picked up King's reins. "If only old Mrs. Blakewell had been here! She would have remembered Mamma."

"Yes, she would have remembered," Stephen reflected soberly. "I don't believe she would have been annoyed as this woman said. But what do we do now?"

Much more cheerfully than she would have thought possible, Jenny answered: "I don't know yet, Stevie, but we'll do something."

Three

The Point

*I*t took them some time to find Brownsville Road, which would lead down into the city. It wound a serpentine way through the south hills about two miles east of the Point, as the junction where the three rivers met was called. After they left the tollgate that stood at the top of the hill, the children crowded onto the driver's seat with Jenny, eager not to miss anything so fascinating as their entrance down into the town.

"Name the three rivers." Jenny challenged them to a lesson in geography.

"The Monongahela," Carlotta began.

"The Allegheny," said Mady triumphantly.

"And the Ohio," finished Stephen. Then suddenly he cried in sheer delight, "And look at them, Jenny!"

A turn of the road had brought before their eyes a broad view of the rivers. From above the wooded wall that formed the south hills, the lowering sun sent down shafts of golden light to illuminate the waters.

"Look at them, Jenny," cried Stephen again. "They're golden rivers—all three of them!"

Jenny and her sisters looked down, entranced. Stephen was

absolutely right. This sunset hour was making three flowing rivers of gold. Nothing else in the town seemed half so bright. Buildings were etched in shadowy outlines compared to the tawny brilliance; bridges hung darkly, suspended as in golden mist across the three rivers.

High upon the hill directly above the Point, stood the Blakewell house, haughtily looking down. It, too, looked dark in silhouette against the sky. Carlotta was the first to discover it now that they were in the long valley below and one had to look up to see it. Little wonder that the house was proud, she thought. Everyone could see it from everywhere in town! Yes, it was an eyrie, commanding a magnificent view of all that lay down here. As if to make it even more a significant part of the city, bright-eyed Carlotta also discovered a sign painted on a long, low-roofed building on the Monongahela shore. Large letters were printed to form the words:

Blakewells'—Boats

This was not a surprise to the Bayards. Their mother had told them many times that the Blakewell riches came from boats. John Blakewell, Sr., had made a fortune building flatboats and keelboats. These had carried migrants and produce on the river from Pittsburgh to St. Louis. When the steamboat was invented, he had kept pace with progress and had had an influential hand in building the first line of packets to operate between Pittsburgh and New Orleans. Now that he was dead, and the business belonged to his son, it had become an ever larger enterprise. Whole fleets of steamboats plying the rivers had been built in the Blakewell yards over on the Allegheny shore. They were familiar sights from the Point here in Pittsburgh to New Orleans on the Gulf. One or two, with their big paddle wheels lying quietly astern, lay at the wharf now. One was named simply the *Blakewell,* and the other *Victoria.*

Carlotta noted these two boats as their wagon rumbled across a bridge. She turned up her pretty nose. "Hmm! the *Victoria!* I—I hope it sinks!"

Jenny turned to her, frowning. "Carlotta Bayard! If I weren't driving this wagon——"

"Well, she needn't have been so uppity."

Jenny thought for a moment before she spoke again, remembering all she had heard as she stood near the window.

"No, she needn't have been, that's true. But we must admit that we must have been a bit of a shock. Four of us and a goat!"

Little Mady defended Carlotta. "Carlotta's right, Jenny. We didn't seem to shock that pretty girl on the stairs."

"No, I know we didn't," Jenny said slowly. "I think she is kind."

"I'll always think of her as a princess," Mady declared, "like the picture of the one in the fairy book you gave me last Christmas."

"That's a lovely way to think of her, Mady." Jenny turned from the girls to look at Stephen. "And Stevie, darling, what do you say about all this? You haven't spoken one word since you pointed out the rivers."

It was true that Stephen had not spoken. But he often fell into silence when he was deep in thoughts of his own. Jenny called it his "dreamer's mood." She knew it was in such moments as these that Stephen dreamed up patterns to ornament glass, as painters dream pictures, and poets dream their verses.

He turned to look at Jenny, then again his eyes sought the rivers. As far down the Ohio as he could see, the waters were shimmering with the same golden light that had captivated him at first sight. Stephen was looking at something imperishable. He, himself, would make it so.

Jenny's voice was tender as she spoke again. "Seeing something wonderful?"

Stephen's answer warmed her heart. "Someday, Jenny, we'll put these three golden rivers on glass."

It was part of Stephen's generous nature to recognize Jenny's help in all that he did or planned to do. Seldom did he say, "I will do this," or "I will do that." Always it was, "We will do this," or "We have done that." It was as though he had a gift of understanding all that Jenny was; as though he realized that she had set herself the arduous task of bringing up this "brood" as well as she knew how, and would stand by them always with her whole heart.

The problem presented to her now was acute. With the passing of the sunset, the world became gray. A magical moment was over. The gold had gone from the rivers, leaving them unfriendly and cold. A chill evening wind came up from the waters. Jenny saw Mady turn up the collar of her cotton dress to protect her throat from the change in the weather. For the first time Jenny realized that here they were alone: strangers in a strange country. Living in Pittsburgh, apart from working for the Blakewells, had hitherto not occurred to her. Without that security, everything loomed formidable. What should they do? Where should they go? Where, in fact should they sleep tonight?

"I'm hungry!" Mady's small hands were pressed to her tummy.

"So am I," seconded Carlotta.

"There are still some apples in the basket." Jenny told them cheerfully. "Better eat those until we decide what to do."

"I'm tired of apples." Mady was disappointed. "We've had them all the way from the farm. They're giving me the stomach-ache."

"I don't really blame you." Jenny looked sympathetic. "I'm a bit tired of them myself. Wait a little longer, Mady. Maybe we can soon milk Sandy and buy some fresh bread."

"Hmm!" Carlotta sighed blissfully. "Fresh bread and—a chocolate cake!"

"Oh, Miss Money Bags." Stephen grinned.

It was dusk when the wagon rumbled down off a bridge and along a cobbled street. Stephen gave a cry of pleasure.

"Look! There's a camping ground!"

"Where?" asked unbelieving Jenny.

"Right at this place they call the Point. There must be hundreds of wagons!"

Jenny's hands gave a glad pull on King's reins. "Hooray!" she said thankfully. "We'll stay here all night!"

The billowing canvas tops of many prairie schooners looked very white in the oncoming darkness. This was a famous stopping place for wagons on the trail. Most of them had come through from the green Appalachian mountains. At the point of these three rivers lay the lovely gateway to the west. Here the broad Ohio lured all who would be pioneers. To start out from here to California, or to be on the way to "take up a claim in Missouri" was common talk on every side. As the farm wagon turned into the grove people were starting campfires, and the good smell of coffee and bacon made the children realize how very hungry they were. Jenny shooed them down from the seat beside her.

"Get busy now and we'll eat. Stephen, you unhitch King.

Give the poor darling his feed bag. He's been so good all the way."

"I'll feed Sandy," said Mady. "She's been good too."

"Ask Mrs. Blakewell!" Stephen laughed.

Jenny took a market basket out of the wagon, meanwhile insisting: "I don't want to hear the Blakewell name again, even in fun. We'll just forget all about it."

Stephen glanced up at the great house on the hill: a blue castle now, hung like a picture in blue twilight. He glanced from it to the Blakewell boat sign.

"You won't be able to forget it, Jenny. Not so long as we're here."

And Jenny, remembering all the searing things she had heard from Mrs. Blakewell, answered briefly, "Well, we don't need to talk about it." Then she ordered Sandy, "Get out of this wagon, Lazy Bones! Let Carlotta milk you!"

Carlotta was taking in everything in sight. She was eager to see this city, to start at once on a quest of her own. She pouted at Jenny's words.

"Let Mady milk Sandy. I'll go for the bread."

Jenny knew what this meant. Carlotta's gypsy urge was on her again. She would have to curb it as time went on. Her little sister had such insatiable curiosity. She loved people and life to swirl gaily all around her. "You may go with Stephen when he gets the bread. Meanwhile, do as I tell you."

So Carlotta fell to her task with the others. Sandy dutifully filled the little pail with foaming milk. Much to Carlotta's chagrin, Stephen found a baker's shop on a cobbled street close by. It needed no excursion, after all, to get a loaf of bread in Pittsburgh. Jenny understood Carlotta's disappointment and placated it by celebrating their arrival with the added purchase of the longed-for chocolate cake. Fifteen cents' extra expense in their time of need, thought Jenny wryly, might perversely enough bring them luck! This was a trait she had inherited from her mother, who had always been one to tempt the gods with gaiety in the face of disappointment.

It was not quite dark when later they sat on the riverbank. The big steamboats passed before them, their paddle wheels making long trails of silvery foam. The boats were taking passengers and produce down to New Orleans, and this was the beginning of their journey. Tomorrow, thought Stephen, he would visit the wharf and watch these boats being loaded. As darkness fell, the children watched the skies turn red. Clouds of smoke from furnaces and mills floated upward, seeming to brush the night with cobwebs that were a fiery mixture of red-gold sparks and purple flames.

"Let's take a walk," suggested Jenny, much to the brood's delight.

They made their way out of the camping ground, leaving Sandy behind in the wagon.

"Which way shall we go?" asked Carlotta, as they came to a winding street.

"This way," indicated Stephen, for no reason at all starting northeast.

It was fun to walk up Water Street along the Monongahela shore. The wharf was still a busy place, even after dark. The children heard workers singing as they busied themselves about the many boats. One great steamboat glittered with lights, apparently about to begin its downriver voyage. People were streaming out of a near-by hotel.

"That must be a fashionable place," said Jenny. "Look at the ladies and gentlemen."

"It's the Monongahela House," said Stephen, stopping to read the sign on the big structure with its white-columned balcony under which carriages drew to a stop.

"Look at the lady on the steps." Carlotta pointed. "She's wearing a pink lace shawl!"

"And the one beside her," Mady chimed in, "has a bonnet covered with roses!"

Jenny hustled them through the bright pool of light that streamed from the hotel entrance.

"Why can't we go in?" asked Carlotta rebelliously. "I'd like to see the lobby. It has fancy furniture and a lot of red carpet."

"It's too crowded now," said Jenny. "Someday we'll dress up and walk in one door and out the other, if nobody stops us."

Carlotta had to be content. She looked back over her shoulder at the well-dressed people milling about the entrance as Jenny relentlessly hurried her on.

"I think that boat will be leaving soon," said Mady. "It would be fun to watch it go."

Stephen stopped a near-by man who was carrying a small trunk down to the wharf.

"How soon will the boat leave?" Stephen asked.

"Not until midnight, sonny. This fooling around goes on for hours!"

"Everything's always too late for us to have any fun," grumbled Carlotta. Then she looked hopefully at Jenny. "Why not stay up for it?"

"Until midnight?" Jenny gasped.

"That's twelve o'clock!" said Mady.

"What of it?" Carlotta asked carelessly.

Jenny took her sister's hand firmly. "Just get it out of your head."

They continued to walk until they had rounded a slight bend in the river. Here Stephen stopped short. "Look!" he directed impressively.

Below them on the river lay a large flat boat. Jenny saw at once that it was fitted out as a glassworks.

"Why, Stephen! They're making glass!"

"Of course they are!" he said, delighted. "Let's go down and watch them."

A few moments later they stood at the water's edge. The boat was fitted out with a furnace, tempering oven and other equipment required to make glass. At right angles to the furnace, "the blower's post," as Stephen knew, stood the glass blower. Between his lips was a long tube which Stephen knew was called "a blow pipe." Soon a glass bubble appeared at the end of his pipe, and the children watched him, fascinated. As he kept on blowing, this glass bubble apparently cooled and had to be reheated to allow further manipulation.

"Watch him," Stephen said enthusiastically. "He'll take it to the glory hole."

The glory hole was a smaller furnace where white-hot fires eddied and swirled. The Bayards watched with round-eyed interest as the glass blower put his pipe into the glory hole and the bubble was restored to the proper temperature for blowing.

When the bubble was blown into its required size and properly shaped, another workman with a punty, which was an iron rod about four feet long, slightly enlarged at one end, placed a small piece of semimolten glass at the top of the bubble. Then he took a piece of steel which had been moistened in water, drew it around the bubble and struck a sharp blow. His blow caused the bubble to separate from the glass blower's pipe, and left it attached to the punty rod with one side open.

"Now it's off the pipe," said Stephen, "and they'll take it back to the glory hole."

Again they watched as the workmen proceeded to do just what Stephen had said would be done.

"You know all about making glass already!" Carlotta burst out, impressed. "You don't need to be apprenticed!"

Jenny laughed at her merrily. "These are only the simple things," she told Carlotta. "The things that are easily seen. We can't see the skill in the glass blower's breathing and timing—and many other things these other workmen are doing. It will take Stephen years to learn it all."

Stephen was watching the next procedure. A workman sat in a chair that resembled a shoemaker's bench with long arms extending. With the aid of a few simple tools he was proceeding to work into the required shape the piece of glass he had taken from the blow pipe.

"Now it's ready for cutting," said Stephen after a little time had passed.

Jenny felt Mady lean suddenly against her. Interested as the child was in this business of glassmaking, her eyes were no longer able to take it all in. They were drooping wearily, even though she rebelled against sleep.

"Poor little Mady." Jenny pressed her sister gently against her. "You're too tired to watch this any longer. We'll have to go back. Come, Stephen, we'll see the rest of all this tomorrow."

Stephen turned and followed them reluctantly. As they came up from the water front, he noticed boys carrying baskets filled with novelty glassware that had been made on the boat. They were selling it along the shore. Tiny glass bottles. A small glass hen sitting cozily on a glass nest. A jolly glass pig which was also a penny bank. All the way back to the camp Stephen talked of nothing else but this floating glassworks.

"I've got to work there, Jenny."

Jenny put her hand on his arm. "We'll see what we can do, Stevie."

As the children slept in the wagon that night, Jenny lay wide-awake wondering how she could manage to begin their new life in Pittsburgh. They would have to have a house to live in. They couldn't live forever in a wagon! Their mother would not have thought it decent.

People here in the camping ground talked much of Pittsburgh clingers. These were houses so-called because they clung precariously to the hills they were built on, rock-ribbed hills above the mills and the rivers. Many of them were little more than tumble-down shacks where poor people lived, but they were up in the sunlight, and on some of the hills there were grassy slopes where one might pasture a goat. Yes, if they were to stay here—and where, thought Jenny, where else could they go?—they must have a clinger. Somehow she would manage it.

Still wide-awake, she counted over the possessions they might sell. Their household belongings were few. All they had brought from their life on the farm were a few necessary pieces of furniture—their mother's rocking chair, the beds and a small bureau. A kitchen table. One or two chairs. None of these could bring very much, worried Jenny. Nor could the basket that contained their odd assortment of dishes, or the small painted trunk that had been their mother's bridal chest. Aside from their selling price, the children held these things very dear. Nothing else remained but the horse and wagon. Sandy couldn't be sold or they would lose their supply of milk.

Suddenly Jenny's heart seemed to skip a beat. Sell their horse, perhaps—sell King? Beloved King, who had been so faithful those hard years on the farm? It would be like selling a part of her own heart. King had plowed the earth for them. He had pulled them about in the wagon, worked tirelessly spring, summer, fall. He had shared with them the long, cruel winters, had drawn their homemade bobsled through almost impassable drifts of snow to buy supplies in town. Always he had been a friend and kind companion. *Sell King?* Jenny felt hot tears running down her cheeks. Why, he had been one of the family. She couldn't sell him—oh, she couldn't!

She heard the haunting whistle of a steamboat departing from the wharf. So it was midnight. The porter near the hotel had said the glittering boat would sail at midnight. Hours later, Jenny was still awake. Her eyes were hot and dry from too much silent weeping. The cold gray light of morning was piercing the mist on the rivers when she at last decided what she must do. King—beloved King—must go.

 *Four*

Jenny Makes a Bargain

Jenny made sure that the children were still asleep before she crept noiselessly out of the wagon. She would do it before they woke, she had decided, and spare the children the pain of parting from their cherished companion. She was not sure that even Stephen could face selling King bravely.

A few yards away the beautiful chestnut-brown horse stood in the early morning light. Jenny clutched her shawl tightly as she crossed the grassy space between them.

"King," she called gently. "King!"

The horse widened his eyes as he looked in her direction. He neighed very softly as he heard her voice. Jenny went close to him and put her arms around his neck.

"King, darling," she began, "I've got to tell you something——"

At the very sound of her voice, King's ears suddenly went up. He had been too close a companion of Jenny's not to know when she was in trouble.

"King, darling," she began again, and the horse nuzzled his head against her shoulder as he felt the wetness of her tears.

She looked into his startled eyes, knowing that he sensed

the seriousness of this moment. Silently she stroked him, trying to gather the courage to go on.

"I know you'll understand," she began at last with all the resolution she could command. "I know you'll understand," she began again, "when I tell you that I must sell you, King. I–I don't want to–you–you——" Her tears were flowing freely now as the animal stood stalwart beside her. "You know I don't want to because I love you with all my heart. But–but there are the children, King. We've got to go on living, got to have a little house, and–and——"

Jenny's voice broke suddenly. For an awful moment all that she had ever learned of bravery under fire, as her father had often termed it, deserted her completely. King stood patiently beside her as she laid her face against him and sobbed. Now an then he tried to nuzzle his head between her locked hands, then feeling her tears, he pressed closely against her, waiting with deep wells of sympathy in his troubled eyes.

"I'll–I'll do the best I can for you, darling. I'll find the man with the biggest, finest wagon who will be able to–to feed you well and keep you in–in comfort." Suddenly her tones held a false note of hope. "Maybe you'll like going west in a wagon train with other horses for company. Maybe you've been lonely with us——"

But that was not true, Jenny knew, as she again stroked King. He hadn't been lonely with them. He had been happy, and he wouldn't be happy again anywhere in the world. She and the brood were "family" to King, just as he had been "family" to them. Bleakly she stood looking at him. Then with a sudden intake of breath, she quickly turned and walked away.

An hour later, it was still only six o'clock, and Jenny had

covered the entire camp. There was no one there to whom she cared to trust him. Carefully she had studied the neighboring wagons and their equipment; the greater part of them were pitifully dilapidated. These people were poor just as they were. As she had come east to search for a new and better existence, they were going west to stake their claims, not merely on riches, but on life itself.

"Lookin' for somethin', young lady?"

There was a creaking of wagon wheels, and a wagon drew to a stop beside her. Jenny looked up into the rugged face of a middle-aged man on the driver's seat. It was a pleasant face; he was smiling.

"Who are you?" asked Jenny.

"Fair enough." He laughed and explained, "I'm Timothy Drew. I own a feed store here in town. Sell feed for horses to these people going west."

Jenny's eyes brightened a little. She liked the sound of his voice.

"Do—do you ever buy anything?" she asked warily.

"Got anything to sell?"

She looked up at him with candor. "I've got a farm wagon—and—and—maybe a horse."

He considered in silence for a moment. "Where?" he asked presently.

"Just over there."

"I'll take a look."

She explained that her brother and sisters were still asleep in the wagon, so he examined it with silent, expert appraisal.

"Now where's the horse?" he asked.

"Over here under the tree."

He followed her to where King stood. He spoke in low

kindly tones to the animal before he laid a hand on him. Jenny felt a little comforted, and, seeing her standing there, King let Timothy Drew examine him, although his big soft eyes were puzzled.

"He's a good horse," Drew murmured.

"He's the finest horse in the world! Just seven years old. In his prime."

Drew stood considering for a moment, then laid a hand on King's flanks.

"I'll give you a hundred dollars," he said. "That is, for the horse and the wagon."

Jenny looked at him steadily. "Thank you, Mr. Drew, but that just isn't enough."

Timothy Drew chuckled. "You're bargaining."

"I have to bargain, Mr. Drew, but all I want is a fair price."

"One hundred twenty then. That's tops."

"One hundred fifty," insisted Jenny.

Again Timothy laughed. "Whoever taught you to buy and sell——" he began.

"My father taught me," Jenny interrupted.

Timothy looked ruefully at King.

"Your father did a fine job. Very well," he decided. "One hundred and fifty dollars."

"Cash, please," said Jenny slowly.

"One the line." He laughed again and took a wallet out of his pocket. "I'll take the horse now and come back later for the wagon."

Jenny looked long and painfully at King. "Yes, you take the horse," she said softly.

"What do you mean?" questioned Timothy Drew, counting out paper bills.

Jenny turned away from him, her mouth quivering.

"You—you take the horse," she repeated, "'cause I—well, I just can't give him to you."

She took the money silently. A great lump in her throat prevented her from saying "Thank you." Suddenly, without another glance at Timothy Drew, she turned and ran past the horse with averted eyes. She tried to run fleetly but the first thing she knew she had tripped over a stone and was lying prostrate on the grass. With a sorrowful neigh, King crossed the few feet between them and stood looking down at her. It was as if he were saying: "Courage, Jenny. Courage!"

The look in his eyes thwarted all that Jenny had tried so valiantly to accomplish.

"King," She murmured. "Darling, darling King!"

Her arms went up around the animal's neck and she lifted herself to her feet beside him. Standing there close to this dearly beloved companion of many difficult years, Jenny realized that come what might she could not part with this living, breathing intelligent creature who had served them all so well. Surely there must be another way out——

She was utterly unconscious of Timothy Drew standing there watching her sympathetically.

"Well?" he asked gently at last, as though he understood. "Do I get the horse or do you keep him?"

Jenny smiled through her tears. "I keep him, Mr. Drew, and here is your money."

"How about the wagon?"

She looked at him hopefully. "Would you—could you—buy it without King?"

"Sure, I'll buy it," he answered heartily. "Give you thirty dollars."

"You're very kind," she murmured gratefully. "I'll bring it down to your store later."

"Fair enough," he said again. Then as he looked at her searchingly, he asked, "Who are you, anyhow? What are you doing here alone and what are you looking for in Pittsburgh?"

They sat down on a near-by bench while Jenny told him her story.

"So you want to work," he mused.

"I've got to work," she said quietly.

"Ever work at a hotel?" he asked after a moment's thought.

"No, but I can cook—I can cook and bake very well—so they say," she added modestly.

Timothy Drew considered a moment, then he scribbled a name on a piece of paper he took from his wallet.

"When you get settled," he advised, "go talk to Anna Houston. She's head of the kitchen staff at the Monongahela House."

"The Monongahela House!" Jenny's eyes brightened. "Oh, I'd like working there!"

"It won't be easy," he warned. "The hours are long and hard."

"That doesn't matter," Jenny said enthusiastically, "just so we can rent a clinger and Stevie can be apprenticed."

Mr. Drew laid a kindly hand on hers. "You're a fine girl, Miss Jenny. Here's good luck to you."

She stood up to take leave. "Thank you for all you've done, Mr. Drew." She smiled at him.

He held out his hand. "You're welcome, young lady. And if things don't work out, let me know. You'll usually find me at my store on Penn Street."

"They'll work out," she promised. "And we'll drop in to say hello. Thanks to you, Mr. Drew, nothing will stop me now."

"Good girl! And now good-bye."

"Good-bye, sir."

She stood beside King, watching Timothy Drew walk back to his wagon.

"You see, King," she said very happily, "there *are* nice people in Pittsburgh."

The sun was shining brightly as she went back to the wagon. She would call the children now and they would have breakfast. She would tell them all about Timothy Drew, but she would never, never tell them how close she had been to selling King. She hoped that King didn't know.

Stephen lay curled up under a blanket at the back end of the wagon. Jenny shook him lightly.

"Stevie, Stevie," she murmured, "it's time to get up and milk Sandy."

"Aw, Jenny, wait!" Stephen turned over.

She pulled the blanket away from his chin. "Can't wait, Stevie. We've got lots to do. Wake up, Mady! Wake up, Carlotta!"

Not one of the three children stirred. Jenny laughed as she finally shook the nanny goat, also still sleeping near by on the grass, her halter tied to a spoke of a wheel on the wagon.

"Sandy! Sandy! Get up! You've got to give us our breakfast!"

It was almost two hours later before they were ready to leave the camping ground. Sandy had been milked, breakfast was over, and King had been hitched to the wagon when Jenny suddenly discovered that Mady was not around.

"Where do you suppose she's gone?" she asked Stephen.

"How do I know?" He shrugged. "She was here just a minute ago."

From a little distance away came the rolling sound of a drum. Carlotta climbed up to the driver's seat and shaded her eyes from the sun with the back of her hand. She stood for a moment concentrating her gaze on a small five-sided building almost at the tip of the Point.

"There's some kind of parade," she told Jenny. "There are boys and girls carrying flags and marching."

Stephen loved parades. "Let's go and see what it is," he suggested at once. "I'll bet Mady's down there."

Mady was there, as Stephen had thought. She was standing near the entrance to the little brick building watching a group of children marching toward the structure with flag waving and fanfare.

"Look!" she called to Jenny.

"What's all this for?" asked Carlotta, as a small boy went by beating a drum.

"This is Fort Pitt," Mady eagerly explained.

"Fort Pitt?" questioned Stephen, as the children followed the drummer boy across the crumbling threshold.

Mady looked serious. "It was built by Colonel Henry Bouquet in 1764. One of the wagoners just told me."

"That's a long time ago," said Stephen. "Almost a hundred years."

"Sure it is," said Mady. "He said it's called the Block House and the site was chosen for a fort by George Washington himself!"

"Oh, my!" said Carlotta, impressed.

Mady thrust out her chin. "In history they call this holy ground. Men fought and died here."

"In a real battle?" asked Stephen.

"Yes," said Mady. "Come see the bullet holes."

All four inspected Fort Pitt and learned that the English and the French and the Indians had battled on this very spot;

that it was General Forbes who had won the victory for George Washington. Although there were spiders and cobwebs inside, they were thrilled at the sight of the musket holes through which the red-coated soldiers had aimed at their enemies.

Finally Jenny spoke decisively. "I think we'd better go or we'll never get started to look for a clinger."

She had high-heartedly made an elaborate plan for the day. It was to be given to finding a clinger, preferably on the south side overlooking the city. Not on Mount Washington where the Blakewells lived, but high above Carson Street to the east. There the hills were dotted with tumble-down houses. Perhaps one of them would be empty—waiting——

They looked all day without success. Either the clingers were occupied, or the rent was frighteningly high.

"I'm sure I don't know what to do," Jenny said despairingly.

"We haven't been to what they call Goat Hill," suggested Stephen, looking up at a hill just to the east of the one they were on.

"Let's go to Goat Hill—" Mady was enthusiastic—"Sandy will feel right at home."

Jenny hesitated. Reports she had heard had not been too encouraging. Most of the clingers there were just shacks.

Goat Hill above Birmingham was not so populous as Jenny had feared. There were several houses there, a bit too large for her purpose, and all of them occupied. She was about to turn and go back down the hill, discouraged, when suddenly an aged Scotchman spoke from his front door: "Dinna ye find a place, lassie?"

"Nothing suitable," answered Jenny.

He looked at her and the children with keen, appraising eyes.

"I'm movin' oot in a few days," he said. "Want to come in and look at this?"

Jenny accepted his offer. The house looked small and comfortable enough even if it did appear to cling to the rocky hillside at a slightly crazy angle. Perhaps it was because the roof was actually crooked.

"It looks like a witch's little house!" Mady shivered in delight.

"I found no witch," said the kindly old Scotchman, "but I did find a good fairy."

"Where?" challenged Mady, enchanted.

"On the shelf above the fireplace." The old man beamed. "No matter how the north winds blow this chimney corner is so warm you niver mind the weather."

A chimney corner. An open fire. Jenny looked far ahead to the onslaught of the snows. Warmth would mean everything up here on Goat Hill. Gaily she herded the children into the little house.

They discovered that it had three rooms. A square kitchen and combination sitting-bedroom adjoining. And up a small flight of wooden steps, a little room under the eaves, for Stephen, Jenny decided at once.

"I like it," Carlotta said forthrightly.

"So do I," said Mady.

"Won't it do, Jenny?" urged Stephen.

"Yes, I think it will," she said.

She was quite unprepared for the view from the kitchen windows. The south one looked down, showing the city on the three rivers; yes, there it lay, an entrancing panorama below, just as it had from the Blakewells'. But the window to the west—Jenny stood before it, startled. It was like a piece of tapestry showing an Old World castle on a hill, the Blakewell house. Jenny watched it, fascinated in spite of herself. One, two, three—yes, four green hills to the west away, the Blakewell mansion was distinctly framed in this little clinger's window.

 *Five*

The River Queen

Timothy Drew did Jenny another good turn that evening. He told her to keep the farm wagon until she and the brood were established in their new house. This would permit them to remain in the camping ground on the Point until the clinger was ready for their occupancy.

Meanwhile, Jenny lost no time. The following morning she walked up Water Street to the Monongahela House. Carlotta had borrowed a flatiron from a neighboring wagon and had laboriously pressed Jenny's plain blue cotton dress with a bit of a white hand-embroidered ruffle at the neckline and wrists. This was Jenny's Sunday dress. She hoped it would be presentable enough to make a good impression on Mrs. Houston when she went to ask for work. She hoped also that the cherry-colored bow she had pinned in her hair would divert attention from the hole in the toe of her left shoe. If she could only keep Mrs. Houston's eyes on her face and not on her feet! Jenny held her head up proudly and pretended she was a fine young lady like Rosalie Blakewell about to sweep into the big hotel.

As she entered the little brick passageway that led to the servants' entrance, Jenny paused to look back at the rivers.

Activity was brisk on the water front. So many steamboats were in port that there seemed to be a veritable forest of smoke-stacks. Boys were piling up kegs on the wharf; captains, pilots and merchants were shouting orders to sweating stevedores. Beyond the rivers were the hills.

Jenny looked up to them gratefully. There was her little clinger bravely tottering on Goat Hill, looking as if at any moment it might tumble down. Jenny felt like blowing it a kiss. Within its walls, she would make a good home. Per-haps—and her eyes sparkled at the thought—if she were given work to do at this hotel, she could buy some calico for cur-tains. If it were not more than five cents a yard—yes, calico curtains in the clinger would delight the children. Calico would make them feel as happy as elaborate rose-point-lace curtains like the Blakewells'. She looked challengingly up at the Blakewell house as if she were actually daring it to object to her starting this new life in Pittsburgh.

The kitchen of the Monongahela House was a fascinating place to Jenny. White-capped cooks were basting huge savory roasts; she saw one lift the lid of an enormous roaster to reveal a leg of mutton simmering in what the cook was bragging was the best caper sauce ever made in Pittsburgh. There was mint jelly and an amazing assortment of relishes such as she had never before seen. They included walnut catsup and horse-radish, Crosse and Blackwell's pickles and John Bull's sauce.

But it was the pastries and desserts that interested Jenny most. While she was waiting for Mrs. Houston she saw a cook bring in a delectable tray of puddings with a little sign to distinguish them from other desserts. White raisin pud-ding, á la Windsor with vanilla sauce. There were lemon pies and ladyfingers filled with maraschino jelly—and if only

Carlotta might have seen the cakes! Three-tiered chocolate cakes with pecan nuts in tiny nests of whipped cream, fruit cakes lavish with figs and dates and cherries, and a frothy white concoction of a cake called cocoanut plarine. Yes, hungry, little luxury-loving Carlotta would have reveled in all this, which was to Jenny strictly exotic food.

Each kind—meats, vegetables, fish, entrées, pastries, desserts—had its own separate department in this busy kitchen; each cook his appointed place to work. All was so well organized there was little evidence of hurry or confusion. Jenny sat quietly beside a huge coal stove and marveled at the order and efficiency of it all. It would be hot to work here in this summer season, she realized, as she saw the perspiring cooks stop for a moment to fan themselves. She moved a little away from the stove, which placed her near an open window.

"Are you Jenny Bayard?" a voice asked from the doorway.

"Mrs. Houston?" Jenny rose and faced an extremely efficient-looking matron.

"So Mr. Drew sent you."

"Yes, Ma'am," said Jenny.

"I understand you are looking for work."

Mrs. Houston took in Jenny's carefully pressed dress, the brave little ribbon bow in her hair, and quite unbeknownst to Jenny, the hole in her left shoe. She smiled at her without condescension.

"I can cook," Jenny was saying, "and I can sew. If there were any openings here——" She broke off abruptly.

"Good at making desserts?"

Jenny smiled. "My little family thinks I am."

"Mr. Drew mentioned them," said Mrs. Houston. "And I hope by this time you've found a place to live?"

Impulsively Jenny told her about their clinger; how eager they were to move into it; and how kind Timothy Drew and the old Scotchman had been to them. For a few pleasurable moments they talked about things that had nothing to do with Jenny's working at the Monongahela House.

Presently Mrs. Houston said: "If you'll come here tomorrow at ten, I'll start you working on my dessert staff."

Jenny looked very happy. "I'm awfully grateful——" she began.

"Don't be." Mrs. Houston laughed. "The working day is long and hard and it gets as hot as blazes in this kitchen. Sometimes you'll be so tired you won't be able to stand. Your salary will be three dollars a week."

Jenny left the kitchen with a warm feeling of security. This work would enable her to move into the clinger without immediate fear. The thirty dollars Timothy Drew had paid for the farm wagon would ensure six months rent being paid. What she could earn at the hotel should buy absolute necessities such as food and a few pieces of clothing. When winter came and they had to buy fuel to keep warm—— Jenny shunted that thought away. She would face the problem when it appeared. And now that she had found her own niche to work in, perhaps Stephen, too, could be apprenticed without further delay. This very afternoon they would visit the floating glasshouse again and talk with the person in charge.

As Jenny walked toward the front of the hotel, she sensed excitement all around her. People were gathering in animated groups at the entrance; little boys on Water Street were racing down the river, calling to the gathering crowd, "Here she comes! Here she comes!"

Suddenly the sound of a steamboat whistle broke over the

waters of the Monongahela and reverberated through the hills. It was a haunting sound that seemed to hold strange and lovely music. Jenny looked in the direction everyone else was looking; she hurried along with the crowd.

"It's the *River Queen!* The *River Queen!*"

Jenny found herself being jostled with others down to the wharf. The *River Queen*, she gathered, must be a very special steamboat, since everyone in town seemed suddenly to be here. Making their way dangerously along the crowded street were horses and wagons, two-wheeled carts, and Conestoga wagons drawn by six-horse teams. The merry sound of Conestoga bells mingled with the steamboat's whistle. Jenny learned from snatches of conversation on every side that the *River Queen* was the finest ship afloat between Pittsburgh and New Orleans; that its captain was one of the most genial and beloved of all steamboat captains. Everyone seemed to be saying, "There's Chris! There's Chris!" pointing, meanwhile, to a tall young lad standing high on the ship's wheelhouse, visible above the heads of countless passengers on the top deck. Jenny learned also from the conversation around her that Chris was the captain's son, a merry, amiable young man everyone seemed to know and like.

The *River Queen* drew close to the wharf. Its two mighty paddle wheels, placed one on either side of the vessel, slightly to the back, plied steadily. They made tracks of frothy white foam on the river, sending sprays of water upwards, slender arcs of silver in the sunlight. This, thought Jenny, watching, must be what people meant when they called a steamboat "a floating palace." Its cabins, railings, the cornices of its pilot-house, were gleaming white and intricately carved. Even the high smokestacks had delicately cut ornamentations of royal crowns. All white and gold was this *River Queen*, her name on the wheelhouse done in glittering gold leaf. She moved regally, built with such rightness and precision that her very set on the waters gave her a look of grandeur. Jenny hoped that someday she might see the inside of such a beautiful boat.

When it was tied up at the wharf and disembarkation began, Jenny still lingered, fascinated. She watched aristocratic ladies from the South come down the gangplank. She took quick mental note of their gloves and shawls and the flowers on their bonnets so that she might relay all this to fashion-loving Carlotta. Such was the hustle and bustle around her that when she finally turned to go, Jenny was unaware that the son of the *River Queen's* captain was standing only a few feet away, surrounded by a bevy of young ladies and gentlemen who all seemed to be talking at once. Such gay words as "party," "dance tonight" and "It's moonlight, Chris," could be heard by anyone standing near by. Jenny was unaware, too, that a carriage drawn by two spirited dapple-gray horses was being driven along the wharf down to the water's edge.

Jenny never knew for certain what actually happened then, but onlookers saw a small boy throw a stone at one of the horses, causing it to rear suddenly and lunge forward. Jenny stood stranded, directly in its path. A frantic man on the carriage seat was shouting, "Out o' the way, missie! Quick! Out o' the way!"

As Jenny hesitated for an instant, uncertain which way to go, the horse was struck by a second stone and reared again violently. Jenny stood paralyzed with fear, unable to move. As the horses seemed to make a direct leap in her direction, she suddenly felt herself swept from her feet, caught up in the strong young arms of a boy who swiftly carried her out of danger. A quick cheer went up from the spectators as he placed her on her feet.

"Are—are you hurt?" he asked breathlessly.

Jenny found herself looking up into the eyes of the captain's son. They were big and brown and concerned about her. Instantly something pleasurable tugged at her heart. She smiled at him gratefully. "No," she answered. "I'm not hurt, thanks to you."

"I'm very glad."

Jenny was conscious that this young man had wind-tousled brick-red hair and freckles on his nose. She noticed also that his shoulders were broad and that he was standing tall, head and shoulders, above her. Now that he realized she was unhurt, he laughed merrily. "Well, I guess I'm no hero after all, but I might have been, mightn't I?"

"I think you were," said Jenny. Then she took a step backward as she saw the carriage door being opened by a servant.

Victoria Blakewell stepped down on the wharf and came toward them.

"Just a moment! What's your name?" Christopher was asking Jenny.

"Jenny——" she began, but was immediately stopped by Mrs. Blakewell's unapologetic voice.

"Christopher." She approached him grandly, her jade-green silk shawl falling a little over one shoulder, her bonnet set at a haughty angle.

"Good morning, Mrs. Blakewell," Christopher greeted her respectfully. "Excuse me a moment, please." Then he turned back to Jenny. "Before you go, Jenny——"

Mrs. Blakewell looked annoyed. She laid a compelling hand on Christopher's arm.

"Rosalie's in the carriage, Christopher. She's rather upset about all this. Go to her at once, won't you?"

Christopher hesitated. He looked at Jenny and spoke again. "May I ask you to wait a moment?"

"Yes—oh, yes!"

He turned and went toward the carriage. Jenny was about to stand quietly aside when Mrs. Blakewell spoke to her for the first time.

"If you're a wise girl," she said very pointedly, "you won't wait for Christopher, even if he did request you to."

Jenny considered her words for a moment. Beyond the elegant figure of this woman she saw Christopher assisting Rosalie out of the carriage. Rosalie was wearing a bright yellow dress as golden-yellow as her hair. It fell gracefully about her ankles, showing only the tips of shining black slippers. She was carrying a coquettish little parasol. It was yellow, too, embroidered in blue. She didn't look frightened at all. Surely her mother had been mistaken, because Rosalie was talking gaily to Christopher, linking her arm through his. Immediately they were surrounded by the group of well-dressed young people who had clustered about him the moment he had come off the boat.

Jenny suddenly remembered that hole in the toe of her left shoe. She looked proudly at Mrs. Blakewell who spoke two weighty words. "You see?"

For a long time afterward Jenny didn't realize what she was supposed to have seen, but the consciousness of that hole in her shoe battled against her resolution to wait for this young man of fashion. Without another look toward any of them, she turned away and lost herself in the crowd.

She walked along, remembering. She was amazed at the

significance the incident had taken on in her mind. All in the flash of an instant Christopher had seemed young and gay and wonderful to her. She was sixteen years old. Surely he couldn't be more than a year or two older! She smiled a little as she thought of his name. Christopher. She liked its adventurous sound. It suited one such as he who had sailed into her life on a ship all white and gold. She fancied he had the glamour of the rivers about him, imagined that his charm and his laughter were the result of happy journeyings in strange and captivating places.

But he must have weaknesses, too, she thought with characteristic humor. Surely no young man could be so compelling and magnetic as she was daydreaming him into being! Immediately she tried to find flaws in her mental picture of him to dampen this sudden ardor. He was not really handsome, she told herself soberly. His brick-red hair would be forever unmanageable and those freckles on his nose would stay there, for keeps, as Carlotta was fond of saying. And perhaps he had played a hero's part, as he had ridiculously called it, merely to show off! He had not seemed to resent it when Rosalie had linked her arm through his. No, Jenny told herself with strict discipline, such a lad as Christopher was not meant for such as she. He was the rich young son of the captain of the *River Queen*. She was Jenny Bayard, currently of Goat Hill, and she had a raggle-taggle brood to take care of.

But as she walked down Water Street she couldn't help wondering if she would ever see him again. And desperately she hoped that he had not noticed that hole in the toe of her left shoe.

 *Six*

Stephen Begins

*J*enny took a handkerchief out of her pocket. "There's a smudge on your nose, Stevie. Let me wipe it off before we go in."

They were standing on the wharf in front of the floating glasshouse. It was late afternoon and Jenny had brought Stephen up along the water front, pointing out the *River Queen* to him as they went by. She had told him nothing at all about Christopher or her meeting with the Blakewells. She had decided not to tell anyone and, if at all possible, to rid her own mind of the whole encounter. Her thoughts, she determined, must all be concerned with her brood. Nothing really counted but Stephen's apprenticeship. It was his career in glass that must be paramount to all other things. Only in his success, thought Jenny, could she find a key to any great destiny for them all.

She looked down at him proudly as she gave his necktie a last-minute adjustment. He looked very presentable in his Sunday coat and cap and best trousers. He was carrying his pattern book. Its pages were filled with drawings of designs he hoped to transform into perfect pieces of fine glassware. There were patterns for a sugar bowl and creamer so fragile they were reminiscent of old French designs for Sévres porcelain. Stephen hoped to paint the finished product with delicate rose-colored tamarisk sprays. A pair of candle sticks were to be done in pressed glass in what Stephen called his laurel pattern. A flint-glass fruit bowl was to be decorated with copper-wheel engravings of apple blossoms and leaves.

"There now, you'll do." Jenny patted his shoulder.

"Do you know who to ask for?" Stephen's voice was anxious.

"Not by name. But there's always a manager."

"Scared?"

"I should say not!" Jenny reached for his hand. "Are you?"

"Not exactly, but I wish it was over. And don't hold my hand or people will think I'm a baby!"

Once aboard the flatboat that was the glasshouse, Stephen was much too absorbed in his surroundings to be either timid or afraid. While Jenny went to make inquiries, he watched the glassmakers working. He saw one man treading the clay for the pot makers. This, Stephen had heard, was one of the first processes in glassmaking, and also one of the most tedious steps in the entire industry. "Treading" meant kneading the clay to the desired consistency so that it could be fashioned into a melting pot to be placed in a furnace. It was done by putting clay and water in a large trough and having a man work the mass with his bare feet until it was the proper consistency. This kneading procedure required almost a month's time. Patiently the worker would go on treading until the clay was prepared; it then passed on to the potmaker, who would shape it into a clay pot with the utmost care. This was done almost entirely by hand in a room that was kept continually warm and moist.

Stephen was still watching the man treading when Jenny returned for him. She was smiling.

"We're going to see Big Dan!"

"Who is he?"

"He's the manager here, and they say he's the best master craftsman in Pittsburgh!"

Stephen followed her, impressed. As they made their way to where Big Dan was standing talking to an engraver, Jenny tried to tell Stephen in excited whispers that this was one of the greatest moments in his life. She had learned that Big Dan had been a maker of the famous ruby glass of Bohemia. A rich industrialist had brought him to Pittsburgh to develop his own fine craftsmanship and to teach apprentices.

Big Dan was an enormous fellow with a great head of shaggy gray hair. He wore glasses and had an amusing way of letting them fall down to the middle of his nose while he peered with the kindliest eyes imaginable at the person to whom he happened to be speaking. His voice was surprisingly gentle for one so huge. His workers said that he "ate, slept, lived and dreamed in glass." His thick-fingered hands that looked so awkward could pick up a piece of the most fragile, hand-blown glassware, tap it to hear it if had the proper metallic ring and put it back in its place as gently as if it were living and breathing. He had the eye of the true artist in his craft, and no experiment that occurred to him or other fine craftsmen was too arduous for him to undertake. A boy who had the qualities of a potential artist in glass was his greatest delight. At no time would he consider having more than four boy apprentices under his personal supervision, and to these four he gave all the richness and intelligence of his own vast experience.

Big Dan did not believe for a moment that Stephen would be all Jenny had intimated in her short, eager conversation with him. Something about her sincerity, however, had captured his interest. This, more than the glowing things she had said about her brother, had made Big Dan consent to talk with him.

"Here we are, sir."

Big Dan turned at the sound of Jenny's respectful voice. "Yes, so I see!" His eyes beamed above his thick glasses as he held out his hand to Stephen. "How do you do, young fellow?"

Stephen's eyes were earnestly glued to this giant of a man on whom he felt his destiny hung.

"So you want to make glass?" Big Dan was asking.

"Yes, sir. Fine glass."

"Know anything about it?"

"I have watched it being made but I've never worked with my own hands. I want to learn to do that first." The boy's face was bright with enthusiasm. "And then after that——"

"After that?" Big Dan encouraged as Stephen paused, afraid that he had said too much.

"I want to design glassware from my own patterns."

Jenny was proud of Stephen's forthrightness. She listened eagerly as Big Dan spoke again with a sudden twinkle in his eye. "Got any patterns?"

Stephen opened his book. "I've brought them with me, sir."

Big Dan threw back his head and chuckled. "Well, you are prepared, aren't you?" He laid his hand genially on Stephen's shoulder. "If you've got all those you had better come into my office and we'll have a look at them."

He led them past the glass blowers and through the hubbub of the factory to his own private quarters at the rear of the boat. In a quiet workroom in his outer office were three boy apprentices. They sat on high stools at a counter built in below a window that looked out on the river. They stared at Stephen curiously as he followed Big Dan and Jenny into Big Dan's private office. One was tall and towheaded. He said something to the boy seated next to him. Both of them snickered.

Big Dan's office was a friendly, orderly place. Shelves along the walls displayed almost priceless glassware. One showed Venetian glass so delicately colored and so beautifully blown that it had an almost ethereal look. Another was devoted to hand-blown glassware from France, particularly goblets and chalices. Still a third was rich and exotic with Big Dan's favorite ruby glass pieces which he himself had made in Bohemia. Many of these were encrusted with gold.

Stephen reveled in this exhibition. He stood staring at the shelves, his eyes large with fascination. Big Dan seated himself at his desk after drawing up a chair for Jenny. Finally he said quietly, "Want to show me your pattern book, Stephen?"

"Oh, yes, sir! Yes!"

' He stood beside Big Dan, laid his book open on the desk. On the first page Stephen had written a schoolboy's composition:

Glass is a hard brittle substance made by melting certain ingredients by intense heat. These ingredients are a melted mixture of sand with two oxides from a group of four—soda, potash, lime and lead. The other ingredients found in glass, such as manganese, tin, arsenic, iron, zinc, etc., are coloring matter, impurities or correctives of impurities.

Glass is usually named from its principal base. The ancient glass was "soda glass." Bohemia's white and English flint are "potash glass." Cheap tableware is "lime glass." Tableware suitable for cutting is "lead glass." The one staple element of all glass, silica, must first be pure and finely pulverized

There are many different kinds of glass such as flint, crown, window, bottle, and plate.

Big Dan read this, smiling. Finally he said, "You get right down to fundamentals, don't you, boy?"

"I try to."

"Well, let's read on." Big Dan turned to the next page.

It showed a pen-and-ink sketch of what Stephen called his fountain pattern. Its principal motif was the five-spray play of waterdrops reminiscent of pictures he had seen of the fountains at Versailles. He had designated this pattern to be done on goblets Blown Three Mold which was a new step in American glassmaking and meant that tableware was to be blown in full-size molds which formed both shape and pattern. Stephen's book indicated that the goblets should be sapphire blue in color.

As Big Dan studied this pattern with interest, Stephen explained: "These aren't all original with me, sir. Some of them were my grandfather's."

"Your grandfather's!"

"We never really knew him, sir," Jenny enlightened Big Dan, "but he was a fine craftsman in France. When Mother came to America she brought his pattern book with her."

Big Dan mused silently for a moment before he spoke again. He turned another page.

"Yes, I can see. There is fine craftsmanship here. Fine craftsmanship indeed."

A quarter of an hour later, Big Dan had perused most of the book. Finally he looked up, his kindly eyes quizzical. As Jenny practically held her breath waiting for his verdict, he said to Stephen, "If you can learn to execute these patterns according to these formulas, son——"

Stephen waited silently, eager for him to go on. After a moment, Big Dan continued, "Someday you'll be a great artist in glass."

"As—as great as you are, sir?" Stephen asked impulsively.

Big Dan laughed. "I hope you will start where I leave off."

"Then you will apprentice Stephen?" Jenny asked impetuously.

"Not so fast, child, not so fast!" Big Dan rose from his chair. "The road to that is long and hard. Stephen may become my apprentice only after arduous work. Like most important men in these times, he must start at the bottom."

"And what is that?" asked Stephen.

Big Dan laid a hand on his shoulder. "You must begin as a carrying-in boy."

"Carrying-in boy?"

"It's simply this," explained Big Dan. "Each workman here has his own special boy to fetch and carry for him—a sort of apprentice who helps him at his own particular job. He will teach you the mechanics of the trade and you will come to learn through him how to work with your own hands."

"I would like that, sir," said Stephen.

"This boat is not the whole of Page and Company," went on Big Dan. "There are additional furnaces on down the river. You'll soon become familiar with all our property."

"I'm sure that I will," Stephen said confidently.

"After you have 'carried in' for several workmen in turn,"

Big Dan continued, "and if you still show promise and want to——"

"Yes?" Stephen questioned, as Big Dan paused.

"Well, then lad, you will finally become apprenticed to me."

Although Stephen was not at all let down, Jenny was a bit disappointed. The fact that Stephen had such a long way to go appalled her.

"How long will it take until Stephen becomes apprenticed to you?" she asked Big Dan slowly.

He answered with a counterquestion. "What does it matter? The important thing is that he will have a practical knowledge of every phase of glassmaking. He should become the technician as well as the artist. Isn't that true?"

Before Jenny could answer, Stephen said, convinced, "Of course it's true, sir. It's what I want too."

Big Dan looked down at him, pleased. "Then you think you can do it, son?"

"I know I can do it."

"At two dollars and fifty cents a week?"

"At two dollars and fifty cents a week."

So the bargain was finally made. As they left Big Dan's office, both Jenny and Stephen felt the importance of the moment. Stephen was conscious that he had finally succeeded in dedicating himself to a career. It would, he hoped, lead him to greatness in the creation of beautiful things. To Jenny, too, it was a moment of consecration. Stephen, with all his youth, and all his talent, was started at last on the long, hard road to achievement. Neither spoke to the other until they were once again on the wharf.

Presently Stephen said slowly, "I think Big Dan is a great man."

"Yes," Jenny answered, "I think he is, too."

"Someday," Stephen went on, "I'll ask him to tell us the story of all that glass in his office."

"Someday, I think, he'll want to."

The following afternoon, she and her brood moved into their clinger. It was a wonderful moment for them all when they drove up to Goat Hill and stopped in front of the tumbledown house.

"We're home!" cried Mady.

"Give me the key, Jenny," caroled joyous Carlotta. "Let's hurry and unpack!"

All four climbed down from the farm wagon and raced up to the front door.

"Look! Here's an apple tree we didn't see before!"

The empty house was as clean as it could be. Jenny and the children stood in the middle of the kitchen surveying their new domicile with all the pleasure of lords of creation. Jenny was delighted with the stove. The old Scotchman had polished it for them until its black iron surface shone like pure ebony.

"It's got four lids!" Mady counted with pride. "Look, Jenny, you can cook a whole meal at once."

"It's a wonderful stove." Jenny smiled.

Carlotta went to the south window. "Know what?" she queried after a moment. "We ought to have a window seat here. We can see the whole city. Even Stevie's glasshouse."

Jenny looked questioningly at Stephen. "Do you suppose you could make a window seat out of a store box?"

"Sure," said Stephen. "All I need is a hammer and nails."

"Or maybe you'd like the window seat there." Jenny glanced at the west window.

"Who wants to look at the Blakewells?" Carlotta said with a grand air of disdain.

Mady was shuffling up the little flight of crooked steps that led to Stephen's room.

"Ooh! It's dark up here!"

"Open the shutters," suggested Stephen. "And when you come down, don't bump your head on that rafter."

"I'll need a shelf for Mamma's clock—" Jenny, too, was taking inventory—"and more shelves for dishes."

"We'll get a lot of store boxes," decided Stephen. "You can buy one for a penny."

Carlotta was standing in the center of the room adjoining the kitchen.

"Come on in here," she called. "Let's choose our corners!"

Choosing corners was an old game with them. They had often played it in the barn on their Enon Valley farm. It simply meant that each was given her own corner and in that particular place each kept the things that were cherished most. From time to time their corners were swapped to lend variety to the routine.

Carlotta's was always ornate with pictures of ladies of fashion torn out of *Godey's Lady's Book*. These she would tack on the wall. Her own special piece of furniture was a tiny bureau with an oval mirror. Always this stood in Carlotta's corner, littered with bits of ribbon and lace, and a silver shoe buckle she had found on the street in East Palestine. She kept it for luck.

Mady's corner was always presided over by Yvonne, a dark-haired French doll that had first belonged to her mother, had been passed down to Jenny and Carlotta and finally to her. Yvonne had once been as lovely as a princess is supposed to be, gowned in a Madame de Pompadour dress. Now she was only a dilapidated shadow of her former glittering self, dressed in calico, but Mady loved her with all her heart. On Mady's particular piece of furniture, a small maple table, stood an oil lamp, a sewing basket neatly arranged and her precious book of fairy tales.

Stephen's corner always had the look of a serious student's. He too had a small table of his own on which he kept his drawing materials and pattern books. The only ornament he cherished was a fine glass paperweight his mother had brought from France. It was beautifully cut. The glass globe enclosed the tiny blue-gowned figure of an angel with golden wings. His mother had told him that it had been made by his grandfather in a celebrated glasshouse in Clichy, a suburb of Paris.

Jenny's corner was no corner at all because she invariably occupied the space in front of the fire. Here she kept her mother's little rosewood rocker and a fireside bench for the children to sit on.

Their corners had just been chosen when there came a knock on the front door. Mady went to open it. She stepped back in pleased surprise.

"Oh!"

Jenny crossed the room to look over Mady's shoulder. A group of women stood there, smiling. The old Scotchman had told the other five families who lived on Goat Hill that Jenny and her brother and sisters would move into his clinger. This neighborly call was their welcome. Two of the families were Polish, two of Irish descent, one German. Old Mrs. Stepnosky detached herself from the group and came forward.

"Welcome to Goat Hill," she said, smiling broadly.

"It's very nice of you to come," said Jenny. "Won't you all come in?"

Mrs. Stepnosky made a gesture of protest. "Aw, no, no! You are too busy now." She peered beyond Jenny into the cluttered room. "I can see—" she laughed—"not even your chairs are unloaded yet! We come again when you are settled. This is just to say hello."

Jenny smiled at this friendly person and introduced her brood. Mrs. Stepnosky then drew each of her neighbors forward in turn.

"This is my nearest neighbor, Mrs. Kowalski," she said. "Her husband works in the south-side mills and she has two married daughters in Poland. As for me," she complained pleasantly, "I have no daughters. Only nine big strapping sons—all working at the furnaces."

"Nine sons!" Jenny gasped, while the other women laughed at her look of amazement.

Mrs. Stepnosky laughed, too, and drew another woman forward to greet her.

"And this is Mrs. O'Brien. Everyone calls her 'Bridgie.' She's not very long out of Killarney and her two sons are puddlers in an Allegheny Mill."

"Puddlers?" echoed Carlotta.

Mrs. O'Brien folded her hands across her ample stomach. "Sure, an' that means that they work at the furnaces too." She smiled.

Another Irish matron took a step toward Jenny at a gesture from Mrs. Stepnosky.

"And this is Mrs. Duffy," the old Polish woman went on. "She lives alone in the nearest clinger." She pointed to a little house several hundred feet away. "She's Widow Duffy but has three married daughters over on the Canal Basin. Their husbands are river men."

"Don't any of you have anyone for me to play with?" asked little Mady blankly. "You're all grown up."

Mrs. Stepnosky laughed again as she drew Mrs. Weimar forward. She was younger than the others and quite pretty with blue eyes like a Dresden doll's.

"This is Mrs. Weimar," said Mrs. Stepnosky. "She has two babies you might like to play with. One is two years old, the other is four. Fredericka and Frederick, she calls them."

Mady smiled at Mrs. Weimar. "I'll mind them for you if you want me to," she volunteered.

Young Mrs. Weimar laughed, showing two pretty dimples which interested Carlotta.

"You'd find them a handful for a little girl your age," she said. "But come play with them when you want to."

Mrs. Stepnosky lifted a market basket from the ground.

"We didn't think you'd have much time to cook supper," she said pleasantly. "We brought you a few things—some of Mrs. Weimar's lentil soup, a coffee cake from Mrs. Kowalski and freshly baked bread from Mrs. O'Brien. And, not forgetting, of course, such a good apple pie from Mrs. Duffy." She laughed as she gave Jenny the basket. "And there's a dandelion salad from me."

"All that for us!" gasped Jenny.

"Sure, an' it's just a little welcome gift, God bless you." Mrs. Duffy smiled.

The other children looked their thanks.

"Apple pie! Umm!" said Stephen.

"Coffee cake!" Carlotta said appreciatively.

"Lentil soup!" said Mady. "That's my favorite and Jenny's."

The neighbors nodded their heads and smiled.

"Good luck to you," said Mrs. Stepnosky.

"Let us help you when we can," said Mrs. O'Brien.

Jenny and the brood thanked them again as they turned away and prepared to depart in a chattering group. So these were their new neighbors! Polish. Irish. German. A part of Pittsburgh's melting pot she had heard so much about, thought Jenny. A kindly, human, wonderful part.

It was late that night when the oil lamps burned low in the Bayard clinger. Their few possessions had been brought inside, Sandy and King had been tied to the apple tree at the door. Except for their mother's and father's portraits which were always placed on the shelf above the fireplace, nothing had been arranged. The beds, however, had been put into place and all the fascinating details of what should go here and what should go there had been planned.

Carlotta literally fell into bed beside exhausted little Mady.

"We ought to have a housewarming," she called to Jenny, who was almost asleep in her bed in the opposite corner.

"What did you say?" called Stephen from his own room under the eaves.

"We ought to have a housewarming!" Carlotta repeated loudly. "And invite all those nice neighbors."

"Sure," said Stephen. "Will you make popovers for it, Jenny?"

Jenny smiled happily in the darkness. "I'll make the best popovers you ever tasted! Now, please, all of you, go to sleep!"

"What we dream tonight will come true," Carlotta babbled. "We're in a new house."

"Don't be too sure," warned Jenny. "That's only a superstition."

"But I am sure," insisted Carlotta.

"Very well, then." Jenny laughed sleepily. "Happy dreams to you all."

As she turned on her side facing the shadowy wall, she suddenly wondered what would happen if she should dream about Christopher and his beautiful packet, the *River Queen*.

 Seven

The Fight on the Wharf

The following morning Jenny began her new work at the Monongahela House. She was feeling very hopeful. Was not all going well in spite of the Blakewells? Were they not cozily established even if things were hard to manage and it would be difficult to make ends meet? They were all together. She and Stephen were working. Carlotta, regardless of her frivolities, would take care of the clinger. Mady could help her considerably. She was amazingly efficient for a little girl still playing with dolls. Jenny, in fact, was coming to think of Mady as Carlotta's balance wheel.

This would also be Stephen's first day at the glasshouse. Jenny could look out of the north window in the hotel kitchen and see the large sign on the boat which read, Page and Company, Glass. It was a wonderful feeling to know that what she was doing here would enable Stephen to start on his way up a glittering glass mountain. She had no doubt at all they would often slip backward during the difficult climb, but at least they were climbing.

Jenny's first hour in the hotel kitchen was spent in getting acquainted with her work and coworkers. Mrs. Houston herself introduced her to the kitchen staff, the pastry cooks and the salad makers, the women who prepared the vegetables, and the men who tended the meat. They were all cheerful, middle-aged people for the most part, and Jenny felt very comfortable with them. It was only when she encountered Helen that she was immediately puzzled.

Mrs. Houston introduced them pleasantly. "This is Helen Corrado, Jenny. She works at the fruit table."

The dark, sloe-eyed Italian girl was perhaps a year or two older than Jenny. She had long dark curls tucked up with a comb under her white cap. She was tall and wore heavy gold bracelets. Her hair and eyes were beautiful, and so was her cream-of-roses complexion, but her full red lips were petulant. She looked at Jenny measuring her coldly with her eyes. No smile touched her lips. She shrugged her shoulders carelessly.

"Hello," she said shortly.

"How do you do," answered Jenny, wanting to talk but suddenly made silent by this girl's hostile air.

Mrs. Houston filled in the pause. "Coming along with the strawberries, Helen?"

"Coming along with the strawberries!" repeated the girl. "Can't you see there are mountains?"

Mrs. Houston laughed. "This is the end of the strawberry season and everyone's ordering shortcake before it's too late." She smiled at Jenny. "Jenny will encounter them, too, when she starts fixing desserts."

Helen looked at Jenny again, but this time not so coldly. Her eyes were suddenly shrewd and sharp.

"So she's to fix the desserts," she said noncommittally.

"For the time being," Mrs. Houston answered.

As Mrs. Houston hurried her on, Jenny was quick to gather

that Helen Corrado, justly or unjustly, had immediately disliked her. She supposed it wouldn't be too long until the Italian girl would make the reason evident. The elation Jenny had felt in beginning her first day's work suddenly seemed to vanish. She would have trouble with Helen, she suspected, but why, or what for, she couldn't fathom now.

As Jenny folded her apron at the end of her first hard day, she decided to go up to the glasshouse so that she and Stephen might walk home together. He could tell her all the wonderful things that must have happened on his first day. She wouldn't mention to Stephen that she had unwittingly made an enemy. Stephen would worry about Helen Corrado.

She had turned off Water Street and onto the wharf at the foot of Ross Street when she suddenly stood still, amazed. Stephen was standing on the wharf surrounded by a half-curious, half-jeering crowd of boys. He had taken off his cap and tie and had his shirt sleeves rolled up to his elbows. Straight, dark-eyed, defiant, he was angrily listening to taunts they were making, lunging forward at a towheaded boy who stood a little apart from the others. Could this be Stephen—really Stephen?

Jenny quickened her steps as she went closer to the group completely oblivious of her presence. What had come over the habitually gentle lad? All of a sudden he seemed to have turned into as rowdy a street fighter as any ragamuffin on the water front.

Jenny heard him saying, "Come on, fight, you towheaded braggart! Are you afraid?"

If Jenny had not been so absorbed in Big Dan the day she and Stephen were in his office, she would have recognized the "towheaded braggart" as one of Big Dan's apprentices. Her

first impulse was to rush to Stephen and insist that he behave himself, to ask him if this was her reward for trying to
teach him the manners of a gentleman. But her instinctive
good common sense came to her rescue. This was Stephen's
battle, not hers. If she forced him away from the intolerant
group of boys he wouldn't have the chance to test his mettle
in their eyes again.

Jenny made a quick detour and stood in the shadow of a
great pile of packing boxes near the bridge of the glasshouse.
She could see every gesture from here, hear every word. Her
heart was fluttering as though it were caged. She was trembling for Stephen's handling of the situation. Would he be a
match for this plainly organized gang? Again she heard him
challenge: "You'd better fight now or I'll put a yellow streak
right down your back!"

"Not on my back, you won't!" said the towhead.

Jenny estimated the boy to be older then Stephen. He was
certainly bigger, and had the look of an old hand at street
fighting.

One of his companions baited, "Go on and fight the kid, Jo!
Beat him to a pulp! Who does he think he's askin' to fight?"

Jo grinned at the boy slyly, winking a deliberate eye. "Can't
you see I'm takin' my time? Let him suffer first. Let him
worry——"

"He can't suffer," jeered his friend, "unless he's got his sister's
apron to cry in!" Then, looking at Stephen's outraged face, he
began to taunt in a singsong voice, "Yer sister had to get yer
job! Yer sister had to get yer job!"

Jenny's whole body quivered with anger. So this was the
reason for the fight! The boys had seen her come to the glasshouse with Stephen and had probably accused him of hiding

behind her skirts. The—the little ruffians! She ached to fly at their throats. Suddenly her heart leaped jubilantly. Stephen wasn't waiting for anyone else to act. He was letting go himself. With one agile leap he sprang forward and aimed a blow at Jo's sneering companion, which sent him sprawling to the ground.

A sudden, surprised murmur reverberated through the whole group. It seemed to go from boy to boy. One with more temerity concerning Jo's leadership than the others had the actual spirit to challenge: "Hooray! That was a dandy! Could you take that, Jo?"

That was Jo's cue for action. So this little upstart was beginning to win his gang's respect! He spat on Tom, lying whimpering on the wharf. Weakling. He'd show this little gentleman—he'd show him! He'd wipe him out!

Jo doubled his fists and swung. Jenny could almost feel suspense hanging in the air. Stephen swung back at Jo. They sparred without hard hitting. Suddenly Jo let go again. He swung his fist against Stephen's chin with such fury that Stephen staggered backward blindly. Jenny felt suddenly as shattered as if she had been the one to receive the terrific blow. She put her hands to her throat to keep from crying aloud. Jo delivered a second blow. The miserable bully! *The bully!* It was not a fair match. He was older than Stephen and had the fighting form of a tomcat, decided Jenny. Jo stood back and swung again. The force of his third blow knocked Stephen down.

One of the boys tossed his cap in the air. "Hurray for Jo!" he cried. "Hurray!"

Instantly Stephen was back on his feet. Jenny closed her eyes at the sight of blood trickling down his chin.

"Oh, so you want more!" taunted Jo.

An outraged cry left Stephen's lips. "I'll show you! I'll show you!"

It was probably his anger that doubled or tripled his strength. Jenny had never known he could be capable of such fury.

As Jo sparred, grinning, certain that Stephen couldn't deliver, Stephen suddenly poised himself with the strength of a young, wary animal. He looked at Jo deliberately. He stood for a moment measuring him from head to foot, unconscious of the blows Jo was raining against him. The boys thought this funny and laughed. Jo was laughing, too, when suddenly Stephen sprang at him with amazing agility and batted him in both eyes. Jo was so taken by surprise that he failed to hit back. He couldn't have seen to hit back if he had wanted to. He was conscious only of darkness pierced by six million stars. Stephen was almost making a pulp of his flaccid face.

"Hey! Stop him!" One boy came forward.

"Got enough, you braggart? Got enough?" Stephen was panting, still aiming blows, left and right, to Jo's chin.

The boy Jo had spat on staggered to his feet. Jenny saw him look at Stephen, astounded. Suddenly he turned and ran. Little coward, thought Jenny contemptuously.

Stephen stood holding fast to Jo, aiming for a knockout blow. He delivered it like a gentleman fighter with hands that were swift and sure. Jo whined. His knees began to bend. Finally he too was prostrate on the wharf.

"Say, how you can fight!"

An enthusiastic lad came forward, followed by an admiring group. Stephen paid no attention to them. He bent and picked up his hat and coat. He put his necktie in his pocket.

"Look at the hero!" someone jeered at Jo as he tried to sit up and rub his hand across his eyes.

The boys were running true to form. They were ready to follow the winner. They surged backward as Stephen turned to look at them. They were not sure just what they saw in his eyes. Few of them knew that it was discernment. Stephen was taking stock. One or two backed farther away.

"Anyone else want to mention my sister?" Jenny heard him challenge.

Not one of the group flickered an eyelash. Stephen suddenly knew he had won in a way that commanded this gang's admiration. Without another word to them, he turned and walked off the wharf.

Jenny overtook him walking across the bridge. He was swinging along with his coat hanging over one shoulder, his cap still in his hand.

"Hello, Stevie." She tried to make her voice sound casual.

"Hello, Jenny." He never glanced toward her.

"Tired?" she asked gently. Then seizing him by the shoulders, she swung him around so that he faced her. "Oh, Stevie, I saw the fight! You were wonderful!"

"You saw the fight!" He stared at her in astonishment.

She took a handkerchief out of her pocket and wiped off the blood that was caked on his chin.

"You look a wreck." She smiled tenderly. "And your face is bruised—and I was so scared for you at first——" Suddenly tears were running down Jenny's cheeks.

"There's nothing to cry about. Aw, Jenny, stop it!"

"I—I will." Jenny sniffled. "And we've got to get home and wash your face."

As they were climbing the crude wooden steps that led up

Goat Hill, Stephen paused and leaned against the trunk of a tree.

"Jenny . . ." he began soberly.

"Yes, Stevie?" She sensed uncertainty in his voice.

"I guess we hadn't better tag around together so much any more." He saw a hurt look come into her eyes, and added hastily. "Not that I want it that way—but during working hours—" he shuffled from one foot to another—"Aw, Jenny, you know what they said."

She understood as she looked at him what he meant. It was not that he was loving her less, or trying to escape from what they had always meant to each other. It was simply that he was endeavoring to make her see that he had to embark into a world of his own, a world in which he was responsible for his own decisions, his own successes, his own failures. In short, a boy's own world with a boy's own visions and a boy's own association with his kind. It was as though they had been traveling on a long, long road together and this was the first time they were forced to go in opposite directions. Jenny said comfortingly, "I understand, Stevie, and you're not to worry. But there's still one thing."

"Well?"

"That—that boy you licked. What are you going to do about him?"

Stephen shrugged his shoulders. "Nothing, I guess. What is there to do?"

"Let's sit down here a little while." Jenny sat on the grassy hill, and drew him down beside her.

"Well?" Stephen questioned again.

"You just can't do nothing about that boy, Stevie. He'll make too much trouble."

"I licked him, didn't I?"

"But that's just the point! Don't you see that he'll be resentful?"

"Then I can lick him again."

Jenny laughed. "So your life at the glasshouse is simply to be one licking after another! How do you think Big Dan will like that?"

"He won't, I guess."

"He won't like it and he won't permit it," Jenny decided. "Either you or Jo will lose your chance to become his apprentice."

"Lose my apprenticeship!" Stephen was startled.

"Big Dan's running a glasshouse, not a prize-fight ring for ruffians."

Stephen considered this seriously before he spoke again. "What do you think I should do?"

Jenny's thoughts went back to things past. "Father was a fighter, a good fighter, Stevie. He fought robbers and Indians out West. Sometimes he fought men who were—well, just men, like himself. And he always had a code."

"A code?"

"After the fight was over, no matter if he won or lost—" Jenny smiled a little—"but I think that Father always won ..."

"Well, what about his code?"

"He'd simply say to the man he had fought, 'You've won,' or 'I've won,' whichever the case may have been. 'Now let's shake hands and forget it. We're both good fellows. Let's be friends.'"

"What happened then?"

Jenny looked at him squarely. "If both were made of the right stuff, they would become friends and go on playing fair from there."

Stephen considered her words. "You think I should say that to Jo, don't you?"

"Father would have, I'm sure."

"Well, then, I guess that I can—but——"

"But what?"

"I think that Jo will be pigheaded."

Jenny laughed again as she stood up. "Well, it won't hurt to find out."

Mady was busy at the stove when they went into the clinger. She was about to lift the lid of a pot to see if the potatoes were boiling when she suddenly discovered them. She stared wide-eyed at Stephen.

"Stevie Bayard! You've been fighting!"

"Sure!" Stevie grinned.

"You've been hit on the chin!"

"Guess you're right."

She dropped the potlid and went to him. "Golly! It's a daisy!"

As she put up her hand to touch it, Jenny caught her wrist. "Don't touch it, Mady."

"Does it hurt, Stevie?" the little girl asked, concerned.

"Not now." Stevie grinned again.

"Who did it?" Mady demanded.

"Jo," answered Stephen.

"Who's Jo?"

"For heaven's sake, Mady, stop asking questions!" Jenny led Stephen to the kitchen sink. "Jo's just a boy at the glasshouse a little too big for his britches!"

"And Stevie hit him!" Mady's eyes were alight with pride. "Good, Stevie, good!"

As he bent over the sink to wash, she scanned him again

very critically. "It must have been grand. I wish I could have seen it. Even your shirttail's hanging out!"

"Where's Carlotta?" Jenny abruptly changed the subject.

"I haven't seen her this afternoon."

"This afternoon!" echoed Jenny. "Where on earth did she go?"

"How should I know?" asked matter-of-fact Mady, accustomed to Carlotta's absences and meandering.

Stephen had washed and changed his clothes and they were just about ready to sit down to supper when Carlotta sailed in. Sailed was quite the word she herself would have delighted in living up to. She was in what she would have defined to herself as "a princess mood." Her eyes were bright as though she had been seeing many wonderful things. One shining red-gold curl was tied with a blue satin ribbon which every now and then she flung back with what she hoped was a grand and careless gesture. The three at the table surveyed her as she stood posing in the open doorway.

"Well?" said Jenny finally. "And where have you been?"

Carlotta crossed the room to her, all excitement and gaiety. "Just wait till I tell you."

"Well, we're waiting," said practical little Mady, as Carlotta paused for effect.

Again she flung back her curls with a new and studied gesture. "I've been to the theater," she announced.

"The theater!" The kitchen seemed suddenly electrified.

"It's over on Fifth Avenue," Carlotta continued infectiously. "I had to walk miles!"

"But how did you get in?" Jenny was amazed.

"I didn't. I just hung around the entrance and watched everything that went on. Once I peeped in at the stage door—"

her eyes were now two burning stars—"and I saw the leading lady in a long white satin dress and white flowers in her hair.

"Tell us more," insisted Mady, her eyes fastened on Carlotta.

Carlotta drew a deep sigh. "She was pale and tall and beautiful and a great big brute of a man was tearing his hair out about her."

"Tearing his hair out!" Mady was fascinated.

Carlotta drew up a chair to the table. She leaned gracefully over its back.

"It was the most wonderful thing I ever saw." She drew another deep sigh. "Someday I'm going to be an actress."

"*An actress!*" Mady's eyes popped.

Jenny looked at Carlotta tolerantly. "Eat your potatoes and bacon," she ordered, "and don't talk such nonsense."

 *Eight*

The Key to the Future

As week followed week, the Bayards' life in the little clinger took on a pattern. The housewarming came off hilariously. Jenny invited Timothy Drew as well as the five families on Goat Hill. The popovers were a big success. They were dipped in hot butter, and even old Mrs. Stepnosky said she had never tasted anything better.

Timothy Drew brought a bag of oats for King. After supper was over he printed a sign on a piece of wood which he and Stephen nailed to the tree at the front of the house. The sign read Horse for Hire. With all the construction work going on in the city, he told Jenny, King could really make money for them. He would earn more than the cost of his feed. Pittsburgh was building—the city was growing by leaps and bounds. In the roaring forties it had thundered ahead, even after the great fire which had destroyed the entire business section in 1845. Every available horse was needed to carry on the work of construction, and Timothy would be in a position to send good business their way. He knew men who would treat King kindly and pay a fair price for his services.

The Bayards were delighted. If King could earn a little

money, they would be able to rent a stall for him in Mrs. Duffy's ramshackle stable. He, too would have a clinger! So the merry evening passed. When the guests left late, the brood was very gay.

"We'll have to have lots of parties!" said Carlotta.

"They're fun," said Mady

"We are lucky to have such good neighbors," Jenny told them seriously.

Jenny was getting along very well under the supervision of Mrs. Houston at the Monongahela House. Her work on the dessert staff became in a way a kind of creative experience; she was learning so much that was new in culinary matters. If it had not been for Helen Corrado's continued hostility, her work would have been almost pleasant. Though her fingers became callused from the endless holding of the paring knife with which she cut fruit and nuts and other candied delicacies, she could adjust herself to wearying tasks. But always Helen seemed to be watching her, watching her furtively like a shadow. She doubtless hoped this would unnerve Jenny and make her complain to Mrs. Houston. Jenny decided to do no such thing. She would meet this girl on her own ground, and someday she would discover what was behind all the mystery.

Day after day went by until the one chosen by Christopher White to give a *bon voyage* party arrived. The *River Queen* was scheduled to make her return trip to New Orleans. The manager of the Monongahela House decided to send a three-tiered marble cake with his compliments for the occasion. The kitchen staff was to bake it. It was to be delectable with fancy swirls of white frosting and, high on the top layer, a pink-sugar model of the captivating queen of the river boats.

The afternoon of the day of the party Christopher breezed in and out of the kitchen like a fresh young wind blowing up from the waters. His enthusiasm was boundless. He praised the fat pastry cook extravagantly, saying that not even down in New Orleans could such a cake have been baked! The best Creole cook in Louisiana would have been jealous at the sight of it!

Jenny saw him stop at Helen's table. The Italian girl similed at him boldly. "Hello," she said slowly, measuring him with challenging eyes.

"Hello, Helen." Christopher grinned. "How are things going?"

"Dullish," said Helen. "Extremely dullish."

"Job going stale?" teased Christopher.

"How would you like to stay in this hot hole all day?" she retorted.

He laughed at the disgusted glance she threw at the entire kitchen, shrugging, meanwhile, very prettily.

"Guess I wouldn't like it much," Jenny heard Christopher sympathize.

Helen flirted with him gaily. "Now if I were a lady, as you are a gentleman—with flounces and furbelows—" she lifted her face to his and laughed—"and a bustle—I should really have a pink lace bustle."

Christopher laughed uproariously while Jenny inwardly writhed. The witch! Oh, the witch! she rebelled. To—to talk to him so—so brazenly!

"Heaven help us when you wear a pink lace bustle!" Christopher bantered as he turned away from Helen. Much to Jenny's dismay he started to walk toward her own table.

Her heart began to beat in triple time. There was no recognition as yet in his eyes. The knife with which she was frosting the cake shook in her trembling hands. As he stopped at a near-by table to speak to one of the salad chefs, her panic became complete. Suppose—just by luck—or some wonderful chance—he should really recognize her and remember that day on the wharf? What would he think when he discovered that she was a servant here in a hotel kitchen? Would he catalogue her, perhaps, in the same low category in which he doubtless classed Helen? If he had thought of Jenny at all since that day, he might, she hoped, have imagined much more romantic things.

Christopher was turning away from the salad table and coming in her direction. She could see that he meant to watch her put the frosting on the big *bon voyage* cake. Christopher, who lived on a ship, laughed and danced and rode in carriages with girls like Rosalie Blakewell! Jenny couldn't bear the possibility of a comparison. Rosalie knew the gay things to say, she knew how to coquette without being brash as Helen was.

Jenny had to escape at once. He wasn't more than a few feet away. Suddenly she dropped the cake knife. It fell to the floor with a metallic thud. As Christopher immediately crossed the little space that lay between them and stooped to pick it up, Jenny turned and hurried away into a smaller kitchen adjoining.

She found shelter behind a wooden cabinet there. Even to her own surprise, she felt sudden tears in her eyes. With a characteristic gesture of discipline, accompanied by a surge of defiance, she brushed them angrily away. She had never felt like this before. What absurd power did this freckle-faced boy hold over her that he could make her act like a child afraid of her own shadow? She sat down on a crate of cabbages and gave herself up to being completely miserable. When Mrs. Houston came looking for her Jenny told her she had a headache and asked permission to go home. Neither Mrs. Houston nor Jenny was aware that Helen had followed Jenny into the kitchen, had watched and heard all that was said and done.

Jenny hurried out the servant's entrance. Once out on Water Street, she refused to let herself look in the direction of the *River Queen*. It lay shining in the sun directly across from the hotel. She was glad that the boat would soon be leaving and Christopher with it. When he was out of the city and there was no possibility of their meeting she wouldn't have to worry about contrasting herself with girls she had no business contrasting herself with anyhow!

For the first time in her sixteen years, Jenny found herself thinking about her own life instead of the life of her brood. After all, she was sixteen, and she had to become interested in the social side of things sometime! But surely there could be nothing but madness in thinking about such a lad as Christopher! No, she told herself stubbornly, his kind was not for Jenny Bayard. Hadn't Victoria Blakewell made that plain enough the very first time she had seen her? As Jenny walked across the bridge she wondered why she felt so thoroughly miserable all over again.

She had come to the south side of the river when she heard Stephen calling her name. "Jenny! Jenny! Wait!"

She turned around wonderingly. What was he doing on the streets at this hour? Had he been in another fracas, she worried, and perhaps lost his job? There was another boy with him, a messenger boy. He appeared to be about the same age as Stephen. He was a good-looking boy with nice eyes.

"Stephen," Jenny began, "why aren't you at the glasshouse?"

Stephen smiled. She could see that he was pleased about something. The messenger boy stood courteously aside as her brother began to talk.

"Don't worry about the glasshouse, Jenny. I've got permission to be out—and I'm so glad we met you here because I want you to meet Scotchie."

"Hello, Scotchie." Jenny smiled at the boy who smiled back in a half-shy, half-friendly fashion. "But you must have another name."

"He has." Stephen laughed. "It's Andrew. Andrew Carnegie."

"Hello, Andrew," Jenny greeted him again.

"I forgot to tell him," Stephen interrupted as the lad stood, a little at a loss as to how to address her, "that he should just call you Jenny."

"Fair enough, Andrew?" she asked.

"Fair enough," he repeated, pleased. His voice had a heavy Scottish accent.

They walked to a near-by building and idled on the steps. Stephen explained how he had met young Andrew delivering telegrams at the glasshouse. They had talked many times before but it was not until Andrew had told him that a Colonel James Anderson was opening a library of four hundred volumes for working boys that they became companions. Every Saturday afternoon the colonel himself would act as librarian for boys like Andrew and Stephen. Big Dan had given Stephen permission to go to the library with Andrew this very afternoon. Andrew would introduce him to Colonel Anderson, who would allow him to borrow a new book every week!

"Just think, Jenny," Stephen said happily, "We can all read now as much as we like."

Jenny was as enthusiastic as the boys.

"Have you had a book from the library yet, Andrew?" she questioned.

"I've had Lamb's *Essays* and Bancroft's *History of the United States*. The history is wonderful." He paused for a moment before he continued eagerly, "And you can get Shakespeare's plays if you want them!"

"We'll get them for Carlotta." Stephen laughed. "Maybe they'll keep her from hanging around stage doors."

Jenny laughed too. "They may make her worse," she ventured. Then she turned a bright face to Andrew. "Oh, this is a wonderful thing! When I think of the long winter evenings ahead——"

Stephen looked at the clock on the bridge. "We've go to go, Jenny. Andrew has to deliver a telegram over here before we go to the library."

"Andrew works hard, I can see."

"I like my work," said young Andrew. "It takes me all over the city."

Jenny gave him a friendly smile. "You're a very good messenger, I'm sure. And when I think of all those books you are reading——"

Andrew looked at her seriously as she paused. "My mother says they'll light the way to what I want to be."

Jenny looked thoughtful. "I'm glad that Stephen has found you," she said finally. "And thank you for letting us know about the free library."

Stephen spoke again as they were about to turn away. "I'll tell you more about Scotchie tonight," he said merrily. "He was born in Dunfermline, Scotland. His father is a damask weaver. There's an abbey in Dunfermline and he——"

Andrew tugged at his arm to stop this enthusiastic outpouring. "We must go or Colonel Anderson will be gone."

"All right, Scotchie," Stephen assented. " 'Bye, Jenny. See you tonight."

"Good-bye, boys." As they turned to go in the opposite direction, Jenny called, "And thank you again, Andrew. Thank you very much."

Jenny walked on toward the steps that would take her up to the clinger, thinking of magical things. All that she had ever heard about books was magical indeed. She remembered now, in detail, her few precious years of "schooling." There had been two winters on the farm when her mother had boarded the teacher from the little red schoolhouse on the hill. His name was John Banks and he had been a tall, spare New Englander with a love of learning equaled only by his love of seeing America as a sort of traveling professor. He had taught in little red schoolhouses from Maine to Ohio. During those winters at the Bayards', he had taught Jenny and Stephen not only the three R's and elementary studies but had planted within them a respect for knowledge beyond their years. All that their mother had endeavored to teach them, he had supplemented with great earnestness. "Good books," he had once told them, "are like a lantern in your hand." They burned with an incessant glow, illuminating the darkness in the corners of one's mind. Andrew too had said, "They will light the way to what I want to be." What did she want to become, Jenny wondered? Really become? Could books help her there? People like the Blakewells read good books, she knew. And a person like Christopher?

Suddenly she stopped and stood as though transfixed by her thoughts. She didn't want to become like the Blakewells. She didn't want to become like Christopher. Most of all she wanted to become *herself.* Her real self. Her best self which reached up for a better life for herself and her brother and sisters.

Books were keys, too. They could open doors. Once the doors were open one could enter into a world of beauty and culture such as the Blakewells were born to. A world in which she could find a private niche of her own and become the best Jenny Bayard individual destiny could design. Having once attained that—then, even Christopher might not be too far away. Jenny was glad she had met that nice boy, Andrew. The books he had told them about would be as a fire on the hearth in her clinger, fire, indeed, to warm and inspire them all. This moment seemed to bring back to her an old Indian song her father had heard among the Acoma Indian tribes in the great Southwest. Part of it went:

All my life I have been seeking, Seeking——

Jenny knew that, if she were to win what she wanted from life for the Bayards, they must seek what was to be found in the world of books as well as in the world of practical achievement. In other words, they must continue the schooling which John Banks had begun. There were "free schools" in Pittsburgh, she realized, but those who attended had to buy their own books, and until she and Stephen earned more money that would be like reaching for the moon.

That evening Stephen came home with a copy of a book written by Robert Burns. Andrew had recommended it "to start with." Robert Burns was a poet of Andrew's native country. In a sense, he would take the brood in the clinger on a delightful trip through Scotland. Jenny opened the book, laid it on the kitchen table in front of her. She turned the pages idly, finally began to read aloud:

> Ye banks and braes and streams around
> The castle o' Montgomery,
> Green be your woods, and fair your flowers ...

"Isn't that pretty?" mused Carlotta as Jenny paused.

"I'd like to see that castle," said Mady.

"Bet Andrew has seen it," commented Stephen.

"Read us some more," Mady begged.

Jenny was about to continue reading when a strange voice greeted them all from the kitchen steps. All four lifted their heads in surprise. A tall, well-dressed man stood looking in. He was what Jenny termed in her own mind, "an aristocrat." He wore a fine brown beaver-cloth suit, cream-colored beaver hat and cream-colored gloves. His ebony cane was monogrammed in gold.

She rose and went toward him. "Good evening, sir."

He was smiling down at her, a magnetic smile with a quality of warmth not unlike her own.

"I'm John Blakewell," he introduced himself. "May I come in?"

"John Blakewell!" Four voices repeated the name in astonishment. Then Jenny suddenly remembered to step aside and let their visitor in.

"We're very pleased to see you, sir," she said.

He came into the clinger exuberantly, seeming bring a gay friendliness with him. He stood for a moment silently surveying them all.

"So you are Marie Bayard's children! I knew she would do a wonderful job!" He looked at Jenny with serious eyes. "I am very sorry I was not at home the day you called on us. You see, I had gone to New Orleans to spend several weeks with my mother. My wife did not understand who you were or what a real connection you had with us." As Jenny was about to speak, he went on, unheeding, "I want to apologize to you. I am sorry things happened that way."

"Thank you, Mr. Blakewell," Jenny said softly. "Please sit down and be comfortable. It is very kind of you to come." She drew up a chair to the table. He sat down and took off his gloves as she introduced the brood.

"This is Carlotta," she told him proudly. "She is thirteen years old and Mady here is eight. This is my brother, Stephen, fifteen now, and I am Jenny."

He extended a cordial hand to each one.

"Are we connected—like you said?" blurted out Mady.

John Blakewell laughed. "Indeed we are, Mady! Your mamma and I practically grew up together in the house up there on the hill. I still have a little music box she gave me once for Christmas."

"A music box!" The girls were entranced. "What does it play?"

He whistled a familiar tune.

" 'Old King Cole Was a Merry Old Soul'!" they exclaimed simultaneously.

"Right!" He laughed. "And someday I'll show you the music box."

Jenny made coffee later in the evening. To the brood's utter delight, John Blakewell put on one of Jenny's aprons and helped to make sandwiches of green apple jelly they had brought from the farm. He seemed to find fun in all that he did, thought Jenny. She did not realize that this was for John Blakewell one of the most pleasant and heart-warming evenings he had known in years. He was finding graciousness and hospitality such as he would not have believed could exist in a poor little clinger with a motherless brood like this.

Stephen interested him tremendously. They spent more than an hour, their heads close together, perusing Stephen's pattern books. Yes, Pittsburgh was making glass, said John Blakewell; it was fast becoming the great glass caldron of the world. But glass in turn would also make Pittsburgh. Stephen was doing well to have been chosen by Big Dan. A great world lay ahead for the boy. Steamboats built by the Blakewells were carrying Pittsburgh glass to New Orleans every day. From there it went to markets all around the globe.

A clock struck on the kitchen shelf. John Blakewell rose, flabbergasted.

"Twelve o'clock! Oh, how thoughtless I am! I've kept you up hours too late and I've broken my promise to Captain White to look in at the party on the *River Queen*." He hurriedly picked up his hat and cane, then laughed as he laid them down again. "I am a blundering idiot! The *River Queen* sails at midnight!"

"Let's watch it go! We can see it from here!" cried Carlotta.

The brood rushed to the south window. Over their shoulders Jenny watched too. The *River Queen* was sailing.

Christopher was sailing with it, but somehow Jenny was not sad. It looked like a ship ablaze with stars as slowly and majestically it moved down the river, a golden light in every window, from its wheelhouse to its smallest cabin. Today she had met Andrew Carnegie. Tonight she had met John Blakewell. Both were giving her keys to a world far away from this little clinger. She and Stephen would find that world and when they had found it they would be ready to enter in. It lay here in Pittsburgh as surely as the *River Queen* was sailing tonight. Jenny smiled her lovely smile as the haunting sound of the steamboat's whistle came up to her from the river like the clear call of a dream.

 Nine

The Star Window

Jenny stood stock-still in the darkness that enveloped the wharf. She was staring at the glasshouse as if she had never seen it before. Stephen laughed at her, teasing, "What's wrong, Jenny? 'Fraid of the dark?"

She continued to look at the glasshouse, and not at Stephen, as she answered, "It isn't the dark. It's everything. I never realized until this minute how wonderful this looks at night."

"It's wonderful all the time," said Stephen. "At least it is to me."

"Look!" Jenny indicated the scene before them, "against this dark river and hills, this glasshouse looks like a picture in your book of legends."

Stephen considered her words for a moment, then his face lighted. "I know which book you mean. It shows the Persian warriors building altar fires." He, too, looked at the glasshouse again. "And all this looks like that picture because the furnaces make it stand out in the night."

"And look at the glass blowers!" added Jenny. "The way they move about carrying balls of fire on their pipes——"

There was truth in what Jenny was trying to point out to Stephen. The glass workers, unconscious of any drama in their work, seemed part of a pattern in which every movement was timed to a certain rhythm. As the gatherer swung his long pipe upward, on its end a ball of fire, he was like the figure of ancient legend who tended the sacred flames of the Persians and kept them constantly burning.

Stephen felt responsive to all this as they crossed the bridge to the boat. His eyes were alight with eagerness. He had coaxed Jenny to come down to the glasshouse with him because he had a surprise for her. When she had protested that he might again be made an object of ridicule by his fellow workers if he dragged in his sister, Stephen had simply smiled enigmatically and said, "They wouldn't dare." Not even blustering Jo had interfered with Stephen's leadership since the decisive day of what had come to be remembered as The Fight.

Four months had passed since that memorable afternoon. During these months Stephen had worked long and hard. As he and Jenny passed the blazing furnaces on their way to the passage that led to the apprentices' room, she thought of him working here day after day in the fierceness of this heat. She could see that it was exhausting to husky, able-bodied men. How much more so must it be to a growing boy like Stephen?

Yet he had never complained. He had worked at his job as a carrying-in boy, had lugged heavy baskets of glass from the factory to the showrooms with the dogged persistence of one preparing himself for better things. He had watched the process of glassmaking, engrossed in it, step by step. He had made the most of every opportunity to help each master craftsman from the gatherer to the engraver, learning how to work with his own hands. He himself had been permitted to "gather" and "work glass" in his spare time, and long ago he had had the beginner's thrill of taking molten glass from the "batch" and making his first pieces. With his own lips he had blown a goblet for Jenny, a diminutive glass pitcher for Mady and a high glass hat for Carlotta. All of these had been received by them with great pride. Stephen enjoyed showering them with such surprises. That the new one he had to show Jenny tonight had not yet been seen by anyone—no other eyes in the world but his own—filled the present moment with excitement for him.

"Better see if all's clear," warned Jenny as they reached the door to the apprentices' room.

"No one's ever here at night," answered Stephen, smiling at her over his shoulder. "Do you think Jo, for instance, would give up an evening's fun to stay here and study formulas?"

"He would if he were a good apprentice."

Stephen laughed at her. "Come off, Jenny. You're sitting up on a perch. And——"

"And what?" she repeated curiously.

"Well," drawled Stephen as he took hold of the doorknob, "if you really want to know—Jo's got a girl."

"A–a girl!" Jenny was wide-eyed. "At his age!"

Stephen grinned. "What's wrong with his age? He's almost sixteen!"

His words struck Jenny with sudden sharpness. "Almost sixteen." Why, Jo, then, was not much younger than she! Why did she feel herself so much older? she wondered. Was it because she and Stephen were working too steadily and had so little time to play? Suppose that Stephen should soon be attracted to a—well, a girl—as she had been attracted to Christopher? The thought seemed new and strange to Jenny. She felt highly perturbed as she followed him into the apprentices' room.

His voice reassured her as he struck a match. "Wait a moment and I'll light this lamp."

Stephen was not thinking of girls, she decided, as she deliberately watched him. Jenny could plainly see that Stephen's world was here, right here in this room. It was governed by the compass and pattern book there on the desk, by the formula in his handwriting on a blackboard hung on the wall. It was governed, too, by the tools he held in his hands when he worked out there at the furnaces, by the wisdom he heard from the master craftsmen, and the questions he put to them. Yes, Stephen's world was a workaday world made beautiful and almost mystical by the fact that he was urged on by a dream that he hoped would lead him to high places.

"Ready, Jenny?" He was standing at a cabinet in the corner, his hand on the knob of a wooden door. His dark eyes were shining with anticipation.

"Of course I'm ready, Stevie! And hurry, will you?"

He paused a little longer, just for effect.

"Stevie!" Jenny implored.

He laughed again, then immediately sobered. Jenny realized that he was nervous, that this—whatever it was that he had created—had a deep and wonderful significance for him.

"I've worked on this three months," he began, as he finally unlocked the door of the cabinet and brought forth his treasure. "You're the first to know about it, Jenny, and I—I hope you will like it."

Jenny was suddenly speechless as he placed it on the table. She had from time to time while window-shopping seen little houses made out of pressed glass, labeled "glass novelties." But Stephen's creation was not a glass house. His dream had taken the form of a little glass church or chapel. Made of blown glass, its tall, slim steeple was silvery clear and there was an enchanting cluster of tiny glass bells in the diminutive bell tower.

But it was not the steeple or even the bells that gave this glass creation its beauty. It was the light which illuminated its whole interior from a window made of bits of colored glass pieced mosaic-like together. It was fashioned in the shape of a medallion, like the lovely rose windows of stained glass in Old World cathedrals. Stephen's pattern was a simple one. It represented a single blue star blazing against a background of rich, barbaric colors. Softly now in the lamplight, the window diffused its jewel-like tones: sapphire-blue, yellow-gold, ruby-red, the green of emeralds. It was all so carefully planned to so minute a scale that Stephen had fitted almost twenty pieces of glass together to make this small medallion. To be sure, it would have many imperfections to a craftsman's eyes, but so pleasing was it to an amateur like Jenny, that the whole effect of a stained glass window was there to a remarkable degree.

"I call it my star window," said Stephen as she stood silently looking at it.

"Stevie——"

"You like it, Jenny! I can see that you do! Aw, don't cry about it! I made it for you to put under our Christmas tree."

"Your star window! It's beautiful, Stevie, beautiful! And just imagine how it will look in Christmas candlelight."

"You think of everything." Stephen smiled his shy smile of delight.

In the next quarter hour, Jenny learned how Stephen had come to make his little glass chapel. It had all begun with a book he had borrowed from Colonel Anderson's library. It had told the history of stained glass windows and Stephen had been completely fascinated by the story. He had learned that many such windows of great pictorial loveliness had been made by eleventh-century monks in dim and ancient monasteries. From this book, too, he had learned that the first step in the making of ornamental windows is the design. A small sketch is first made from which several copies are taken. It is then enlarged to the full size of the window and properly colored. The copies are cut into small paper sections and pieces of glass are cut out like these sections of the pattern. After this, the glass is selected, and the various colors are painted upon the glass to suit the general design. Stephen's choice of colors included the ones that Jenny had noted, sapphire-blue, yellow-gold, ruby-red and the green of emeralds.

Then had come the design for his star which he had applied with mineral paint on these sections of glass already tinted. This, he had learned, would fuse into the glass when it was heated, after which all the glass bits would be taken to the kiln and fired. When all the sections were assembled on the uncut pattern, he had followed instructions and had compared it with his original drawing. In joining the pieces together he had made a frame of lead for each piece, so that the lines of leading would add to the decorative quality of his scheme. This, he realized, would intensify the brilliance of the colors of the window when it was in place against the daylight. When each piece was finally leaded he had placed it over the pattern until the window was assembled as a whole. Then had come the soldering process which he had also done painstakingly and well.

At last he had cleaned his small window with whiting

and placed it in position above what might have been the altar in his little glass cathedral. This then—this small medallion window—with its star upon its panes of colored glass like something mystically alight, was the result of more than a hundred hours of toil.

Jenny fingered it reverently, noting that the entire chapel from the shining glass base to the tip of its silvery clear steeple was only about twelve inches high.

"Do these lovely little bells ring—really ring, Stevie?"

"Listen!" He pulled a tiny bell rope.

The tinkling sound of fairylike bells was suddenly drowned by a hearty voice booming behind them. "Well! Well! So it's you, lad, and Miss Jenny!"

They turned simultaneously to face Big Dan.

"Good evening, sir." Jenny was delighted to see him.

"I'm glad to see you, too sir," said Stephen. "There's something I've been wanting to show you."

"So?"

Big Dan's eyes twinkled as his spectacles fell down over his nose. He had not yet discovered the little glass chapel in front of which Stephen was standing. He laid a friendly hand on the boy's head.

"Always this lad is intense," he said teasingly to Jenny. "Always intense about something!"

"Perhaps there's a reason," said Jenny proudly. Then as Stephen moved away to reveal his handiwork on the table, she added, "Look!"

"Ach!" Big Dan exclaimed. Then as he approached it, "Stephen, my lad," he said almost tenderly. "Stephen!"

"No one has seen it except Jenny, and now you," Stephen explained.

Big Dan looked at it silently for a moment, then he took it up in his hands, those hands which appeared so clumsy and were yet so capable of handling the most fragile objects with the gentlest care.

"A chapel," he said at last, as though commenting wonderingly to himself, "A chapel with a medallion window!"

"I made it for Jenny to put under our Christmas tree." Big Dan held it up to the lamplight.

"The steeple, Stevie . . . ." He ran sensitive fingers along the spire. "It's mercury-brown and very smooth. It has a good silver sheen." He stopped speaking suddenly as a guilty look came into Stephen's eyes. "Come, now," he finally insisted, "tell me how this was done."

Stephen smiled. "I worked three days for your master engraver, sir, for which he gave me a bit of quicksilver. I added that to my batch to give it that special shine."

"Quicksilver!" echoed Jenny.

"I knew it," Big Dan mused. Then he explained to Jenny, "If quicksilver is added to molten glass you get this brilliant silvery glitter. I have heard that in one case, the workers added handfuls of silver dollars to the mass and the result was a silvery glass more wonderfully mellow than any we had ever dreamed of. But the pity of it is," he chuckled, "we cannot keep adding handfuls of silver dollars!"

Jenny watched Big Dan as he turned the little chapel so that he might examine the window. He held it critically up to the light, noting the blue of the star, studying the way in which the infinitesimal glass panes were fitted together. Quickly he realized that while there was much here that was faulty, there was also something of great value. Stephen's urge, he decided, had been stronger than even he himself had realized. This boy had the rare and precious gift of great imagination. As he continued his inspection, speaking never a word, Jenny saw Stephen shifting uneasily. She, too, became tense.

Finally Big Dan lifted his eyes and looked soberly at them both. "Come into my office," he said. "There's something I must say."

They followed him into the inner room. He lighted a lamp on his desk. The light played softly on his precious pieces of fine glassware on the shelves along the wall. It made Stephen's medallion window flash with all the colors of a thousand sparkling jewels. Still Big Dan held the fragile little chapel in his clumsy hands. Presently he sat down and faced the two eager young people waiting for him to speak.

"Well, lad," he began, "this is what I've been waiting for."

"What you've been waiting for, sir?"

Big Dan placed the chapel on his desk in front of him, leaned forward and folded his great muscular arms.

"Through all these years of glassmaking," he went on soberly, "I had hoped to find a boy who would have not only the potentialities of a fine craftsman but the added quality of the artist. One who could feel and work and dream in glass, who could somehow breathe into its substance not only the necessary ingredients to make it flawless and beautiful, but also something of the spirit. Something that would somehow say we are not merely on this earth to do what we can with what little we have, but that out of that little we are charged to create as much as we know how of beauty. You have done that, Stephen, in this."

"It's very kind of you to say so, sir." Jenny's face was aglow.

"I'm not being kind," continued Big Dan. "And as time goes on, Stephen will find me a hard master." He looked at Stephen, unsmiling. "You've got to study, boy. You've got to study the history of glass from its very beginning in ancient Egypt almost two thousand years before Christ. You've got to learn the methods practiced in Phoenicia, Rome, Venice, and by the guilds in France. You've got to study architecture and to see the great pictorial windows in Old World cathedrals. And when you can't 'think glass' another moment, you've got to begin to create what will come to you out of all this maze of thought. Someday—" again Big Dan fingered the little glass chapel—"you will bring great honor not only to your craft but to your country."

"My country!" echoed Stephen amazed.

"Glassworkers in France," Big Dan explained, "were often gentlemen of nobility. They contributed much to art and history. America is in need of great art to speak for her industries. Here in Pittsburgh is the heartbeat of them all. Here we make the things that will build all that vast country across the Mississippi. Right here on these three rivers the saga of the West begins. Listen to it, Stephen, my boy. Speak for America in glass."

There was silence in the room when Big Dan ceased speaking. Jenny reached for Stephen's hand and they stood like two starry-eyed children at the beginning of a long journey. They were both seeing strange and wonderful things.

Finally Jenny spoke impulsively. "Is Stephen apprenticed to you now, sir? Really apprenticed, I mean?"

Big Dan's seriousness faded.

"He's apprenticed to me up to his neck—" he chuckled—"beginning tomorrow morning."

Jenny looked at the calendar on his desk. "October 7, 1850," she murmured softly.

Big Dan rose from his chair and placed the little chapel on the shelf next to his famous ruby glass.

"We'll leave this here for the present," he said. "I'd like to exhibit it at our glass show. Not as perfection, you understand—" he smiled again as he looked at Jenny—"it's the spirit of this thing that counts."

"I understand," she said.

Stephen said nothing at all. He merely stood there, listening. He had said all that he could say to Big Dan when he had fashioned his little star window.

 *Ten*

Rosalie's Carriage

October 7, 1850

Smoke, accompanied by fog, shrouded the city down in the valley. Fog so thick you could cut it with a knife, so Jenny said. But she and Stephen stood above it, at the head of the steps leading down from Goat Hill, feeling high and glad for the sunlight up here on the hills above the rivers, feeling it as a golden badge of courage shining for them alone on this, Stephen's day.

They made a dramatic descent this morning. As on the day they had had their first glimpse of the rivers, each felt that this hour was writing something indelible on their hearts. Just as Stephen had felt a touch of grandeur in making his little star window, they both felt it now. Today would mark, they were sure, the beginning of a steep ascent to achievement. Much of their feeling was due to the serious quest imposed on them by Big Dan. The sound of the faraway places he had mentioned had alerted them like a bugle call. "Egypt . . . Phoenicia . . . Venice . . . Rome . . . you've got to see the great pictorial windows in Old World cathedrals."

Even Jenny, in all her ambitious dreaming, had never carried her plans for Stephen that far—Egypt, Phoenicia, Venice,

Rome. And today—this very morning in dingy, dirty, downtown Pittsburgh—their way was pointed in these directions with the straightness of an arrow.

When they walked across the bridge, the rivers below were lost in fog. So were the buildings of the city. They were able to see within only a small circumference around them. The smoke and grime in the fog made Jenny's nose and throat burn.

"If Pittsburgh gets any smokier," she said hoarsely, "I shall have to be like a lot of girls and wear only black dresses."

"I don't like 'em."

"I don't either," she laughed, "but it's becoming a practice. A black dress with a white frill for trimming shows the dirt less than a lighter one."

"But look how often you'd have to wash the frills."

"Guess you're right. It's just as much work one way as the other."

"I'd like you to look pretty," Stephen astonished her by saying. "To wear bright colors like Rosalie Blakewell."

Jenny smiled a bit ruefully. "If only I had an Azalea to do the laundering, I'd wear them all the time."

They came to the Monongahela House and prepared to go in different directions. Jenny put her hand on Stephen's shoulder.

"Good luck, Stevie. Good luck in all you do today, and don't fall off that apprentice's stool. It looks awfully high."

"If Jo can manage to sit on it," Stephen laughed, "I guess I can."

"Going to show him your star window?"

"Not unless Big Dan says so. And anyhow he's got it on his shelf with all his ruby glassware."

"That's where it belongs. Up there with the best."

"Aw, you're just prejudiced."

"Not prejudiced, Stevie. Proud."

"Wait for pride till we get to Egypt." Stephen grinned.

"Don't worry. We'll make it." She looked at him critically. "And before you go into Big Dan's office, be sure to wash your face again. And don't forget your neck. It's grimy."

"I will. See you tonight."

She called after him as he turned to go. "I'll be late getting home tonight, Stevie."

"Why?"

"I've promised to take Carlotta shopping."

He came back to her for a moment. "You're going to buy her the new dress?"

"Not the dress, Stevie darling, only the trimmings. We're going to make up the goods she bought before we left the farm."

"But I heard you tell her yourself you're almost out of money."

Jenny smoothed out the frown on his forehead. "I didn't have much, but King has earned ten dollars, thanks to Timothy Drew."

"But you never buy anything for yourself," he protested.

She explained Carlotta's situation. "I'm not just humoring her, Stevie. She really needs the new dress. Since she's learned the folk dances of the mill people, it would be too bad if she couldn't be in their show. It's a church benefit, you know, and Mrs. Kowalski says she can dance the mazurka better than her girls could when they were young."

"I guess she should dance, if it's a benefit." Stephen looked at Jenny's neatly mended shoulder shawl and the darn in her stocking. "But I still think you should buy yourself something."

A strange, new thought occurred to Jenny. Why was Stephen so suddenly concerned about her appearance? Could it be he was taking stock of other girls and comparing her shabbiness with the pretty things they wore? Jo's girl, for instance, or Rosalie Blakewell? It was odd that he had mentioned Rosalie's clothes this morning when they talked of black dresses. Jenny felt a swift heart pang. Every day her world seemed to become a little more complicated than it had been the day before. She wished this business of growing up would not descend on them so swiftly. She would have to respect Stephen's young judgment if she bought only as much as a ribbon for her hair! She smiled at him gaily.

"I'll buy myself a new lace collar, just to celebrate this first day of your apprenticeship."

"I'd like that, Jenny. And buy a blue velvet bow to go with it."

"Away with you!" she laughed. "You'll tempt me beyond endurance! And we'll both be late for work if we don't hurry!"

He turned and walked quickly away, laughing as he went. She watched him vanish into the fog that obscured the entire shore line and blotted out the glass house in an eerie mantle of gray. Down here in the flats it was hard to remember that up on the hills there were warmth and sunlight. Jenny shivered in the early morning dampness and drew her shawl more closely as she hurried across the street.

She was glad when she entered the big busy kitchen of the Monongahela House. Always there was good cheer here: an atmosphere of friendliness in the shining copper kettle singing on the fire, in the smell of good food being cooked by experts. She was becoming rather expert herself, much to Helen's open chagrin. Mrs. Houston had hired a new Viennese pastry cook. He was teaching Jenny how to make Viennese desserts. He was a dreamy-eyed old man who had once owned his own restaurant in the city on the Danube. His mind was a storehouse of memories, from which he drew fantastic tales of Old World castles, the mad King Ludwig of Bavaria and his Isle of Roses, and the madcap little Elizabeth who everyone said would one day become the Empress of Austria. She was more beautiful, so the pastry cook said, than any angel in heaven.

He was very fond of Jenny and always called her "Jenny *Liebling.*" When she did something wrong in mixing or baking he had a lovable way of throwing up both hands and crying out, grieved: "*Ach Gott!* Jenny *Liebling!*"

Jenny loved working with old Franz. Since she had brought the brood to Pittsburgh, it seemed that all the rest of the world had suddenly come closer to them. Big Dan and his glass from Bohemia. Anna Houston from England. Franz and his pastries from the storybook world of Vienna. The castles of Scotland and Andrew Carnegie. Carlotta and her wanderings among the Irish, German and Polish families on Goat Hill. And again in this kitchen, the sloe-eyed Helen whose family came from Italy, and who, as time went on, still kept watching Jenny like a hawk. Yes, Jenny and the brood were finding many worlds here within a small world of their own.

Old Franz was waiting for her this morning. When he saw her come into the kitchen he suddenly beamed with delight.

"Jenny *Liebling! Ach,* you are late on such a morning!"

"And why such a morning?" she laughed.

He put on his pastry cook's cap upside down, fumbled with his big white apron.

"Wait!" Jenny stopped his next words gaily.

"And why should I wait, yes?"

She reached up and straightened his stiffly starched cap. "Because your cap is upside down and you look very funny."

"I shall not look funny tomorrow night. And neither shall you."

"And just what happens tomorrow night?"

"The *River Queen* will be in port and the Blakewells are giving a party in their big house on the hill." Old Franz failed to notice that Jenny was suddenly pale and her lips parted as though she were breathing unevenly as he rattled on: "You and I are to make the pastries and to go up there to help the servants." He rolled his eyes ecstatically and boasted, "We shall make our pink whipped cream puffs—and ah, such pink whipped cream puffs! Yes, Jenny *Liebling?*"

She made a valiant effort to agree with him. She would not, she mentally resolved, let old Franz or Mrs. Houston, or anyone else for that matter, know what her feelings were toward Christopher.

The last time she had seen him she had run away and wept, sitting on a cabbage box. Then she had pleaded a headache and gone home, utterly defeated by her own emotion. That could not happen again. It must not. As she had sternly told herself then, Christopher of the *River Queen,* and she, Jenny Bayard of Goat Hill, belonged to two different worlds as surely as if each was existing on a different planet.

His world was a luxurious one, but her world was also good. It had Stephen and his wonderful talent, it had warmth and affection in their clinger and extravagant young dreams of what they would someday become. If she accepted this with the pride it deserved, surely she could go even into the Blakewell house and do her job with dignity. It wouldn't be fair to Mrs. Houston to refuse to go. Her job was "pastries and desserts" and if it required going to the big house up there on the hill, she would somehow make herself go.

There were nine chances out of ten that she wouldn't even see the party. Rosalie would be busy with her guests, and surely Christopher would not invade the kitchen domain. And even if he did, she had to get over this silliness about him sometime. Perhaps if she could see him as a young man among his own kind she would not have this crazy "desire of the moth for the star" interest in him. Yes, she would go with old Franz to the Blakewells'. If she saw John Blakewell, well and good. She knew where she stood with him. And if she saw Rosalie, Christopher or even "uppity Mrs. Blakewell" as Carlotta called her, she would have to cope with that situation when it arrived. So Jenny planned her line of conduct bravely and refused to listen to a still, small, mocking voice that seemed to come from somewhere in the region of her heart.

She and Franz were still planning Viennese delicacies when Carlotta appeared that afternoon. So eager was she to go shopping that the fact that she had come fully forty minutes too soon concerned her not in the least. She arrived hatless, her hair romantically piled in a cluster of curls on the top of her head, a pair of bright green cotton mittens on her hands, and a green leather belt clasped around her small waist. She felt that she looked beautiful and in some indefinable way she actually did. Perhaps it was her very aliveness, or only that shining red-gold hair, of which she was so proud, that made an aureole around her lovely little heart shaped face.

"I'm ready, Jenny," she caroled blithely.

Jenny surveyed her, unimpressed. "Sit down, Carlotta. You've come too early."

Carlotta didn't sit down. She fidgeted. "But I want to go to Horne's!"

"Horne's!" echoed Jenny.

"They've got trimmings by the mile. And you should see the colors!"

"Horne's is a good store," said old Franz.

"It's a very good store," said Jenny. "I would love to shop there with Carlotta." She turned to her sister gravely. "But did you bother to ask what their trimmings might cost? Or don't you know they cater to the carriage trade?"

Carlotta smiled impishly. "Market Street was lined with carriages. You should have seen the coachmen helping ladies across the puddles! I saw one girl in a gray chinchilla suit——"

Jenny realized that Carlotta was off, and if she didn't immediately stop her the entire kitchen staff of the Monongahela House would be entertained by her comments on fashions.

She took off her apron and looked at old Franz. "I wonder if I might leave now and make it up by coming in a half hour earlier tomorrow morning?"

Old Franz shook his head and smiled indulgently at Carlotta. "Sure, Jenny *Liebling*, you go. I'll finish these desserts."

Carlotta hugged him unceremoniously. "I like you, Franz. And you may call me 'Carlotta *Liebling*.'"

He looked enormously pleased as he grumbled, "*Ach Gott*, Carlotta *Liebling*, you better go put on a hat or you'll catch your death of cold."

Jenny took a little old head shawl down from a hook. "Put this on," she ordered Carlotta. "Franz is right."

As they left the kitchen, both were completely unaware

that Helen's eyes followed them. She smiled a little to herself, and in that smile lay something like truimph.

As they walked up to Market Street, Carlotta babbled incessantly. She had looked at trimmings in many stores, she told Jenny, but only at Horne's could she get the bright yellow and red strips of insertion that she wanted for her dancing dress. The Poles and Hungarians adored bright colors. When she danced the mazurka she wanted to look as though she had come straight from one of their native villages.

They had entered the store and gone up to a counter when Carlotta suddenly nudged Jenny. "Look!"

"Now what?"

Carlotta indicated a girl standing near by. There were twelve clerks in the entire store and three were outdoing themselves to wait on her. She was looking at a glamorous bolt of pink net embroidered with tiny glittering silver sequins. One clerk had partially unrolled it and it was cascading over the counter like a fragile pink cloud.

"It's Rosalie Blakewell," Carlotta told Jenny. "And look at her clothes! A green velvet suit trimmed with leopard!"

"Quiet! Do you want her to hear you?"

Carlotta quieted but she was too late. Rosalie had undoubtedly heard. She turned away from the counter and approached them with a smile. Jenny noted the grace with which she held out a velvet-gloved hand.

"I couldn't help hearing my name," she said graciously, "and I'm awfully glad to see you both."

"Thank you," said Jenny, smiling.

Rosalie drew them aside in the aisle. "I've been begging father to bring me to see you ever since that night he had so much fun at your house. He's been wanting to bring me, too, but he was away on business and since he's come back we scarcely ever see him ourselves. He's so awfully busy building boats."

Jenny was glad to hear this. Somehow she had worried a little because John Blakewell had not been to see them since the night he had missed the party on the *River Queen*. She didn't believe he had been offended, nor could she believe that he had forgotten them.

"I wish you would come," Carlotta said impulsively.

Rosalie looked at pretty Carlotta, her eyes sparkling with enthusiasm.

"I'll tell you what let's do. Let's hurry and buy what we want, then let me drive you home in my carriage."

"Oh, Jenny, let's!" Carlotta was bubbling over.

Jenny yielded graciously enough but she had the feeling it wouldn't be an easy thing to do. It would be entirely possible for Rosalie to hurry her shopping. All she had to do was pick and choose, but Jenny had to count pennies. Luckily, however, the clerk showed her trimmings marked down as remnants, so she bought them quickly. She would wait, she decided, for a more appropriate time to buy the lace collar she had promised Stephen to get for herself.

Rosalie's own little carriage with its smart pair of dapple-grays drew up to the entrance as they left the store. A young boy sat on the driver's seat holding highly polished reins. Inside, the carriage was upholstered in rose-colored plush, lovely enough for a princess. There was a carriage robe of soft white fur.

"Oh!" Carlotta uttered one musical syllable as they stepped into it.

"You like my carriage?" Rosalie laughed.

"Like it!" Carlotta settled herself in the seat with undisguised joy in luxury.

Rosalie explained that the carriage had been a birthday present from her father on her sixteenth birthday. She was so utterly free from artificiality that Jenny delighted in hearing her talk. She had been right in her first estimate of Rosalie Blakewell, she decided now. Rosalie was like her father. Gay, generous, filled with sheer joy in living.

"Did you buy the pink net?" Carlotta asked curiously.

"Yes, I thought it rather pretty."

Rosalie told them she wanted a pink net scarf to go with a blue satin dress she would wear the following evening. Jenny didn't tell her that she knew about the party; that she would be working in the kitchen downstairs while Rosalie danced with Christopher in the drawing room.

Jenny leaned back on the rose-colored seat as the carriage crossed the bridge and made its way through murk and fog toward Goat Hill. It was like a separate little rose-colored world in here, safe and lovely and protected. If she didn't look out through the shining glass windows at the wet, muddy streets and dingy buildings, the inside of this carriage made her feel that there was no workaday world to combat, that life was a perpetual sunrise heralding a beautiful day. Jenny heard Rosalie laugh gaily as Carlotta rambled on vivaciously. Suddenly she closed her eyes. She had no business scolding Carlotta for her luxury-loving tendencies, no business at all, she thought whimsically. This rose-colored carriage was going ridiculously straight to her own head!

 *Eleven*

Jenny at the Blakewells'

*L*ittle Mady was standing in the doorway of the clinger when Rosalie's carriage drew up in front. She was waiting for her sisters to come home. Her eyes fairly popped out of her head when the boy climbed down from the driver's seat, opened the door ceremoniously, and Carlotta descended from the carriage with a distinct air of grandeur. Mady had a swift glimpse of a rose-colored interior like the inside of a tufted-velvet candy box. Then Jenny stepped out and her eyes popped again.

"Heavenly days!" Her voice was a whisper of wonder.

A moment later Rosalie emerged, and Mady was entranced by the picture she made in her green velvet suit and bonnet, her incredibly golden hair hanging in clusters of curls to her shoulders.

"Heavenly days!" Mady said again, and stood blinking as though this lovely carriage in front of their crooked little house was casting a spell on her.

Being Mady, however, she couldn't blink very long without attempting to investigate. She fairly flew down the steps and out into the street. "Oh, what a beautiful carriage!"

Carlotta looked at her sympathetically. She felt rather sorry for Mady because she had missed the ride.

"Why don't you sit in it?" she suggested. "Miss Rosalie won't mind."

"May I?" Mady's eyes were dancing with anticipation.

"Climb in and sit as long as you like!" answered Rosalie, laughing.

Jenny laid a detaining hand on Mady's small shoulder. "Are your hands clean?"

"Of course they're clean. Look!"

Jenny inspected them carefully. She was taking no chances with that rose-colored upholstery.

"They'll do, but don't stay out here too long. Miss Rosalie's coming in to have a cup of tea."

Mady was thrilled with delight. "Everything happens so—so unexpected!"

Unexpected as it was, the tea was a great success. Rosalie liked the little clinger as much as her father had. There was no condescension about her whatever. She had none of the gracious-lady-inspecting-a-hovel air. She liked the clinger because it was homey and there was no formal restraint. One could laugh, or even cry—she felt certain—without worrying about being "indelicate," "emotional" or "indiscreet"—all favorite terms of her mother's. And oddly enough she felt a warmth here that did not seem to come from the heat of the kitchen stove or even the steam from the teapot. She did not define it as family closeness or the love of one human heart for another, but in a subconscious way she realized that this was what it actually was. This little clinger family was held together by the deep affection possible only when human beings have shared troubled times and hardships which seem insurmountable.

That was one thing being rich made one miss, Rosalie thought a little sadly. "Without great sorrow," a line in her copy book had read, "there can be no great joy." Rosalie looked around her. The children in this shabby little house knew both, she was sure, in a way she had never known.

"More tea?" Jenny filled her cup.

"Thank you," said Rosalie. Then as she sipped it gracefully, she questioned, "What do you all do on Saturdays?"

"Saturdays?" repeated Jenny.

"Well, say, on a Saturday afternoon."

"I clean house," said Mady with a grimace.

"I do the marketing." Carlotta frowned.

Jenny laughed at the grim resignation in their voices. "And I work at the hotel," she explained. "Saturday is our busy day."

Rosalie looked incredulous. "Don't you ever have a holiday?"

"Sundays," said Jenny, "after church."

"Any particular church?"

Carlotta interrupted as Jenny was about to answer. "We like the little one on the South Side in the mornings, but sometimes on Sunday evenings we go to the big First Presbyterian Church in the city."

"And we go early," supplemented Jenny. "The children like to watch the sexton light the hundred candles in that big crystal chandelier."

Rosalie smiled. "That's quite a famous fixture. General O'Hara presented it to the church, so Father says 'as a token of a glowing desire to promote the luster of this enlightened society.'"

"My goodness!" said Mady, impressed. "I didn't know all that went with those candles."

Rosalie looked at the little heart-shaped gold watch pinned

to her ribbon belt. "Mercy! I had no idea it was so late! I must be leaving!"

Jenny held out her hand as Rosalie rose to go. "Thank you for bringing us home in your carriage."

"We'll have to do this again." Rosalie pressed her hand warmly. "It was fun, wasn't it?"

As Rosalie settled herself in the carriage, Jenny was thinking how surprised she would be if she knew that tomorrow evening Jenny would be coming up to the Blakewell kitchen with old Franz. She had no idea why she had not told her, apart from the fact that she wanted any friendship that might grow between them to be begun by Rosalie. It was not that she felt inferior, or that she was putting up the formal barrier that exists between mistress and servant. The fact that she would be at the Blakewells' only as part of her work on the staff of the Monongahela House made her no servant of theirs at all. It was simply that her work was one thing, and any contact she might have with Rosalie was another. Jenny didn't believe in mixing the various channels of her existence unless they inevitably flowed together.

Carlotta sighed as Rosalie waved and the carriage moved away. "Sometime I shall have a carriage of my own," she vowed.

"With a rose-colored lining and two dapple-grays," added Mady.

Jenny remembered their words the next evening as she walked up to the Blakewell house and saw the carriages in the driveway. There was none so pretty or graceful of line as Rosalie's, nevertheless they all looked quite in keeping with what must be the background of her friends. Jenny wondered if Christopher had arrived in a carriage and if so, which one.

Walking toward the house, she studied its many windows, all ablaze with candlelight. A group of laughing young people was being welcomed by Samson at the front door. Jenny heard the soft swish of silk and velvet. She could almost smell the fragrance of the hothouse flowers the girls wore in their hair. As they went into the hall she caught a glimpse of a golden circle of light made by the crystal chandelier with all fifty candles burning. Its prisms reflected the candle flames until the whole graceful fixture became as tremulous and beautiful as a thousand twinkling stars festooned on silver chains.

Jenny remembered with a tug at her heart the first day she had come here. How high had been the hopes of her little brood, how fascinated Stephen had been by the intricate workmanship of that chandelier! It seemed faraway and long ago and yet what little time had actually passed and how really far they had come since then!

She was glad now that Mrs. Blakewell had forced them to create their own little world apart from all this. In their very fight for existence in their clinger they had somehow gained greater strength and sufficiency than she now felt they could have mustered here. Surely her mother would have thought so, too, and would understand how Jenny could feel even grateful to Mrs. Blakewell for her lack of understanding that day they had arrived. She wondered if Mrs. Blakewell knew that Mrs. Houston had sent her to help in the kitchen tonight. Jenny was glad she had no one to answer to but Franz. She knew that she could please him.

She made her way to the kitchen door at the back of the house. Franz had already arrived. He was in earnest discussion with Mrs. Blakewell's housekeeper concerning the arrangement of the pastries on the flower-tinted Sèvres china plates, and the time they should be served. He looked up, pleased, as he saw Jenny unfolding her little white apron.

"Ah, Jenny *Liebling*, it's good you have come."

"Am I late?"

"No, you are not late." He smiled. "But there are so many plates and so many cream puffs!"

"Not to mention the chocolate bonbon cakes and the angel-food squares and the queen's fruit tarts," said Jenny, as she went immediately to work.

Aside from the housekeeper there were five servants bustling about the big kitchen. It was pleasant to be busy with so many party concoctions, now and then to catch the sound of laughter from upstairs, and to hear the strains of the new waltz music everyone was talking about. It was Viennese dance music. Old Franz had a name for it. "Strauss," he said. "Johann Strauss!" And then he gave a rapturous report about the great waltz king of the city of his birth.

Jenny was decorating a cake with tiny sugar bluebirds when John Blakewell entered the kitchen. It was his habit to look in on the servants when there was a party in the house. They loved to see him come because he was always gay. The older servants tempted him with choice samples of the feast which would be served upstairs later in the evening. Tonight he and Jenny discovered each other simultaneously. He strode across the room to her, beaming with welcome.

"Jenny! It can't really be you!"

The gladness in his voice and his genuine pleasure in her being there warmed her heart.

"Oh, but it is, Mr. Blakewell! Mrs. Houston sent me to help Franz with the pastries."

"Wonderful!" he murmured. "Wonderful!" Then with extravagant praise, he added, "I have never seen such gorgeous pastries in my life!"

Old Franz practically purred. He took as much pride in being the perfect pastry cook as Big Dan took in making fine glass. Jenny smiled as he and John Blakewell entered into an animated discussion of how he had made the cakes they both considered works of art.

Finally John Blakewell turned back to her. "I want you to come with me, Jenny. There's something I must show you. Take off your apron and come upstairs."

"Upstairs!"

"And why not?" he asked pleasantly.

She looked at him with troubled eyes. She couldn't very well say that she did not want to risk going where she might run into Christopher. John Blakewell saw her glance furtively down at her dress and then touch her hair, embarrassed. Immediately he understood. He was an unthinking fool, he upbraided himself. Naturally Jenny would feel this way with all those young things upstairs dressed in fancy frills and furbelows! He spoke again smiling.

"I want to show you something you'll like. And if you don't want to go through the parlor we'll be really adventurous and go up the back stairs!"

Jenny could have hugged him. She took off her apron instead. He held out his hand to her gaily. Together they crossed the kitchen, went up a few painted steps, and opened a door to a winding stairway.

The moment John Blakewell opened that door Jenny had a strange feeling. Immediately she had the sensation that she had been here before. If he had told her that he and her mother (little older than she was now) had often sat and talked on these stairs, she would not have been surprised. Her mother had lived in this house nine years, long before Mrs. Blakewell had known that it existed. The thought seemed to make it strangely familiar to Jenny, as though she, too, had been a part of it.

Her feeling became even stronger when they had climbed a second long flight of stairs and John Blakewell stopped by a door to a room at the back of the house.

He turned to her, his infectious smile suddenly tender. "This was your mother's room, Jenny. It is almost the same as when she was here and I wanted you to see it."

Jenny was silent for a moment, then she said very softly, "I think that I want to more than anything else I know of."

He opened the door and went in first. She watched him strike a match and light a kerosene lamp. It seemed to set the room aglow. Softly its radiance touched the four-poster bed with its crisp, blue-flowered canopy, a washstand with a blue-flowered bowl, and a charming little dressing table with an oval mirror in a maple frame. This room was not an outsider's room, Jenny thought instantly. It was a room that had been loved, and showed her mother to have been a respected and intimate part of this household. She remembered things she had been told about her mother's life when she had lived in this house. Happy memories seemed to linger still in this room. Was it because of such contentment that her mother had embroidered in needlework that motto hung on the wall—"Count only happy hours"? And was it because of these words that Jenny did not feel quite so poignantly the sadness she might have felt, but only warmth that seemed to embrace her?

John Blakewell watched her kindly as she walked slowly across the room to the window. Red skies at night! The red skies of the mill district! How often her mother must have stood here and looked out at their magnificence, then at the three rivers in the valley far below. It came to Jenny while she stood there that it was little wonder she and the children felt so vibrantly a part of it all—the city, the rivers, the hills and even this Blakewell house. All had been part of their mother's life; perhaps hereditary memories had carried it into theirs. She turned to John Blakewell, glowing. "I love this room because I know she was happy here."

He came to her, gently cupped her face in his hands. "I like you for saying that, Jenny, and I hope you will be a good friend to Rosalie. She told me abut her visit with you and how wonderful it was for her."

"Wonderful for her!"

He smiled, and, for the first time since she had known him, his smile held a suggestion of sadness.

"I believe that in her heart Rosalie is lonely. She's had only formal contacts with people." Jenny wondered if he had arrived at this conclusion because Mrs. Blakewell was so strictly formal, as he continued, "You are real as your mother was, Jenny. Real and strong and true."

She looked at him steadily, thinking what his wife's reaction would be if she knew what he was daring to say to the riffraff with which she classed Jenny.

"Thank you, Mr. Blakewell. You're very kind to me."

"Nonsense," he said, and seemed suddenly happy.

Strange, thought Jenny now, that people like the Blakewells should have heart's need of clinger people like the Bayards. Old Marsha Blakewell must have needed her mother or there would not have been a room like this in her house. Rosalie lonely, living so gaily! How odd, marveled Jenny. *How very odd!*

 Twelve

Christopher

They heard a gay ripple of laughter as they left the little bedroom and went into the hall. Rosalie was standing at the top of the winding, white stairway surrounded by a bevy of girls in party dresses as flower-tinted as a garden.

"Oh, how exciting!" Rosalie was saying. "Just to think that Elizabeth dared!"

A dark-haired girl with a red rose in her hair laughed mockingly. "Who wouldn't dare to elope with David? I would myself!"

Jenny involuntarily drew John Blakewell back into the shadow of a curtained window. Romantic strains of music came up from the parlors below.

A girl in yellow fingered a beribboned program tied to her wrist. "There's the first dance! And I for one am not going to miss it!"

"Nor I!"
"Nor I!"
"Nor I!"

There was the rustle of satin as they picked up their skirts and hurried down to the landing on the stairs. Rosalie fol-

lowed them, laughing. Suddenly when she reached the landing she made a dead stop.

"You go on down," she told the others. "I'll be with you in a
moment."

She came back up into the hall. The light of many candles
in cut-glass brackets on the wall seemed to make a blue illu-
sion of the blueness of her party dress. It made the sapphires
surrounding an old-fashioned cameo necklace burn with the
deep blueness of a flame. And, as always, her hair was a golden
halo as incredibly lovely as a veil of golden mist. Jenny caught
her breath as she was once again made suddenly aware of
this fragile girl's beauty.

"Rosalie!" John Blakewell intercepted her as she was about
to pass them.

"Father!" Discovering Jenny, Rosalie held out both hands.
"And Jenny! Well, I am surprised!"

"Jenny's helping in the kitchen. She was sent to help with
the pastries. And I've just been showing her what used to be
her mother's room."

Rosalie looked at Jenny sympathetically. "Sounds like a
wonderful evening for you."

"It is!"

"But how could it be?"

Jenny laughed at Rosalie's chagrin. "Just to see all this, I
guess."

"Want to see *my* room?"

"I'd love to."

John Blakewell looked pleased. "Run along then. Meanwhile, I'll drop in on your mother."

Rosalie put a silencing finger lightly against his lips. "Don't
tell her I've left my guests!"

"I don't know a thing about it!" He grinned understandingly as he strode down the hall.

Jenny said soberly as Rosalie flung an arm around her waist, "Perhaps your mother wouldn't approve of my being in your room."

"Don't think about that," Rosalie surprised her by answering.

Once across the threshold, Jenny forgot to worry whether or not Mrs. Blakewell would approve or disapprove. This bedroom of Rosalie's seemed dedicated to all the lovely things a girl every dreamed of. It was so feminine, so enchanting that Jenny had the same impulsive longing luxury-loving little Carlotta would most certainly have had: "Oh, for a room like this of my own!"

From the ivory-framed French cheval-glass mirror in which one could see one's whole self to the fireplace decorated with dancing silhouettes, it was entrancing. The French Provençal furniture was painted with pink and blue garlands of flowers; the ivory bed was the shape of a swan and had been brought by Rosalie's father from an exposition in Paris. The dressing table with its flowered satin skirt sparkled with cut-crystal bottles of eau de cologne and fine perfumes. When Rosalie opened the door to her wardrobe, Jenny actually gasped. Little quilted satin hangers held dress after dress, countless, it seemed, for every occasion. A dozen slipper trees stood in a row—and when it came to hats and bonnets! They seemed a bewildering array of flowers and ribbons and saucy little feathers curled like the plumes of Empress Eugénie.

"Now, let's see, where's that green satin?" Rosalie moved the hangers about. "I never know where anything is, so Florabelle tells me."

"Who's Florabelle?"

"She's supposed to be my personal maid but she's never around when I want her."

Jenny smiled. "A little like Carlotta, I'd say."

"Glory be! Here's that dress!"

Rosalie took the green satin frock out of the wardrobe and held it up for Jenny's inspection. "Like it?"

"It's beautiful!"

Rosalie laid the dress on the bed. It was the green of the sea and had tiny puff sleeves that were mere caps, a heart-shaped neckline, softly draped. Small pink flowers adorned the tight-fitting basque waist, and the skirt fell in glistening flounces and folds.

"Think it would fit Carlotta?" asked Rosalie. "It's too small for me and I'd like her to have it."

"You would! How very nice!"

Rosalie smiled reminiscently. "She'd take to it, I think. Her interest in fashions seemed endless."

Jenny eyed the dress critically. "I think I could alter it to fit her."

Rosalie swept it up from the bed. "Take it home with you tonight."

"Carlotta will parade like a peacock, and——"

Her words were interrupted by a knock on the door. Rosalie opened it to a pretty little girl in a maid's apron and cap whom Jenny suspected at once must be Florabelle.

"Your mother's looking for you, Miss Rosalie," she said softly. "She's on her way downstairs."

"I'd better fly," said Rosalie.

"And old Franz will be looking for me." Jenny moved toward the door. "Many thanks for the dress. And for showing me this lovely room."

"I've loved it," said Rosalie. "I'll see you later."

As Jenny made her way back down the kitchen stairway, she could hear music played to waltz time. If she had gone down the front stairs as John Blakewell had at first intended, she might have had a glimpse of Christopher, she thought wistfully. She hugged the dress she was carrying close to her heart.

Suppose, she dreamed daringly, just suppose this was her dress and she was arrayed in it for the party, standing on that landing where those other girls had stood. Suppose she was waiting for Christopher to lead her in the waltz! Jenny drew a deep sigh. By this time, she was sure, Christopher would have quite forgotten that morning on the wharf. And if he were actually upstairs dancing, it would be with Rosalie or perhaps that glamorous girl in yellow. Jenny sighed again as she took hold of the kitchen doorknob and entered the hub-bub of the basement floor.

Old Franz lifted reproachful eyes above a three-tiered plate of fruit tarts.

"*Ach*, Jenny *Liebling*, you have deserted me!"

Jenny smiled at his melancholy. "But Franz, I've been seeing wonderful things! The room my mother used to have here——"

His eyes were suddenly tender as he put an awkward hand on her shoulder. "*Ja*, that was wonderful, Jenny. And remember, *Liebling*, no one ever dies. Your mamma—no one——"

"I believe that too," she said softly.

"And what else did you see?"

"Pretty girls in party dresses, and Rosalie's lovely room. And she gave me this dress for Carlotta."

Old Franz's eyes twinkled. "*Ach*, I should like to be around when the little minx puts it on!"

Jenny folded the dress and crossed the room to the kitchen cupboard where she had hung her apron. She put the dress on the shelf and tied the strings of her frilly little apron around her waist. A mirror hung on the cupboard door. As she looked into it, adjusting a maid's cap on her curls, she thought again of the music and dancing upstairs. She thought again of Christopher. Suddenly she frowned at her reflection.

If you were working for anyone else but old Franz, she thought, you would be properly scolded for not keeping your mind on your work!

She turned away from the mirror and went slowly back to the pastry table. Old Franz pushed an empty tray toward her. "Put the chocolate cakes on this."

In the busy hour that followed, Jenny had the curious sensation of having a double self. One part of her was upstairs dancing with that haunting young man she had seen only once in her life, the other part was down here in the kitchen working with trays and pastries, polishing pink glass plates on which they were to be served.

You're having a bad case of hallucinations, she reprimanded herself mentally. After all, you *are* down here and it's down here you belong!

But the hallucinations seemed to continue the whole evening. Sometimes they had only the soft, roselike quality of a young girl's dream; then as the sound of a new melody drifted down to Jenny's listening ears, they became like storm clouds, one with the protest in her heart. Rosalie. The other girls dancing in their party dresses. Jenny suddenly longed for all that too. No, it was not quite all that. Wildfire burned her cheeks as she confessed to herself that most of all she wanted to see Christopher again. The very fact of his proximity was making her heart turn cartwheels. She punished herself by wishing that the party was over and that she was free to go home.

So the busy evening passed. Mechanically she sorted pastries, bonbons and salted nuts, and refilled the big crystal punch bowls, brought down from the dining room, with hot, strongly spiced lemonade. When the servants began to serve the charming little supper, she had already taken off her apron and received Franz's permission to leave.

"You look white, Jenny *Liebling*," he said sympathetically. "You need more sleep than an old man like me. *Ach*, run along home now, like a good girl."

When she protested that there was till much work to be done, he patted her shoulder, saying gravely, "Your little brood will be waiting—away with you now!"

The house was still ablaze with lights. The enchanting music of another waltz could be heard as she closed the kitchen door and went out into the night. She felt lonely and depressed as she left the circle of its warmth, but it did not occur to her to be afraid. She was accustomed to walking in darkness. There had been no gas lights on the farm, and it was not really pitch-dark tonight because there was a moon. A crazy little crooked moon that rocked in and out of cloud banks like a merry little boat tossing about on a star-spangled sea. And below her was the drama of the city, lighted with blazing furnaces that made the moon and the street lights seem dim.

She walked at a good pace, carrying the little cardboard box of pastries Franz had salvaged for her to take home. She was glad that she had the children to go home to. How awful it would have been, she thought, if there were no little brood and she had had to leave that big house with its music and dancing for a clinger that was empty and forlorn. Jenny shivered, growing clammy and cold at the thought.

She was walking around a bend in the road when she heard the sound of horses' feet velvetly clopping along in the dust. A carriage was coming down the road behind her. She was about to step aside to let it pass when she heard the driver give the word to the horses to stop. Suddenly her heart seemed to skip a beat. Here she was on this isolated road, and in spite of the moon it was almost midnight! The emotional intensity through which she had passed this evening, coupled with the surge of fear now racing through her, made Jenny clutch her little blue shawl with cold fingers. She kept walking on steadily, afraid to look back.

"I beg your pardon——"

It was another voice now, not the driver's, a gentleman's voice, she was sure. It had a vaguely familiar sound and yet—— She turned quickly about. By the golden light of the carriage lamps, Jenny saw Christopher sitting forward on the carriage seat about to open the carriage door. A moment later, he stood facing her on the road. He made a slight bow, speaking meanwhile, with charming respect.

"I saw you leave the Blakewell house, miss, but you had already gone through the gate by the time my carriage was ready. It's very late and if you would allow me——"

As Jenny turned her face toward the full glow of the carriage lamps, he stopped speaking suddenly. Then, after a moment's close scrutiny he continued with young and gay impetuousness, "Say! You're not a stranger! I've seen you before! No—don't tell me now——"

Something like magic kindled a quick glow in Jenny's heart. This tall, merry lad with thick bright hair and a freckled nose held an absurd and lovely power over her without even half trying! She stood smiling up at him shyly as he went on, "You vanished that day on the wharf, you know, simply vanished in thin air!"

"I—I didn't——" Jenny began to protest.

He held out his hand in a friendly fashion. "Let me help you into the carriage. Tell me where to take you, then we'll get things straight."

Once inside his carriage, Jenny sank back against plush upholstery that was the gray of old silver. It was finished with deep maroon leather bands which highlighted the flawless mahogany trim of the woodwork. As she heard Christopher give orders to his driver to proceed to Goat Hill, she felt suddenly transported to a world of wealth and well-being to which she would have never dared to aspire. This was not *really* happening, she thought, half-bewildered. I am not *really* in Christopher's carriage, for all the world like Cinderella in her glass coach! It can't be, it just can't be! I'm dreaming one of Mady's fairy tales! The sound of Christopher's voice made her realize the truth of her situation—yes, it was all real and actual.

"I call it gross ingratitude," he was bantering, "to run away from a gentleman who practically saved your life. Shame on you, Miss Jenny!"

"Miss Jenny." So he really remembered her name! That, too, seemed strange and rather wonderful.

"I—I wasn't ungrateful." She took his words seriously.

Christopher laughed as he stretched his long legs, leaned back in the seat and made himself comfortable. "Don't look so conscience-stricken," he teased. "I'm only joking."

Jenny wished that she had a gay gift of speech. Rosalie had it, she knew. So, in a way, did Helen Corrado. Appropriate words seemed to fall so easily from their lips. Her own lips were hot and dry and her tongue seemed tied into knots! Why wasn't she like them, she wondered? Why couldn't she think of the right thing to say?

Christopher's face was turned toward her thoughtfully. "Now, why did you run away? Honestly, I mean?"

A rush of confusion overwhelmed her. She couldn't very well confess that Rosalie's mother had bluntly asked her to leave the wharf, or that she had really gone because she had had a hole in her shoe! She looked at him helplessly while rosy color crept up from her throat toward her chin.

"It doesn't matter," he laughed. "Really, it doesn't. You're not in a prisoner's box, you know. But I can't help but wonder where you were hiding at Blakewells' tonight, because I didn't see you at the party."

Jenny hesitated a moment before she said slowly, "I wasn't at the party. I work on the pastry staff at the Monongahela House and I was sent to the Blakewells' to help with the desserts."

"Then you were down in the kitchen all evening?"

She nodded a bit defiantly, speaking meanwhile with a certain pride which she didn't realize sprang from her consciousness of the difference between his social status and hers. "Yes, I was down in the kitchen."

He looked at her steadily. "Wonderful," he breathed. "Why, that's wonderful."

"Wonderful?"

"Isn't there something wonderful about being of use to someone?" His eyes twinkled merrily. "And I don't mean to sound like a preacher!"

Jenny laughed as she answered, "I have to be of use to someone. I've a little brood to take care of."

"Brood? Tell me about it."

So the ride in the carriage became a sort of introduction to their respective lives. When they arrived at the clinger, it was Christopher, however, who had learned more about Jenny than she had learned about him. He was adept at asking questions without seeming at all to pry. He drew her out with a young and almost courtly kindliness that was both heartwarming and gay. By the time his carriage stood still, she had learned that he had left the party early because there was so much yet to be done on board the *River Queen* before it could sail the next day. His father relied on him for the prompt dispatch of much of the ship's business. As he laughingly told her, he was up to his neck in shipboard routine. He had been lucky to sandwich in the party at all.

When he gave her his hand to help her out of the carriage, he smiled at her warmly. "You look very pretty, Jenny, in that little shawl, with your curls blowing——"

"Very pretty." Jenny's heart was racing again. She felt radiantly happy. To think that Christopher thought that she looked "very pretty" when all those girls at the party had worn silks and satins and velvets with lace!

"Thank you," she said softly.

He held her hand a moment longer before he let her go, saying, "It's very late. But I hope to see you tomorrow."

"Tomorrow!" she repeated incredulously.

"The ship doesn't sail until afternoon." He looked down at

her earnestly. "Please let me come and meet your family. We're going to be friends, you know."

Jenny was glad there was only the glow of the carriage lamps to see by. She wouldn't have wanted Christopher to see the sudden light she knew must be shining in her eyes. She answered in a low voice, "Yes, I hope we'll be friends."

"Let's count on it," he urged.

The little girls had heard the carriage stop in front of the house. When Jenny came up the walk, Mady's and Carlotta's heads popped up simultaneously just above the window sill. By the light of the oil lamp she could see their wide-eyed amazement. Jenny being brought home by a beau in a fancy carriage! They stood in their nightgowns and bare feet, entranced, as she opened the door.

"Who is he? Who is he?" they demanded together, rushing to her at once.

"He looked as handsome as Hamlet," added Carlotta.

"What do you know about Hamlet?" asked Jenny gaily.

"I heard all about him at the theater. Maybe he *is* handsome, but he's not as tall, I'll bet, as that fine young gentleman——"

"What fine young gentleman?" Stephen was coming sleepily down from his little room under the eaves.

Jenny faced her brood and laughed. "I should scold you all for not wearing your slippers—but I'll tell you first that the young gentleman was Christopher White, whose father owns the *River Queen.*"

"*The River Queen!*" It was as though she had dropped a bombshell.

"He was at the party," she explained, "and overtook me in his carriage as I was walking. He was good enough to bring me home."

"Oh, my!" breathed little Mady.

"It's fate, that's what it is, just fate," Carlotta decided, convinced.

"Maybe you think so," Stephen almost growled. "It was just circumstance, wasn't it, Jenny?"

Jenny looked, concerned, at the cloud on Stephen's face. Then she, too, spoke with conviction. "Why, yes, Stevie darling, it was just circumstance."

Then Jenny made hot chocolate for them and served the pink whipped cream puffs old Franz had given her. The sea-green dress Rosalie had sent had to be inspected with infinite care, each bit of lace, every ruffle. That this could be for Carlotta! She held it close to her saying fervently, "Thank you, God, for ruffles," repeating the words again and again until Mady insisted she shouldn't take so much of God's time. They would have babbled on all night, it seemed to Jenny, when all she really wanted to do was crawl into bed and relive those moments in Christopher's carriage.

Early next morning, they were still babbling and Jenny was gayer and happier than she had ever been in her life. Carlotta eyed her shrewdly, and then said, "You've changed since last night, Jenny."

"Changed?"

"You laugh quicker, and you are prettier!"

"I think so too," decided Mady.

"She's always laughed and she's always been pretty," Stephen defended Jenny as she was about to speak. "She hasn't changed a bit."

All through this hubbub, it had been Stephen alone who had kept his own counsel. Secretly he also recognized a change in Jenny. He wasn't sure that he liked it. Why should the

Blakewells or even this Christopher intrude on their life in the clinger, and, as Stephen suddenly feared, perhaps try to change it? He didn't want it changed, he thought rebelliously, especially if it changed Jenny. All he wanted her to do was to stay exactly as she was until he himself could someday give her all the good things of life. It was not really a selfish attitude. The reason underlying Stephen's thoughts was a quick and natural fear that Christopher might only be amusing himself with Jenny, and in due time, would revert to girls like Rosalie Blakewell who were an integral part of his own world. Stephen and Jenny had managed together since their parents had died. He had taken a quite masculine pride in their own self-sufficiency.

In the hours that followed, however, Stephen was forced to dispense with much of his resentment. Not only did Christopher add to the general merriment by coming to the clinger as he had promised, but he immediately took such a wholehearted interest in Stephen's glassmaking that the boy felt rather ashamed of himself for his first reaction. Christopher, it developed, knew many interesting things about glass as well as steamboating, as he called it. With a boy like Stephen he adopted no lofty big-brother airs. He was as matter-of-fact with him as he was with John Blakewell or Big Dan.

Christopher's interest in glass was largely associated with buying and shipping it on the rivers. His father's boat rarely sailed without a consignment from some Pittsburgh maker to be carried on the *River Queen* to New Orleans. From there it was merchandised through the South and some of it was sent abroad. He enlightened the Bayards with stories of how he collected glass oddities in the famous French Quarter of New Orleans. Shop after shop, he told them, displayed glass of such beauty and variety that it would make them gasp with excitement. He had bought a moonstone glass pitcher there for his mother when he was eleven years old. She had died when he was twelve.

All in the space of an hour, Christopher won the hearts of the brood. Jenny felt as though a light was going out in the clinger when he rose to go.

"Don't go yet!" protested Carlotta.

"I'm sorry but I must," he answered. Then as he looked at Jenny, he said, "I'd like to stay and teach you how to make French drip coffee for supper, but the *River Queen* sails at sunset and my father insists that I be aboard."

"I'm sorry you're sailing so soon."

"This trip is what we call a week-end berth." He smiled. "We're going back to New Orleans as fast as we can get there. We're carrying rush cargo for Christmas merchandising."

Carlotta looked at him candidly. "I'd like to see the *River Queen*. All three decks and every cabin."

"Carlotta!" Jenny scolded. "You're practically asking Christopher to——"

"She's only a step ahead of me, Jenny. If there were time today, you'd all be seeing the *River Queen* now. But the very next time we're in port——"

"Heavenly days!" anticipated little Mady.

"I shall wear my new dress," said Carlotta.

Christopher laughed as he bid them good-bye. He delighted Stephen by promising to bring him some very special glassware from the French Quarter the next time they were in port. Finally he turned to Jenny who was standing near the doorway.

"Jenny," he requested, "walk a little way with me, won't you?"

"Of course."

Mady ran for a shawl. "I'll go too!"

Carlotta grabbed her by the wrist unceremoniously. "You weren't asked," she said pointedly. "Don't you think you should wait until you are?"

Mady looked crestfallen as Jenny and Christopher went out together. Either they had not heard her speak or, as Carlotta suspected, had not wanted to.

Mady turned to Stephen, demanding, "Do you suppose he's Jenny's beau?"

"Certainly he's her beau," said Carlotta.

"Does a fellow have to be a girl's beau because he takes her for a walk?" growled Stephen. "Besides, Jenny doesn't want a beau. She just likes company."

"I don't believe it," Carlotta said flatly.

"Neither do I," agreed Mady.

And Stephen suddenly looked ill at ease.

Goat Hill was bright with autumn sunshine, and here and there gay foliage flaunted vivid colors. There was the gold of oaks, the scarlet of young maples, the crimson of sumac. Above, the sky was the bright Ming blue of a Chinese plate and far below the rivers sparkled like fairy-tale rivers flowing in silver light.

"Here we are," said Jenny, as though they had come to the parting of the ways.

"Yes, here we are," repeated Christopher raptly, "and look at all that down there in the valley—rivers to the sea——"

Jenny gazed at the city below, the smoke-begrimed town at the tip of the Point, then at the long length of the rivers curving between red and gold wooded hills. She turned to Christopher with shining eyes.

"There's a light in your face again, Jenny. Sometimes you look all bright as though a candle burns in your heart and lights you up from inside."

"That's nice to hear, but it's nonsense, really. I was thinking only of what you said."

"Meaning?"

She indicated the panorama below. "Rivers to the sea."

"Well, aren't they?"

"I guess I haven't a sailor's eye," she said slowly. "I've become too much in the habit of thinking of them as Pittsburgh's own rivers, and especially Stevie's . . . ."

"And why Stevie's?"

"The first day we saw them they were all gold from the sunset and Stevie called them 'three golden rivers,' and someday, he said, he'd put them on glass."

"Ambitious lad, isn't he?"

"He has reason to be. Even Big Dan——"

"I know Big Dan," interrupted Christopher. "And if he believes that Stevie has talent, the boy very definitely has."

"Ask him sometime."

"It's all pretty wonderful, Jenny."

"What is?"

"The way you handle that little brood. But don't you ever think of yourself?"

"Why, yes, I think of myself. I think of myself a lot."

His eyes were filled with admiration. "You were prettier last night than any parasol girl at the party."

"Parasol girl?"

Christopher laughed as he threw his brown beaver hat on the grass. The wind immediately tousled his hair and made him look as he had the first day she had seen him.

145

"That's what I call them, Rosalie and her friends. They're rich and pampered and all of one piece."

"Rosalie isn't."

Christopher liked her quick defense of the girl who had everything by comparison.

"Well, maybe she isn't, so much," he admitted, "but that isn't her fault or theirs. They're all schooled alike."

Jenny leaned on the wooden bannister of the steps. "And how were you schooled, Christopher?"

"I had a mother—" he began—"well, a mother who must have been very much like yours. She taught me the kind of honesty your mother must have taught you. That men and women and boys and girls are to be judged for what they are, not what they may have gained by advantages at birth." He looked away from her as his eyes became sad. "My mother didn't live to see Father grow rich on the rivers. Seven years ago when she was till living, Father was still the captain of a flatboat that carried only iron ore and coal."

"And he went from that to the *River Queen?*"

Christopher smiled. "This is the golden age on these rivers. Steamboating's now at its peak. And Father made friends with men who had money and believed enough in his integrity to launch the *River Queen* at their own risk. So——"

"So?" she repeated, fascinated.

"Well, Father actually knew these rivers. All the ports between Pittsburgh and the Gulf were familiar to him, and all the treacherous currents between. He made the *River Queen* so proud and respected a steamboat that it took him only four years to become its owner."

"Your father's career sounds like a dream," she said softly.

Christopher laughed and his hand touched hers where it

lay on the bannister. The sudden contact made Jenny's heart flutter, but she concealed that from him with all the skill she could command.

"It isn't a dream. It's simply what's happening now in America. There's a boom on from East to West and North to South. This whole great country's on the move. That's what is making America, this migration and settlement. And that's what is making Pittsburgh. America is as far West now as the Pacific. Somewhere there's room for everyone and everyone's special talent."

"This boom will make Stevie too," Jenny decided, delighted.

"Yes, you can count on that, I think." Suddenly Christopher's seriousness vanished and he resumed his characteristic merriment. "You're a little schemer, Jenny."

"Why so?"

"You've got the pioneer spirit. It will put your brood where you want them to be."

"The pioneer spirit. I hope I have it. It sounds rugged."

"And, forgetting the others for a moment, what do you want out of life for yourself?"

She thought hard before she spoke. "Schooling, I think, Christopher. That is, I want that first."

"Schooling! You mean you want to study books?"

"What's wrong with that?" she asked defiantly.

"Nothing, why, nothing, of course. Only——"

"Only what?"

"All the young ladies I know ask for other things. Pretty clothes and carriages, parasols and parties, beaux and——"

She interrupted him eagerly. "I want all those too!"

Suddenly he understood, "But you want schooling first," he

mused. Then he added, "So you can meet these parasol girls on their own ground."

Jenny nodded a quick assent.

"In other words," teased Christopher, "you want what they call 'elegance.'"

"That's it," she agreed, "exactly it."

"And then?"

"Along with Stevie," she finished, "I'll make my bid for the world."

Christopher looked straight into her eyes. "I said you had the pioneer spirit. Make a bid for it, Jenny. I dare you!"

She looked away from him, fearing that she had revealed herself too much. What was there about him, she wondered, that had immediately claimed her confidence? Down in the valley the *River Queen* whistled. Christopher picked up his hat from the grass.

He took both her hands. "We've told each other a lot," he said.

"Yes, I guess we have."

"That makes us really pals, Jenny."

"Yes, it makes us really pals."

"You're a lady now without that 'schooling,' but go after it if you want it. My mother thought it important for me and Father carried out her program. Believe me, Jenny–" he laughed–"I had tutors–tutors up to my neck! And when I come back——"

"When you come back?"

"We'll talk about it some more and we'll see what's to be done about that thing called 'elegance.'"

 *Thirteen*

New Fancies and Footlights

Crimson-cheeked with excitement, Jenny watched Christopher go down the steps. Yes, they were friends, "really pals," as he had said, and they *had* told each other "a lot." Somehow what he had said about his early background had established a kinship between them. He was no longer only the fine young gentleman, son of the *River Queen's* captain. He had been a ragged little boy on a flatboat. Yes, she saw him two ways now. Christopher, a little river urchin, with a mother "like hers," and also Christopher, the fashionable young man sought by "the parasol girls." Unconsciously, she curled her lips a little mockingly. They—none of them—would ever understand him as she did. It would simply be quite beyond them to realize what had gone into the making of him, what it really was, perhaps, that made him so merry, but also a bit contemptuous of their easy way of living. But she, Jenny Bayard of Goat Hill, knew the answer. In all that he had told her, she visualized him with his mother and father in a long, uphill struggle not very much different from her own. Flatboat or clinger, what did it matter? They, like the parasol girls, were "one of a piece."

She saw him turn at the foot of the steps. He took off his hat with a romantic gesture and bowed almost down to his polished boots. As she waved to him in farewell, she wondered if he were mocking her a little about "that thing called elegance."

It had not as yet occurred to Jenny that Christopher's life on the rivers brought him into contact with all sorts of people. The down-and-out, as well as the fashionable, professional gamblers and wasters, aristocratic Southern ladies, and women who lived by their wits on one boat after another. He had contact, too, with the French and Spanish of New Orleans and the bayous, the plantation owners downriver, sailors, waifs and stevedores.

Christopher knew them all, firsthand, and that knowledge had given him a wisdom beyond his nineteen years. So when Jenny had made such a point of elegance, it had amused as well as touched him. Poor little wistful Jenny, he had thought, looking out from the door of her clinger, seeing Rosalie and the parasol girls move in a sphere she thought unattainable until she had had that precious "schooling."

And she was right, Christopher had realized. Look how he had been tutored, for instance, since he had lived on the *River Queen!* One tutor for Spanish. Another for French. A third for mathematics. Still others to teach him to fence like a gentleman, box according to the rules. And much to Christopher's masculine disgust, he had even had a dancing master! All the things necessary to the making of a "gentleman" had been left in carefully written directions by his mother. She had instructed his father that these were the things one must learn to become a part of a world far beyond their own in money, manners and gentility. So, Christopher had thought, how well he could understand Jenny! Hadn't he had many similar experiences? Here was a girl who could really be his friend. The whole world would be enchanting to her because as yet she had seen little of it beyond her own fight for a bare existence.

But Jenny, watching Christopher until he was out of sight, knew nothing of all this in his thoughts, and could only guess if she were right in her judgment of him. Or if she had been too hasty in thinking that they were somehow alike. She had better keep her two feet on the ground, she reprimanded herself.

No matter what Christopher's world had been he certainly lived as a young gentleman now. In spite of a feeling of closeness when he had stood beside her on this hill, Jenny now forced herself to believe that she had no special kinship with him. She would save herself trouble if she would forget all this nonsense and get back to the business of plain living. Would it not be definitely to her own advantage just to wait and see if all this rose color dissolved in mist? So Jenny built up defenses against Christopher as she walked slowly back toward the clinger. Again he was on the *River Queen* and she was here on Goat Hill. And, as far as she knew now, here she would remain for a long time to come.

Mady was in a near-by grass patch with Sandy as Jenny came back up the path. When she saw her sister coming toward her, she left the little nanny goat grazing, and hurried to Jenny eagerly. "Jenny——"

"Hello, Mady-kins." Jenny touched the little girl's straight hair affectionately.

"Has Christopher gone?"

"Didn't you hear the *River Queen* whistle?"

"I guess I did," Mady said, solemn-eyed.

"Why so gloomy about it?"

Mady twisted in her hands the rope she had used to tether Sandy. All of a sudden, she sighed. It was a big, deep sigh that took most of her breath. "Gloomy!" she repeated. "I think you would be the one to be gloomy."

"Why?"

Mady came to the point. "You wouldn't let me go with you, and Carlotta says it's because Christopher is your beau. Now he has gone, so you ought to be gloomy."

"Nonsense!"

"I think Carlotta is right."

"And Stephen?" asked Jenny, purposely gay to draw her sister out. "What does Stevie say about this?"

Mady considered before giving an answer. "Well, Stevie is rather dumb."

"Dumb!"

"Just about this."

"Meaning?"

"Well, he says you just like company."

Good boy, thought Jenny, good boy!

"Well, who's right?" demanded Mady,

"Stevie's right, Mady."

Mady looked as though she didn't know whether to be glad or sorry. "Honest and true?"

"Honest and true. Now tie up Sandy and come back to the house."

When they reached the clinger, Jenny saw that Carlotta had put on the sea-green dress and was deeply engrossed in admiring her reflection in the mirror on her bureau. She was unaware that Mady and Jenny had come in. Jenny was instantly struck by the dramatic appearance of her little sister as she stood there posing, her red-gold curls a brilliant contrast to the sea-green sheen of the dress, which put sea-green lights in her eyes.

"Oh, Carlotta!" Mady was charmed by her sister's beauty.

"Like it?" Carlotta whirled around to face them with the natural grace of a dancer.

Jenny thought it wise not to add to Mady's admiration with too much enthusiasm. Carlotta would soak up flattery like a sponge.

"It's very pretty on you, Carlotta," she said quickly. "Better take it off now so you won't get it wrinkled."

"I'm not taking it off." Carlotta's eyes danced as she smiled. "We're having more company."

"Who? Who?" caroled Mady. "First Christopher, then—?"

Jenny saw that Carlotta was deliberately building up to drama. She paused impressively, threw her curls back over her shoulder, said in a hushed kind of voice, "First Christopher, then Francesca——"

"Who's she?" demanded Jenny.

Carlotta reached for Jenny's hand, a gesture which always forecast a confidence.

"I'll have to tell you in a hurry because it's almost time for her to be here. Francesca is an actress."

"*An actress!*" Mady was delighted.

"Go on," directed Jenny calmly.

Carlotta smiled a guilty little smile. "I didn't always tell you, Jenny, but I've been spending a lot of my time down at the theater. I've come to know the company—John, who plays the hero, Marie Anne, the heroine, and Francesca, who does the older parts——"

"Is Francesca *old?*" asked Mady disappointed.

Carlotta looked witheringly down her nose. "Francesca will never be old. She's what stage people call 'ever young.' She says so herself."

"But why is she coming here?" Jenny wanted to know.

Again Carlotta paused most impressively. "She wants me to play a part in the show."

"What?" Even Jenny was astonished.

"You—on the stage! Oh, my!" Mady sank down backward on the bed.

"And why shouldn't I?" asked Carlotta.

Jenny said very gravely, "Because I won't let you. I simply won't let you."

For the first time in her life, Carlotta looked at Jenny with eyes that blazed with defiance.

"We'll see!" she challenged. "We'll just see!"

"I guess I haven't been careful enough," Jenny said slowly. "I shouldn't have let you go to that stage door."

Carlotta faced her squarely. There was no defiance about her now, only calm assertion of what she intended to do.

"I'll always go to that stage door whether you scold me or not. There's something about even peeping in at show folks from the alley that—that—" she saw another warning look in Jenny's eyes, but went on heedlessly—"well, it draws me like a magnet!"

From her small storehouse of wisdom in managing this sister, Jenny knew enough to conceal her very real feeling of consternation. She realized it would only make things worse if she opposed Carlotta too much. She would see this so-called actress, she decided. She would talk to her and discover what really lay behind this new, disturbing happening. Carlotta could and would very easily shut up like a clam and leave

Jenny entirely in the dark as to what she intended to do. That, realized Jenny now, would be dangerous for them all.

"Well?" Carlotta's voice was still demanding.

"I'll talk to Francesca," promised Jenny noncommittally.

Carlotta became immediately radiant. "I knew you wouldn't fail me! You never do!"

"There's a carriage! Another carriage! And it's stopping at our door!" Mady drew back the curtain.

Carlotta slapped her fingers. "Don't let her see you spying," she ordered. "That's Francesca, I'm sure."

A moment later, Francesca was really getting out of a hired carriage and bidding the driver who helped her to wait.

"My! She looks like a queen!" Mady's eyes were big with interest.

"Why shouldn't she?" said Carlotta, pleased. "She's played queens' parts more times than you could count!"

Over their shoulders, Jenny watched Francesca approach. She was a tall and stately woman, theatrical-looking, of course, but there was about her a fine, mellow dignity which was especially evident in her lined, characterful face. Francesca was no ordinary woman, Jenny could see at a glance. Nor was she "common," as actresses were often reputed to be by strictly conventional people. Jenny took note of her hair, which was dyed, but not dyed flamboyantly. It was the darker brown of a used copper penny, combed back in wings from her forehead. Her hat was wine-colored velvet trimmed with white ostrich feathers, her dress was velvet and wine-colored too. She wore a short fur cape and carried a silver-fox muff. When she had almost reached the door of the clinger, she paused for a moment and held a lorgnette up to her eye with the air of a grand duchess.

"Isn't she wonderful?" Carlotta asked breathlessly.

"Can't she see well?" asked Mady naïvely.

"Of course she can see," growled Carlotta. "She just wants to be sure she's in the right place."

"I'll go to the door." Jenny turned away from them and walked across the room. "Won't you come in?" the girls heard her say a moment later. "You are Francesca, I'm sure."

Francesca entered regally. She looked statuesque in the small room. After a moment's silent survey of Jenny, she smiled, and her smile was the kind that drew one toward her.

"You are Jenny, of course." She looked around the room. "And this is the little clinger I've heard so much about."

Jenny wondered just how much she had heard and what Carlotta had dared to tell her. "It's a small house," she said pleasantly, "but it suits us nicely."

Francesca looked beyond Jenny into the kitchen adjoining. "It's even cozier than I thought it would be."

Little Mady pushed a chair forward. "Won't you sit down?" she said shyly.

Francesca smiled down at her, patted her cheek. "You couldn't be anyone else but Mady. Carlotta says you're a wonderful little housekeeper."

"She—she does?" Mady was enormously pleased.

"Of course I did," broke in Carlotta. "Francesca knows a lot about us." She turned to their guest with her radiant smile. "Let me have your cape and muff and Jenny will make tea."

"Thank you." Francesca removed her cape and gave it to Carlotta as Mady eagerly reached for the muff. "Tea will be very nice indeed."

Mady buried her face in silver fox to feel the warmth of the soft fur.

"This is beautiful," she breathed. "I hope I'll own a muff someday."

Francesca laughed as Carlotta added, "Mady hopes to have a muff and I hope to have a fan." She curtsied gracefully in front of Francesca. "Tell me, do you like this dress?"

Francesca studied her for a moment. "I like it," she said whimsically, "but I wouldn't want to tell you how much. It makes you look like a whirlwind in petticoats."

Jenny turned at the kitchen doorway to admonish her impetuous sisters. "Now don't rattle on and bore Francesca while I make the tea."

As she put the kettle on, she realized that her thoughts were racing. Christopher had barely gone, leaving her in strangely new and lovely turmoil, when Francesca had appeared to add to her problems. Francesca was undoubtedly a woman of distinction. Jenny seemed to remember now seeing her name on posters around town, announcing the new plays.

But Francesca's world was alien to theirs. Carlotta, at thirteen, was too young to identify herself with the stage or any other career for that matter. It was her business now to study and learn, as Stephen was doing, to let things happen to her slowly, not with sudden glamour.

And yet as Stephen had seemed to lean toward all that was creative in glassmaking, so Carlotta had always been like a bright bird, flying high over mundane things. Even as a little girl when solemn-eyed Mady dressed her dolls and tried to coax Carlotta to play house, Carlotta was always off somewhere on some shining quest of her own. Jenny remembered now the day Carlotta had brought home the autumn leaves. She had carried them into the farm kitchen—brilliantly colored boughs with leaves that were aflame.

"Look!" Carlotta had said with a lilt in her voice. "This is how I should like to dress. As trees do in the fall."

Even then, at the age of nine, she had looked like a wood-sprite standing in the open doorway with her hair as bright as the leaves she carried and her eyes as green as the fields beyond. Yes, thought Jenny, worried now, Carlotta had always acted without even knowing she was acting! Perhaps it was as natural to her as Stephen's designing in glass was to him. Perhaps that was what Francesca had seen in the hungry-eyed child at the stage door. Jenny sighed as she poured water from the kettle into a china teapot. If only she knew what was right to do—if only she knew! She even wished that Stephen was here, that she might talk to him about all this. Sometimes in his grave boyish fashion he stumbled on much that was true, and was surprisingly wise in his counsel. Mady had told her that he had gone to the library to meet Andrew Carnegie. He wouldn't be back in time, Jenny was sure, to share in Francesca's visit.

While Jenny had been making the tea in the kitchen, Carlotta had placed a small table in front of the fireplace in the adjoining room. She had laid a hand-embroidered cloth on it and put out the new pink glass plates Stephen had brought from the glasshouse. She had told Francesca with pride that Stephen had helped to make them in the charming star-and-thistle pattern.

When Jenny brought in the teapot, the sugar and creamer and cakes, Francesca was saying: "The play is called *Fashion*, Carlotta."

"*Fashion!*" echoed little Mady impulsively. "Why, that just suits Carlotta. She loves everything about fashion!"

Francesca smiled indulgently. *"Fashion* is a social drama, my dear. It was written by Anna Cora Mowatt, one of the few lady playwrights of our time."

"What's a playwright?" asked Mady, her eyes glued to Francesca's face in utter fascination.

"Anyone who writes a play is called a playwright," Carlotta explained. "Now let Francesca do the talking!"

For the next half hour, even Jenny was charmed by Francesca's talk. The whole glittering world of the theater was opened to them—actors and actresses seemed to appear before them like figures on a magic carpet. Francesca's stage experience was varied and rich. She had played Shakespearean parts in the Old Vic Theatre in London. She had also played in Paris, but the American theater, she insisted, was the breath of life to her. She knew it was crude and only beginning here in this youngest of all countries, but the theater, too, had to be developed like everything else in this amazing land. She was proud to be one of the early crusaders. She mentioned such Yankee plays as *The Forest Rose* and *The People's Lawyer.* She was proud that she had played with such male celebrities as James H. Hackett and John E. Owens. She leaned most of all toward social satire and that was why she was glad for *Fashion.* It had first been produced at the Park Theatre in New York, March 24, 1845, and represented the peak in social drama of the period. Mrs. Mowatt, Francesca said, had already outrivaled her forerunners, Mercy Warren and Charlotte Lennox, in writing such a provocative piece about the current American scene.

"What part will you take in the play?" Carlotta asked eagerly.

Francesca's voice took on the very essence of "culture." "I, Carlotta!" She looked through her lorgnette, and shrugged her shoulders. "Why, I shall be Mrs. Tiffany!"

This manner, she informed them, was quite "in character" and couldn't be done, so Francesca hoped, in better form by Fanny Kemble herself!

"Who's Fanny Kemble?" questioned Mady.

Francesca looked at the girls in amazement. "Is it possible— is it really possible that you haven't heard of Fanny Kemble?"

Jenny was apologetic. "We've never seen a play, Francesca, and know nothing at all about players. It's only Carlotta——"

As Jenny paused, Francesca interrupted with the serious- ness of a sage. "Fanny Kemble, my dears, is a fine English actress. The greatest actress of our time."

She rose from her chair impressively, and walked up and down the little room with a soft swish of her velvet skirts. "There's never been a Juliet—never, my dears, in theatrical history—played as Fanny Kemble can play her."

"Have you ever seen her?" asked Carlotta, taking note of Francesca's very regal gestures.

"She came to American three years ago in company with her father. She was an instant success in New York."

"That's where I shall be a success." Carlotta tossed her head with pride. "Yes, I shall succeed like Fanny Kemble."

Francesca turned and studied her shrewdly. "Then, my dear, you'll begin right now."

"Oh, no! No!" Jenny protested weakly.

Carlotta's belligerence flamed again. "You let Stevie do what he wants to do. Why shouldn't you let me?"

Francesca stared at her hard. "I think, Carlotta, that you and Mady had better run off by yourselves for a while. I should like to talk to Jenny alone."

After a moment's hesitation, Carlotta moved toward the kitchen door. "I don't want to, but I will if you say so."

Mady followed her, disappointed. She, too, had wanted to stay.

When they had gone, Francesca sat down again at the table. "Believe me, Jenny," she said sympathetically, "I know what your problems must be and exactly how you are feeling now."

Jenny leaned forward wearily. "It's just that I know nothing—really nothing about the theater. I know my mother used to say that it was a 'precarious profession.' Now with Stevie, it's different—he's chosen something solid."

Francesca touched her hand gently. "What you don't seem to realize, my dear, is that Carlotta hasn't chosen anything, really——"

"Then what do you call this? A little girl thirteen years old——"

"Perhaps," Francesca went on wisely, "*this*, as you put it, is being chosen for her."

"I don't understand," said Jenny, bewildered.

Francesca, too, leaned forward, eager to explain. "I didn't mean to tell you because Carlotta hoped I wouldn't. But don't think I came here merely because I happened to see a hungry-eyed child haunting the stage door and hiding in the wings."

"Hiding in the wings!" Jenny was horrified by what she hadn't known about her little sister.

"Everyone in the company saw her. At first they took it to be only childish curiosity—until they saw her eyes."

"Carlotta's eyes *are* beautiful," Jenny admitted involuntarily.

"They are not only beautiful—they are expressive. So are her face, her hands—her whole body. She doesn't act—she *is*."

"Go on," said Jenny, impressed.

"One day last week in rehearsal," Francesca mused reminiscently, "a play called for a flower vendor's part. One of the actresses was ill. Someone suggested we look for Carlotta, who would be sure to be in the wings. Artie, our prop boy, found her, starry-eyed as always, standing quietly—very quietly, Jenny—in back of a tree we use for scenery."

As Jenny was about to speak, Francesca silenced her with a gesture. "You mustn't scold Carlotta, Jenny. One thing that impressed us all was the absolute 'quality' of the child. She was never bold, never forward—she was just *always there* as reverent as if she were in a church—even before bad actors."

"She should have told me all this," Jenny said, a bit hurt.

"She would have, I am sure, but not until she felt quite ready."

"What about the flower vendor?" Jenny asked soberly.

"Artie brought her onto the stage. Our director told her what to do. She was simply to carry a basket and cross the stage, calling, 'Lavender, pale lavender! Violets and nosegays!'"

Jenny's eyes sparkled. "She must have been lovely."

"She had loveliness, yes," agreed Francesca, "but there was something more. Our director had the word for it. He said she was 'electric.'"

"Electric." Jenny repeated the word very softly.

She made that little flower vendor, an inconsequential part in the script, vivid and vibrant and quite unforgettable." Francesca looked beyond Jenny at the dancing flame of the fire. "I say that something inside her *sings*."

"You—you mean that she's destined to be an actress?" Jenny's voice was incredulous.

"I fully believe that the child has inner compulsion. She's alive and courageous, and, I repeat, 'electric.' She can very well be molded into a remarkable woman—or she can very easily be betrayed by her own strong will and vanity." Again Francesca's voice held a note of sympathy. "Carlotta's not an easy little person to have within your keeping."

"But what am I to do?" asked Jenny. "I still say she's too young to start a career on the stage."

Francesca sighed a little as she toyed elegantly with her tea cup. "That's where so many mistakes are made. We want to keep our fledglings—fledglings. We simply can't bear to see them try to fly away from the the home nest." The old actress leaned across the table, surveying Jenny with kindly eyes. "Whatever you do to your brood, sweet Jenny, you mustn't keep them waiting to make their start. You are wise in handling Stephen. You allow him to develop his talent at a very early age. Life is so short, and the road is so long—and that is something our fledglings instictively seem to know while we shut our eyes to it."

Jenny considered a moment. Then she asked quietly: "What do you want me to do about Carlotta?"

 *Fourteen*

Broken Things

A fter Francesca left the clinger, Carlotta still kept a fine sense of elation. Mady, too, was excited.

"To think that Carlotta will be an actress!" The little girl seemed to move in the golden aura of the glow of what had happened to her sister.

Jenny, however, was still perplexed. She felt none of the sureness or exhilaration she had experienced when Big Dan had talked to her about Stephen's career in glassmaking. That had been something she could understand and evaluate. This nebulous world of Francesca's, this theater, still remained as foreign to her as something on another planet. The phrases Francesca had used—something inside Carlotta sings, the hungry-eyed child, let Carlotta try her wings——even these seemed overromantic and meaningless when applied to things in the workaday world. Stephen's work demanded no such extravagant phrasing. Neither had Christopher's background nor his present career in steamboating.

Yes, the theater was strange to Jenny, and all the people connected with it. Again she had a feeling that Carlotta was growing away from her. She was running on eager feet into a world so different from her present life in their clinger that, somehow, Jenny shuddered. Had she been right in yielding to Francesca, she wondered? Had she been right in allowing this fledgling to fly?

Furtively she watched Carlotta, who was busy now at the kitchen stove. In even so simple a thing as putting a frying pan on the fire, Jenny had to admit, her sister had grace. Nevertheless, Jenny sighed. It could so easily be with Carlotta as Francesca had said. "She can very well be molded into a remarkable woman or she can very easily be betrayed by her own strong will and vanity." And Jenny remembered, too, that Francesca had also said, "Carlotta's not an easy little person to have within your keeping."

"You're solemn as an owl and I don't like it a bit!"

Carlotta was conscious that Jenny was lost in thoughts of her own, and was speaking forthrightly.

Jenny collected her thoughts. "I was just thinking . . . " she began.

Carlotta pouted prettily. "Think happy thoughts then," she ordered.

"Well, I should say so," said Mady. "When Carlotta's as famous as Fanny Kemble ——"

"Oh, Mady, hush!" Jenny rebuked her harshly.

Carlotta very much resented her tone. "You don't think I'll be another Fanny Kemble," she said very coldly. "But I'll show you. I'll show everybody!"

Jenny stroked Carlotta's curls. "There's no need to be hostile, Carlotta. We're all just a bit upset because too much is happening. I believe you can do whatever you set your heart on doing."

Carlotta was not one, as Mady always said, to hold spite.

"I'm sorry I was cross," she said softly. And when Carlotta apologized it was as Mady said, too, "everyone just melted."

Jenny was glad when the kitchen door opened and Stephen came into the house. He was carrying two books.

"Guess I'm late," he said, putting the books on a chair, "but I stayed to see a boxing match."

"Who was boxing?" asked Mady.

"Michael O'Toole and Marty O'Hara."

"I don't know them," said Mady quaintly.

"Neither do I," said Stephen, "but both of them were good."

"Was Andrew there too?" asked Jenny.

"Sure," said Stephen, smiling. "He knows all about the game from the Greeks on down."

Carlotta picked up the books and read the titles: *Ivanhoe*, by Sir Walter Scott and *Poems* by Tennyson.

"Think you'll like them?" questioned Stephen as he moved to the kitchen sink.

Carlotta said loftily, "I'm not sure, but I'll read them. I'll be reading a lot from now on."

"Golly–" Stephen laughed–"you've turned a new leaf."

Mady was the first informer. "She's turned a lot of things. She's going to be another Fanny Kemble!"

"Another who?" Stephen picked up a towel and started to dry his face.

"Another Fanny Kemble," Carlotta repeated with pride.

Later in the evening, Jenny had time alone with Stephen. Mady had promised young Mrs. Weimar to mind her two children while she went to visit her sister in Allegheny. Much to Mady's delight, Carlotta had offered to accompany her to the neighboring clinger. She would read "The Lady of Shalott," she planned, while Mady watched Frederick and Fredericka. The music of the poem had intrigued her.

> On either side the river lie
> Long fields of barley and of rye,
> That clothe the wold and meet the sky;
> And through the field the road runs by
> To many-towered Camelot . . .

Carlotta could very well fancy herself "the fairy Lady of Shalott" watching

> . . . through the mirror blue
> The knights come riding two by two . . .

So while she and Mady went to the Weimars', Jenny and Stephen remained at home in front of their own fireplace.

"Something's bothering you, Jenny." Stephen had been watching her as she sat mending one of Mady's aprons.

She looked toward him and smiled. "How do you know?"

Stephen shifted the papers on which he had been drawing designs. "You look so sober and you aren't talking. I think you're worrying about Carlotta."

"I guess I am, Stevie." Jenny laid Mady's apron aside. "What do you think about all this theater business?"

"I'm glad it's happened."

"You—you are!"

Stephen nodded his head with conviction.

"Something had to come of it sometime and it might as well be now. She just couldn't grow up having it like a fever—'stage fever,' as you said Francesca said. This should either make her outgrow it or do her some good."

Jenny considered his clear-sighted opinion. "Maybe you're right."

"You hope she outgrows it, don't you?" he questioned anxiously.

"It's just that it's so different from anything we're used to that I feel uncertain, I suppose."

Stephen pondered for a moment, then spoke again with certainty. "Carlotta's different too. She's always been."

"Oh, well, Stevie, let's not worry." Jenny finally smiled. "Maybe it will be as you say—that she's only stagestruck and will outgrow it. As you say, too, we've got to find out sometime and it may as well be now." She picked up Mady's apron and began stitching again. "How are things at the glasshouse these days?"

"Very, very secret, Jenny."

"Secret!"

Stephen got up and moved to the fireplace to prod lazy coals with a poker.

"Big Dan has asked us to submit our final designs for a contest. The best one will be chosen to decorate the glass used at the glassmakers' big annual banquet."

"But the banquet won't beheld until spring!"

Stephen shrugged as he went back to his seat at the table. "Designing and choosing take time. The gilders and engravers and even the glass cutters try their skill at thinking up patterns." Suddenly he flashed her a wide, engaging smile. "I'm not the only artist among them. And I'm not sure I'm the best!"

"Good," pronounced Jenny.

"Good?"

"It will make you try harder to do your best work," she explained. "Fair competition is good for us all."

"Oh, I'll try hard," Stephen said quickly, adding with a sense of humor, "I've got to beat my rival, Jo."

Jenny smiled at him affectionately. "Got any plans for your design?"

"None that I'm telling. Even to you."

"That's all right. I like surprises. And if what you design for the banquet is only half as beautiful as your chapel——"

"It will be," he promised. "And I'll soon be bringing the chapel home. I told Big Dan we want it for Christmas."

"It's hard to realize," Jenny mused a moment later, "that Christmas isn't far away."

"Seven weeks," said Stephen promptly.

"I wish we had more money." Jenny sighed.

"We will have someday," Stephen assured her. "Maybe we'll own a house like the Blakewells' or even a steamboat like Christopher's father's."

Christopher! The sound of his name on Stephen's lips made Jenny think excitedly of what he had said only this morning. "And when I come back we'll talk some more about that thing called elegance." She wondered now what he had really meant, and what he hoped to do about it with a poor clinger girl like her. Elegance. She would have as far to go toward any real achievement in that as Stephen had toward his glass mountain or as Carlotta would have on her long flight toward fame.

Two weeks later Jenny was to have a slight indication of what Christopher had meant. A letter from New Orleans was delivered to her at the clinger. He had addressed it to Jenny but along with it came a package addressed to Stephen. Jenny opened the letter first. She read it to the brood as they all sat in front of the fire. It began gaily:

Dear Brood:

Here am I down among the bayous many miles away from you. The *River Queen* is anchored at the levee here in New Orleans and I have just come aboard with news. The whole city is going mad with excitement over a young Swedish singer named Jenny! She was brought here by that great showman, P.T. Barnum, and already has had a highly successful concert tour in New York's Castle Garden and points between.

She is only in her twenties—almost as pretty as your own Jenny!—and sings more sweetly than a nightingale. I understand she will sing in Pittsburgh sometime in the spring, and you all must hear her. I don't suppose the Jenny Lind craze has reached there yet, but everywhere she has been, they tell me, songs and polkas are dedicated to her and poets sing her praises. Down here in New Orleans you find Jenny Lind gloves, Jenny Lind bonnets (Carlotta should see them!) Jenny Lind riding habits, Jenny Lind shawls, mantillas, robes, chairs, sofas and pianos! And that isn't all. There are Jenny Lind flasks done in glass with her picture enameled on them. I am sending a few along to Stephen. Some are blue, some are amethyst, some emerald-green glass. I hope you like them all.

I'll be writing again in a few days. Meanwhile take care of yourselves in the clinger and think of me as eager to see you all again. Good-night, dear brood, and may God bless you.

Affectionately,
Christopher

"Isn't he wonderful?" Carlotta's eyes were shining.

"Wonderful!" scoffed Mady. "He's a prince!"

"Nonsense," said Jenny, partly to hide her own thrill of pleasure. "Christopher's—well, just Christopher."

"Open the package and stop all this gushing," said Stephen.

The Jenny Lind bottles were a delight to him. There were three of them in varied shapes and sizes. All had different portraits of the lovely young singer. Stephen was intensely interested in their craftsmanship. They had been blown in full size two-piece molds from bottle glass of various colors.

The one in cornflower-blue appealed to Jenny most. It had a three-quarter view of the singer, turned to the left, wearing a lace bertha. There was a large wreath encircling her, and above, the inscription, "Jenny Lind." Jenny held the bottle up to the light. The cornflower-blue glass reflected the silver of the sun, making it an exquisite thing to see.

"A Jenny Lind bottle," said Jenny softly. "This is what Big Dan must have meant when he told you to 'speak for America in glass,' Stevie."

"I guess it is," the boy agreed enthusiastically.

"What do you mean by America in glass?" asked Carlotta.

Jenny examined the bottle again. "In days to come," she explained, "this bottle will be valuable. It will be a historic flask because it portrays an incident in American history."

"Such as what?" asked Mady.

"Such as the coming of a famous Swedish singer to America."

"I like the bottle and I know I'd like Jenny Lind," said Carlotta, turning up her nose, "but all this talk about history makes it seem com—com—compli——"

"You're trying to say complicated," said Stephen. "But if you stop to figure things out they wouldn't seem complicated at all. Jenny Lind *is* social history."

They put the bottles on the window sill where their colors could be reflected in sunlight by day and firelight by night. Cornflower-blue. Emerald-green. Amethyst. They struck an almost exotic note in the poor little room.

A few days later Jenny learned that she was not the only one who knew that Jenny Lind was contemplating a visit to Pittsburgh. Ecstatic reports were circulated that "sometime after Christmas" she would appear in a downtown concert. The Monongahela House buzzed with the news that the singer's manager was arranging for her to stay there during her sojourn in the city. Preparations were already being made for her in gala fashion. Mrs. Houston told the kitchen staff that one of their specialties would be "Jenny Lind pudding" in the young artist's honor. The recipe was said to have been created by Jenny Lind herself. According to reports she was inclined toward domesticity in spite of her glamorous career.

Next to Jenny in the clinger, it was Carlotta who was most interested in the coming of Jenny Lind.

"She's a singer, I know," Carlotta told Jenny, "but she must be an actress too." Then, quite unconscious that her remark had given Jenny a daring idea, Carlotta added, "People all say that she was just a poor girl too. I wish that I could talk to her and find out how she got there."

"Got where?" asked Mady.

"To the top of the heap as a singer and actress," answered Carlotta.

"She's probably well-schooled," said Jenny.

"Well, I'd just like to know," decided Carlotta.

All the next day Jenny found herself thinking that some-how she, too, would like to know what had gone into the making of Jenny Lind's success. What kind of schooling comprised the background of such a fabulous career? Jenny was not so ignorant that she did not realize exceptional talent came first, but she realized, too, that even the best God-given talent had to have proper direction.

Suppose, she thought now, that Carlotta had God-given talent too. If this were so, Jenny wanted to be sure that it would be given the right direction—just as Stephen's talent was being wisely directed by Big Dan. Francesca's interest in Carlotta was a fine thing, Jenny thought now, but how were they to judge whether or not it was charting the little girl's course as it should be charted? They should really have, Jenny decided, a parallel case to go by. Carlotta's wish to talk with Jenny Lind became a signal toward action to Jenny. She, her-self, would try to meet the singer at the hotel. She would try to learn for Carlotta what had gone into the making of Jenny Lind's career. Maybe then she could be certain she was right in giving in to Francesca and letting her fledgling fly. Perhaps if she talked to Mrs. Houston . . . .

The older woman was sitting at her desk as Jenny entered her office. "Good morning, Jenny," she said crisply.

"Good morning, Mrs. Houston." Jenny sat down in a chair at the opposite side of the desk.

"Something on your mind?" Mrs. Houston smiled.

Jenny scarcely knew how to begin. It had not occurred to her until now that it would be presumptuous for her to ask Mrs. Houston to arrange for her to talk with a visiting celebrity—especially one of such magnitude as the great Swedish singer! It came to her as she sat there facing Anna Houston that some other reason would have to be given for her to get out of the kitchen!

Mrs. Houston was watching her curiously. "Well, Jenny?" she questioned, obviously not wanting to lose too much time.

"I—I want to talk about my work . . ." Jenny began, then paused.

"You like your job, don't you?" Mrs. Houston asked efficiently.

"I like it very much," Jenny answered quickly, "but I also like the whole hotel. I should like to become as familiar with as many jobs as I can."

Anna Houston smiled again. "You mean waiting on tables, or being a parlor girl, or looking after the linen closets?"

"Even making beds," Jenny added, and also smiled her charming smile.

"In other words," said Mrs. Houston, "you would like to branch out into every phase of the work so you'll be in line for better things."

"That's it," said Jenny, suddenly feeling a bit guilty because that really wasn't it at all.

Mrs. Houston picked up a ledger which lay on her desk. She turned the pages slowly.

"There's nothing now that I know of," she said finally, "but there may be after Christmas."

"How about room service?" Jenny dared to ask. "I like fixing trays and I know I'd like delivering them."

Mrs. Houston made a short notation in the ledger with a pencil. "See me after the holidays, Jenny. It may be arranged."

A moment later she stood up, a signal for Jenny to go.

"Thank you very much," said Jenny. "You've been very kind."

Mrs. Houston patted her shoulder, "I like ambition, Jenny.

There's room at the top for everyone who has the interest of her work at heart."

Jenny felt a twinge of conscience as she left the little office. Well, at least, she hadn't lied! She *did* like her job. And she would like trying another that would give her further knowledge of how the big hotel was managed. Of course, if it hadn't been for Carlotta and her wish to talk to Jenny Lind . . . .

So absorbed was Jenny in her thoughts that she hadn't noticed Helen Corrado coming down the corridor behind her. Helen's mocking voice stopped her short. "Hello there, Ambition!"

Jenny turned to face the girl who looked at her with angry eyes.

"Want a warning?" Helen asked.

"A warning?" echoed Jenny, completely at a loss to understand.

Helen came a step nearer Jenny with a swift, catlike movement. "I overheard what went on in Houston's office because I made it my business to. Oh, don't look so shocked—you're not so perfect!"

For a moment Jenny wondered if Helen had some inkling of her plans to talk to Jenny Lind. Then she realized immediately that this was impossible. Jenny Lind didn't enter Helen's thoughts—it was only Helen Corrado she was interested in. She went on pouring out words as Jenny listened.

"About the room service job you asked for—well, don't think you're going to get it! I've wanted to be in room service ever since I've been here. And if you get there first, there's going to be trouble." She moved still closer to Jenny and snapped her fingers in her face. "Tons of trouble! That's my warning!"

Before Jenny could answer, Helen turned and left.

So, thought Jenny blankly, trouble again! It seemed to be ever-present, in every direction she turned. Well, she thought now, thrusting out her chin, she'd have to find a way to meet it, or she and the brood could easily be defeated in their struggle for existence. Between now and Christmas, she was thinking, there was much to be accomplished. And just let Helen try to stop her in what she aimed to do!

In the intervening days, the golden haze of Indian summer had felt the onslaught of winds from the north. The innumerable hills surrounding Pittsburgh had reaped a whirlwind of falling leaves. Goat Hill was covered with a sere brown carpet that crackled underfoot. The days became the gray days of a bleak November, days without sun, without shadow, sometimes without even light. This was especially true of the city at the Point. Often Jenny came down from Goat Hill into the fog to find oil lamps burning at high noon and business places illuminated by gaslight.

On the Thursday before Christmas came the first snow. It was already evening and quite dark when Jenny left the Monongahela House. She had had a hard day. Helen had annoyed her. First she had made Jenny wait three hours for fruit that was to go on her cakes. Then Helen had told Mrs. Houston Jenny had used salad bowls to mix cake frostings in. Mrs. Houston had not been too kind about the incident. She had accused Jenny of slowing up the kitchen's efficiency when it had been actually Helen's fault. As Jenny thought more about it, she realized that there had been a coldness toward her in the older woman's attitude. Had Helen been working secretly to undermine Mrs. Houston's kindly feeling toward her, Jenny wondered now?

As she climbed the steps to the clinger, the snow changed

to biting sleet and flailed her in the face with the sharpness of a razor's edge. She could see the circle of light from the lamp on the kitchen table before she reached the clinger. She could also see the open door and little Mady nearby endeavoring to push snow off a woodpile with her hands.

"Mady!" Jenny called in surprise.

Mady sniffled and took off wet mittens. Her snub nose was blue with cold.

"Carlotta's down at the theater," she explained resentfully. "Stevie didn't come home and I've got no wood for a fire. The house is cold."

"You've let the wood get wet," Jenny said crossly. Her own hands were freezing in her thin cotton gloves and her threadbare winter coat was little protection against the gales that swept across the hill.

"I've let the wood get wet!" protested Mady, suddenly in tears. "I'm supposed to watch everything while—while Carlotta dances her head off and you and Stephen are always working!"

She wiped her nose woefully on her sleeve. Suddenly Jenny realized how valiant little Mady had been since they had lived in this clinger. What she had said was true, all true. Carlotta *was* always off somewhere, she and Stephen *were* always working, and eight-year-old Mady had, uncomplainingly for the most part, done household chores. She had had no outlet as Carlotta had in her wandering, or as Stephen had in the enjoyment of his work. No outlet, even, like Jenny's whose life had at least been varied. Jenny was suddenly stricken to the heart. She put her arms around Mady, who was now weeping copiously.

"I'm sorry I scolded you, darling. You've been doing more than any little girl should be expected to do. Never mind the old wood. Dry your eyes and come into the house and I'll make you a cup of tea."

"There's—there's no hot water." Mady shivered.

"Come on in, and we'll see."

The clinger was just as cold as Mady had said. The sleet beat against the windows with an angry sound. There was nothing but ashes in the stove and nothing Jenny could do forced them to ignite. She was about to strike a match and burn a few old newspapers when the outside door was opened and Carlotta entered vibrantly as though blown in on a gust of wind.

"Hello!"

Her eyes were alight and she looked warm and glowing. She stood wrapped from head to foot in a faded gray blanket she had thrown over her light-weight coat. She had taken the blanket from her bed before leaving the clinger, realizing that her coat would be little protection against the wildness of the weather.

"Where have you been?" demanded Jenny. "You should be ashamed to leave Mady here without any fire—and——"

Carlotta smiled whimsically. "You can stop scolding, Jenny. I wouldn't even be here if it weren't for Mady. I came back especially to take her with me."

"And where do you think you're going?"

"Surely you haven't forgotten that this is the night of my first rehearsal? I've been down at the theater—just waiting to start for hours. I've even put on my costume—look!"

She took off the blanket and her coat. She was arrayed in a dance dress Francesca had given her from the wardrobe of the theater. The bright yellow of the skirt and the red-gold of her hair seemed to light the clinger with sudden fire. She was so lovely to look at that both Mady and Jenny forgot the cold for a moment and felt somehow warmed.

"My, you're pretty!" said Mady. "Why, you're beautiful!"

"I think so too," said Jenny.

Carlotta sparkled at their praise. "That's what Francesca said. And she wants to tell you herself how well I'm doing in the play." She looked at the clock on the shelf. "The rehearsal begins in no time, so we'd better run."

"But I'm too hungry," objected Mady.

Carlotta wrapped herself in the blanket and strangely enough the clinger seemed suddenly dark.

"There're sandwiches and coffee backstage. You can eat there."

"Sandwiches and coffee! Oh, yum!"

Jenny stood in the doorway of the clinger and watched them trudge off into the snow. Little Mady looked rather grotesque because she had put on a coat of Stephen's which he had outgrown and discarded. Carlotta had a hard time keeping the bulky old gray blanket from flapping wide open. They were both wearing warm stockings Jenny had knitted for them, and fairly decent overshoes for which she was thankful.

Nevertheless, as she closed the door and felt the coldness of the house, it was hard for her to feel really thankful for anything. Winter had caught her unaware. Only Jenny knew that the clinger was cold because there was no money to buy even a small supply of coal. She hadn't told Stephen that all she and he and King had been able to earn just wasn't enough. After all, there were four of them—four to feed and four to clothe and the rent had to be paid—and—and—well, everything! Suddenly weary Jenny laid her head on the kitchen table and let the tears come.

For a long time she sat there, her shoulders shaking with

uncontrolled sobs. Then, as the clock on the shelf struck seven, she lifted her tear-stained face. Something had to be done, she scolded herself. She just couldn't sit here and freeze and let the children freeze when they came home! Frost flowers were already on the windows. In a few more hours the clinger would be weighted down with snow. Jenny dried her eyes and flew into action. She put Carlotta's old shawl around her shoulders and her own threadbare coat over that. She tied a frayed woolen scarf of Stephen's tightly around her head. Then she took a basket from under the sink, and also went out into the blustery night.

She had remembered that there was an abandoned coal mine not very far from the foot of Goat Hill. Perhaps if the snow were not yet too deep she could go there and gather up enough coal to tide them over tonight. Tomorrow the children could gather more, and so until better days——The wind was rising as she went down the wooden steps. It seemed to delight in frisking sharply around the curve of the hill and blowing sleet in Jenny's face. Soon the sting and the sharpness brought fresh tears to her eyes.

When she reached the mine, its darkness terrified her. She should have waited for Stephen, she thought desolately. Together they might not have minded these queer shadows. There were little hills of slag and cinders at the entrance, under the snow, but it had not yet covered the larger pieces of coal that lay protected just inside the opening. Jenny was not "a scared cat" as Mady would have put it, but it took all the courage she could summon to go into the darkness of that cavern and stay there long enough to fill her basket.

In the following two hours, she made four trips from the clinger to the coal mine. Her back ached and her legs were ready to give way under her as at nine o'clock she lugged in the last basket. She had washed her face and combed her hair, and was starting the fire, when Stephen came home. Something about the way he closed the kitchen door made her get up from her knees on the hearth and look at him questioningly.

"Stevie!" The word seemed to catch in her throat because she saw that his face was white and misery lay deep in his eyes.

He came toward her, not answering.

"Stevie—what on earth has happened to make you look so miserable?"

He took off his coat and mittens, laid his cap on a chair. He didn't seem to notice that the clinger was cold, that the fire had not yet burst into flames. Jenny went over to him.

"Stevie, darling, tell me."

For the first time since their mother had died, Jenny saw tears in Stephen's eyes.

"It's my chapel," he said slowly. "It's broken in a thousand pieces."

"Your little chapel—broken!"

He sat down dejectedly in front of the fireplace. "The cleaning woman knocked it off the shelf when she was dusting Big Dan's office."

Jenny knelt beside him. "Oh, Stevie, how awful! Now it won't be in the glass show."

"You should just see it. You wouldn't even know that it had a star window, the colored glass is in such bits."

"When did this happen?"

"Only this afternoon, I guess. I was going to bring it home tonight. It's almost time to trim our tree, and Big Dan said I could borrow it."

She put her hand over his sympathetically as the fire suddenly came to life. But the welcome sight of its dancing flames did little, it seemed, to cheer him.

"It's hard for you, Stevie—and it's just as hard for me because I loved the chapel too."

"I know you did, Jenny."

"But it seems that life is filled with broken things—especially for people like us. The only thing we can do is to learn how to mend them."

"The chapel can't be mended, nor the star window. It took me weeks to piece it together. Why, just to get those colors on glass——"

"Yes it would have been pretty, Stevie, darling. But we've got to think what Mother always said when things seemed to be at their lowest." She looked into his eyes and saw that he remembered, while she continued softly, "Mother always said, 'We've got to pick up the pieces and keep going right on. There's nothing else we can do.'" Jenny suddenly sat up straight as though giving him a challenge. "Right on, Stevie, do you hear?"

His eyes were bright with reminiscence as well as with tears as he looked at their mother's picture on the fireplace shelf.

"I'll go on," he promised. Then, as his tears began to splash in big drops on Jenny's hand, he gave a frustrated little cry. "But, oh, Jenny, why couldn't they have stayed with us longer?"

And because Jenny, too, felt frustrated, her own eyes filled with tears. Achingly, she, like Stephen, wanted her mother and father tonight. Surely they could have straightened out the troubles which seemed to be descending. Gently she wiped Stephen's tears away, looking meanwhile at the pictures: the kindly, strong face of her father and the lovely countenance of her mother. They would have whispered, "Courage, Jenny," at a time like this, she felt sure. They had fought a good fight, had left their children memories of what it had meant to be surrounded by a great love. Always they had found a way to pull through difficult times together.

"Courage, Jenny." The pictures suddenly seemed to speak, to bring her parents very close. It was as though she were actually hearing their dear, familiar voices. Stephen's eyes were brooding as if he, too, felt their nearness and dearness. Nothing, not even death, could ever dissolve those precious family ties. Love had been transcendent among them. It was something that reached out and up and beyond all earthly things. Jenny felt a strange, wonderful consolation. Her mother and father were with them tonight, right here in this room. Yes, they were returning in spirit from some far, sunny place to give their children courage. With her whole heart she clung to this belief as she spoke again to Stephen.

"They understand and they're with us, Stevie. They trust us to be brave and strong. You see, we've got to make them proud of us."

"Yes, we've got to make them proud."

"They'll always be wherever we are, please believe that, Stevie. Nothing can ever change that now."

And as they sat there, comforted, somehow even the firelight seemed to say that this was so.

Fifteen

Christmas Eve

*I*t was two days before Christmas and Jenny stood at her work table in the Monongahela House sorting Christmas cookies. Old Franz was watching her over his spectacles, his artistic sense delighted because she had a natural instinct for combining colors.

"Ja, that's pretty, Jenny *Liebling!* Those pink peppermint tops beside the blue candy ones. And the big red Christmas cartwheel cookies with the little ones iced so white!"

"Go away with you, Franz." Jenny laughed at his enthusiasm.

Never in all her life had she prepared for such a Christmas as this one at the hotel. They had made mountains of various cookies in every size and shape and color. They looked decorative, indeed, as she was arranging them now, calling off their names to Franz who was cataloguing them for Mrs. Houston. Christmas honey bear cookies for children. Pink peppermints. Anise and Christmas cartwheels. Holly wreath cookies and pecan delights. Chocolate chips and Viennese spice drops. Orange and lemon-flavored squares. Macaroons and sweetheart cookies made out of candied cherries, dates and nuts especially for the parasol girls. Then there were the popcorn balls! Hundreds and hundreds of popcorn balls made festive with red cherries and springs of holly.

"There were three hundred and one when we counted last," said Jenny.

"*Ja,* three hundred and one," repeated Franz.

She began piling the popcorn balls into pyramids. One pyramid toppled over and the balls began rolling across the table, threatening to fall on the floor. She and Franz had a wild scramble to catch them. So absorbed were they in this business, they were both quite oblivious that Christopher had come into the kitchen and was standing just behind them.

Jenny looked up blankly as she heard him say: "That's a good catch!"

"It's—why, it's you!" She wiped her sticky hands on her apron.

"Of course it is," Christopher bantered. "And you look very much surprised. Didn't you know the *River Queen* was in port?"

Old Franz answered for Jenny. "Young man," he pretended to grumble, "we work in this kitchen. We do not watch for steamboats!"

Christopher laughed at Franz and comically wrinkled his freckled nose. "Yes, I can see that you work. I've never smelled so many good things to eat in my life."

He looked at the fowl—chickens, ducks and turkeys—ready to be roasted, at luscious pink hams already turning on their spits, at sides of roast beef, smoked and brown, about to be cut hot or cold. He smelled the savory sauces fragrant with herbs and wine, saw vegetables in such quantities he couldn't begin to count them. Candied fruit was piled high. There were tubs and baskets of apples and oranges and lemons and great purple bunches of grapes. Mincemeat pies were steaming and there were so many plum puddings that Christopher was flabbergasted. He turned back to Jenny.

"Surely you are never hungry!"

"Well, hardly ever," she said rather seriously.

As Franz left them to work at the stove, Christopher came closer to the table. "Say, Jenny, are you glad to see me or aren't you?"

She went right on building pyramids because she didn't want him to see how joyous his coming had made her.

"I'm very glad, Christopher."

"That's not good enough. You're only lukewarm."

"Oh, but I'm not!" Another popcorn ball rolled across the table. She tried to catch it and missed.

"Why don't you play billiards with them?" teased Christopher.

"We don't play billiards in this kitchen."

"That's better."

"What's better?"

"You laughed. I like to see you laugh." As she made no answer, he rambled on, "Oh, Jenny, Jenny, you've got to have fun. And I have such plans!"

"Meaning?"

He looked around cautiously before he replied. "Can't we get out of here for a while?"

"You mean leave the kitchen?"

"Yes."

She looked very tempted but shook her head. "We're busier than a beehive."

"Who cares?" he said recklessly. "Christmas is just around the corner and we're having a party on the *River Queen* such as you've never seen in your life. It's our first Christmas on the boat up here in the North, and I've ordered a snowstorm and all the trimmings." He paid no attention as she stopped working and stood looking at him in amazement. "And you and the brood are coming, Jenny. You're going to dance and sing and be so gay even your little Carlotta will think she's dreaming!"

Suddenly he reached for her hand, looking cautiously, meanwhile, around the room. Everyone on the staff appeared to be busy. Even Helen pretended to be. Neither Jenny nor Christopher realized she was trying to catch every word that passed between them and was furtively watching every move.

"Couldn't you stretch a point and gossip a moment in private in there?" Christopher indicated the smaller kitchen where she had found refuge the day she had sat on a cabbage crate and cried.

Again Jenny looked tempted. Finally after a careful glance at the other workers, she allowed him to lead her into the room adjoining. "There!" she said, facing him. "Are you satisfied?"

"Not satisfied, but better pleased." He smiled down at her merrily. "Now promise you'll come to my Christmas party."

"But, Christopher!" Jenny's eyes were two sparkling stars.

"No excuses, please. None of them will do."

She thought of herself and the brood at such a party as he had mentioned. A curious little group in rags compared to the silks and velvets she knew would be worn there. No, it wouldn't be any good. She just couldn't face it.

"Christopher, you don't understand——" she began seriously.

"Poppycock! I understand so well I can tell you why you hesitate!"

"Oh, you can, can you?"

He smiled at her knowingly. "Cinderella has no fairy godmother and refuses to go to the ball without a gold dress and glass slippers."

Jenny looked so crestfallen Christopher broke into a gay peal of laughter.

"Christopher, hush!" she begged, fearing the kitchen staff would hear.

"I'm right, am I not?"

"Not exactly." She looked away from him, realizing now that he really wanted her to come to the party and that she, just as much, wanted to go. But again she thought of the parasol girls. She imagined the Christmas Eve dress Rosalie Blakewell would probably wear. No, it wouldn't do for the Bayards. She just couldn't compete with Blakewell elegance, couldn't let Christopher actually see the difference between them and how she would look in comparison, followed by her poorly dressed little brood.

"Well, why am I not exactly right?" Christopher's voice was impatient.

"Because the children are going caroling and I promised to go with them."

"And you'd miss a party for that!"

Jenny lifted her head a little proudly, and challenged him with her eyes. "Your kind of party I would."

"What's wrong with my kind of party?"

She sensed a sudden belligerence in his voice. Impulsively she laid her hand on his arm.

"Christopher, you know—you realize—or you ought to—that we just don't belong in that kind of company."

"Poppycock! You're prettier than any of them."

Jenny's smile was sparkling. "Thanks. That's a lovely thing to hear, but I just won't expose you to ridicule."

"No one would dare to ridicule me!"

Jenny thought back to the day she hadn't waited for him on the wharf.

"Don't you think," she asked quietly, "that Mrs. Blakewell might?"

"Well, if that's how you feel——" Christopher turned away from her coldly.

"Christopher——"

He had almost reached the door to the larger kitchen.

"I haven't said what I wanted to tell you." Jenny said almost shyly.

He looked down at her but he didn't smile. "Well, what is it?"

"We were all so pleased to get your letter," she said very softly, "and so delighted with the glass you sent from New Orleans. It was wonderful of you even to think of writing to us."

"Why shouldn't I?" he almost growled.

Jenny went on speaking because she detected a softening in his manner. His growl had been only half-hearted.

"We loved hearing about Jenny Lind. Do you know that she will stay here—right here in the Monongahela House—when she comes to sing in Pittsburgh?"

"She has to stay somewhere," Christopher conceded rather ungraciously.

Jenny lifted her eyes to his. Even Christopher in his present mood was not too blind to see the half-hurt, half-eager light in them. "Thanks, anyhow, for writing. Thank you from my heart."

Suddenly he reached down and cupped her face in both his hands. She could feel his warmth and vigor as he said, almost angrily, "You're welcome, stubborn little Jenny Bayard. You're very welcome indeed. And someday—" he paused a moment before he repeated—"someday, I hope I'll be able to talk some sense into your silly head!"

With that he turned and left her standing alone in the kitchen. Even Jenny didn't know that her eyes were shining, deep wells of light. Strange, she was thinking, almost triumphantly, you can sometimes gain a point just by risking the loss of one!

Christmas Eve brought the snowstorm Christopher had ordered. A lovely picture-book snowstorm with silvery flakes falling so softly they seemed to bring a hush to all the world. Christmas Eve. To Jenny and her brood it was like an angel's song. The Christmas tree in the clinger stood brightly shining with candlelight, trimmed with festoons of pink and white popcorn. From its topmost branch a little white angel with tinsel wings looked down on them and smiled. If Stephen thought about the absence of his glass chapel with its star window, he stoically gave no sign, and Jenny also kept silent about it.

She and Mady and Stephen were waiting for Carlotta to finish dressing. They were all going to the Christmas Eve services in the First Presbyterian Church. Later they were to join the group of young minstrels who would go about the city singing Christmas carols. Some called them "minstrels," others "waits" after the old English custom, still others thought of them as "carol singers." Jenny had not told the children that Christopher had invited them to a party on the *River Queen*.

She realized how deeply disappointed they would be that she had refused to go. She was still glad that they were not going. She still believed she had been right in not risking a contrast between them and the parasol girls.

She stole a glance at herself in the mirror. The dress she was wearing was sapphire blue. She had made it out of an old one of her mother's. It had been a party dress once, fashioned of shimmering satin, and, Jenny remembered, given to her mother by Rosalie Blakewell's Grand'mère Marsha. Her mother had stored it away in her trunk along with other remnants from the days when she had been a seamstress. It was from this trunk also that Jenny garnered many odds and ends of materials to supplement her own sewing.

The dress made Jenny's eyes look doubly blue and did flattering things for her hair, which she had caught up in a cluster of curls and tied with pink satin ribbon. Christopher would still have said, and rightly, that she was prettier than any of the parasol girls. But until she could have their schooling and their elegance she would refuse to go among them.

Stephen looked at her happily. "You're pretty! You look like the belle of a ball!"

"You've never been to a ball." Jenny laughed. "But you're a handsome lad yourself in that hand-embroidered waistcoat."

"How about me?" Little Mady was turning this way and that, furbelowed and flounced in a bright yellow hand-me-down of Carlotta's. "I've always wanted to wear this dress and have my hair fixed in curls."

"You're prettier than any of us," Jenny delighted her by saying.

Carlotta finally turned from a complicated process of beautifying herself in front of her bureau.

"Look at me!"

She was wearing the sea-green satin frock that made her red-gold curls so entrancing and showed only the tips of her slippers with satin bows which Jenny had cunningly fashioned from her store of odds and ends. The skirt had seven flounces, which gave it a party-dress look, but that was not the highlight of Carlotta's appearance this evening. Mady looked spellbound.

"Heavenly days!" she fairly shrieked. "Carlotta's patched her face!"

Stephen and Jenny, too, were amazed at the little black patch Carlotta had applied to her chin. It made her pretty lips look provocative. So velvety black was it in texture that it gave her roses-and-lilies complexion the pearllike glow of fine porcelain.

Jenny suddenly laughed. "Carlotta! You little silly! Take that thing off!"

"Why should I? Francesca wears one, don't she?"

"Doesn't she," corrected Jenny. "And what is suitable for her as a woman is not for you as a young girl."

"It makes you look stagey," Stephen volunteered.

"Maybe that's what I want," asserted Carlotta.

Jenny attempted diplomacy. She did not want to antagonize her firebrand of a sister on such a night as Christmas Eve.

"Just don't wear it to church, Carlotta. It *is* theatrical, as Stevie says. And members of the church are required to take a pledge to abstain from the theater."

"We aren't members," Carlotta reminded her.

"Even if we're not we don't want to be conspicuous and get ourselves talked about. Suppose—just suppose Christopher, for instance, should hear unfavorable reports about us now that he's back in town."

This remark of Jenny's swayed Carlotta. She had come to think of Christopher as being representative of the whole fashionable set she was always reading about in *Godey's Lady's Book*.

"Well," she said grudgingly, "maybe I'd better not wear it to church."

"Take it off and let's go," Stephen urged impatiently.

The night seemed magically blue and white as they went out into the snow.

"Oh, it's up to my ankles!" said Mady in delight.

"And it's drifting higher," said Jenny.

"Look, do you see what I see?" Stephen was pointing down to the wharf where the *River Queen* lay splendidly alight. Through the misty white blur of the snow, it seemed a dream ship afloat on a dreamlike river.

"I wish we could be aboard," Carlotta said wistfully. "They must be having fun tonight."

Jenny laughed at Carlotta's deep and sudden melancholy. "We will someday," she said comfortingly, remembering with a thrill of pleasure Christopher's threat to "talk some sense into her silly head."

When they reached the wharf, carriages were stopping on the river front. Parasol girls and their beaux were alighting and walking toward the gangplank of the *River Queen*. Jenny and the children could hear they gay voices, their laughter. Holiday laughter.

Carlotta was envious. "Huh!" she mocked. "Guess we're not good enough for Christopher, even if he does write us letters." She paused and surveyed the glittering scene. "Just look at all those carriages!" She straightened herself up tall. Defiance was sharp in her eyes. "Well, someday they'll line up for me! You just wait and see!"

"Line up for you!" Mady was incredulous. "What for?"

"To see me on the stage, stupid," Carlotta promised, and believed it.

Jenny took Carlotta's hand. "Have you forgotten," she asked gently, "that we are going to church? And don't say again that we're not good enough for Christopher. There's nothing of the snob about him."

Carlotta turned away reluctantly as they walked on. Ahead they could see the snow-covered steeple of the church. The bell in the tower was ringing happily and joyously. It made Jenny think that all was as it should be on this Christmas Eve.

The church was crowded to its doors. Here, too, was light and color and motion. The sexton was renting hot bricks to pew holders who were moving about in as gala attire as the parasol girls on the *River Queen*. The hundred-candle chandelier shed its sparkling iridescent light on many distinguished members who sat quietly in their pews listening to the chorus of singers in the choir loft. The Bayards stood with others at the back of the church. They were enchanted by the singers. Jenny wished that Stephen had such a voice for singing.

The chorals spoke the universal language of the soul. First they were softly sung, so very softly that the singing seemed to come from faraway. Then it mounted in a crescendo and seemed to break in rapture. Even unschooled Jenny realized now what people meant when they spoke of the greatness of Handel and Bach. She didn't recognize the selection from Bach nor did she know she was listening to bits of Handel's beautiful *Messiah*. Nevertheless she understood that she was hear-

ing melodic lines of exalted beauty. They stirred her to wonderment.

She turned to look at Stephen, who was standing beside
her. He, too, was rapt. Jenny wondered if this superb music
made him think of his glass chapel with its jewellike star
window, so much like this music in spirit. Surely it was in the
cathedrals from which he had drawn his inspiration that music
like this had first been sung. Bach. Handel. Stephen. Jenny
felt no temerity in acknowledging the same creative force in
all. Bach and Handel had already achieved greatness. Stephen
had yet only his dream of greatness.

Jenny remembered fragments of Big Dan's talk the night
they had shown him the chapel. "You've got to see the great
pictorial windows in Old World cathedrals," and "Stephen,
my boy," he had said that evening, "speak for America in glass."
Yes, thought Jenny now, Stephen's art was like this church,
this music, consecrated to all there is in the human heart that
makes it reach upward for better things.

When the service was over, Jenny found it hard to dispel
the solemn mood that had descended on her. It was Carlotta's
gay voice that brought her back. "There's Francesca, Jenny!
Let's say hello to her!"

Before Jenny could answer Carlotta was dashing down the
church steps and hailing Francesca as she went down the
walk. Francesca was delighted to see the Bayards. This was
her first meeting with Stephen and she was immediately
drawn to him. Jenny was impressed again by Francesca's
mellow dignity and charm. Even though she wore the black
patch on her chin Carlotta had so wanted to imitate, she had
still the air of a great lady about her. And it seemed inborn,
not something theatrical added by her life on the stage.

"You ought to come to the theater, Jenny, and see Carlotta," Francesca said gaily. "She's helping us paint scenes at present."

"So she told me." Jenny smiled.

"Jenny ought to see backstage," Carlotta added. "I'll make her come."

"Good," said Francesca. "And now I'll have to hurry back and study lines. There's a matinee tomorrow, you know." She smiled at them graciously. "Meanwhile, my dears, Merry Christmas!"

"Merry Christmas!" they called as she walked away through the snow.

"We'd better find the carolers," said Stephen, "or they'll go off without us."

The group of minstrels was congregating at the church door. They were young people from all over town. Some of them belonged to Pittsburgh's Swedenborgian Society, a famous music-loving organization. Carlotta had met them in her wanderings, and she had promised to bring her sisters and brother to add to their number Christmas Eve.

> God rest you merry, gentlemen,
> Let nothing you dismay,
> For Jesus Christ, Our Saviour,
> Was born upon this day

Through the softly falling snow the minstrel group trudged singing. On a dozen different designated corners, they paused to let their fresh young voices ring out in the night. Jenny and the children enjoyed all this merriment. It was not too cold, and snow had completely transformed the grimy roofs of downtown Pittsburgh. It lay on them softly like white fleece, making chimney pots ice-blue and glittering in the light of the pale moon. A make-believe town it looked tonight, with its cold slate-gray rivers flowing between snow-powdered hills.

It was almost midnight when they moved toward the place of their last serenade. Jenny was startled to see the leader walk down along the wharf toward the *River Queen*. A few moments later they were all standing at the foot of the gangplank beginning to sing their loveliest carols to the loveliest boat on the river. They had sung "O Little Town of Bethlehem," "Silent Night," and "Hark the Herald Angels Sing," when Captain White appeared on the deck. Jenny shrank back as she saw that Christopher and many of the guests were assembling behind the captain. Clearly the minstrel voices sang on. Caught by the spell, those on the *River Queen* listened.

Raggle-taggle for the most part, the whole group of minstrels was in sharp contrast to the silk- and velvet-clad people up there on the boat. Yet each group had color. Perhaps the minstrels had more than color, thought Jenny; they had a certain picturesqueness as they stood singing in the snow. Many of them, like Stephen, wore brightly colored mufflers and red mittens.

Then Captain White, followed by Christopher, came down the gangplank.

"A hearty welcome to you," he called. "All of you will please come aboard. There's hot punch and cakes and something more."

Jenny immediately made a quick motion toward flight but Carlotta was too fast for her.

"Jenny! What on earth are you thinking of? We're all to go aboard the boat!"

"You go. I'll wait."

"Wait?" Carlotta was puzzled. "Where will you wait? And why?"

Jenny looked up toward Water Street. "The Monongahela House is open. I'll wait for you in the lobby."

"You'll do nothing of the sort." Christopher's voice surprised her. He had come up behind them and overheard.

"Christopher, please!" begged Jenny.

There was a sudden, determined look in his eyes. "You might as well get over all this nonsense now. You promised to be friends with me."

Jenny felt his hand at her elbow propelling her toward the gangplank. Stubbornness now would be ungraceful, she was wise enough to know. So, much to the brood's delight, they followed the others up the gangplank and onto the deck of the *River Queen*.

When they entered the grand salon, they discovered that there were two groups of musicians, one at each end of the ballroom, two hundred feet apart. The Bayards blinked at the great expanse of red carpet, the graceful gilded chairs and two gilded pianos. At the foot of the staircase that curved down from the top deck stood tables spread with white cloths and set with crystal and silver. These were loaded with such delicacies that Mady and Carlotta simply stood and stared, both suddenly hungry. Five crystal chandeliers twinkled with the dancing light of five hundred candle flames, and two enormous Christmas trees glittered with tinsel stars. Large mirrors along both walls twice reflected their light until the ballroom seemed to be of three shining dimensions. There were festoons of holly everywhere and garlands of mistletoe bright with red ribbon bows. The fragrance of pine was like incense.

Christopher led his group of guests to where his father was standing waiting to receive them hospitably. He looked genial and fun-loving like Christopher, and Mady admired his mutton-chop whiskers. She fancied he looked like Santa Claus and felt immediately at home with him. His voice was quite the boomingest Jenny had ever heard and his manners were as jovial as they were correct. It was easy to see that he, too, loved life and people, and that he enjoyed making them happy. And with it all, as John Blakewell often said, "Captain White is nobody's fool."

He took Jenny's hand with a slight bow. "So this is Miss Jenny." He smiled at her warmly. "I'm very glad to meet you, little missie. That rascally son of mine has told me so much about you, I warned him he'd better produce you soon or I would think you a myth!"

He turned from Jenny to Mady. "Welcome to the *River Queen*, child! I've a special fondness for little girls in yellow."

Carlotta laughed her lovely laugh. "And for little girls in green?" she asked.

He winked at her slyly, liking her immediately because she was tall for her age and there was something minx-like about her. To her utter delight, he bowed again.

"Little girls in green," he said, "never fail to capture my heart."

To Stephen he gave his hand and a clear look of interest. "Welcome, Stephen. I've learned that you are first apprentice to my good friend, Big Dan. We'll meet later, young man, and talk about glass. And now, please enjoy yourselves."

He turned away from them as Christopher made a move to help Jenny and the girls take off their coats. "I've got to introduce another Stephen." Captain White smiled merrily as he left them. "He's a minstrel too."

They watched him go to the musicians' platform where a tall young man joined him. A moment later he was facing his guests, saying, "My friends, I give you Pittsburgh's own composer, who composed the waltz you are now about to hear." He was interrupted by a burst of applause before he could continue. "The young man, as you know, is Stephen Collins Foster and his famous waltz is—'Open Thy Lattice, Love.'"

He paused for a moment and the musicians played a few lovely strains of the serenade. Suddenly everyone in the room was singing:

> Open thy lattice, love,
> Listen to me!
> The cool balmy breeze
> Is abroad on the sea!
> The moon like a queen,
> Roams her realms of blue,
> And the stars keep their vigils
> In heaven for you.
> Ere morn's gushing light
> Tips the hills with its ray,
> Away o'er the waters
> Away and away!
> Then open thy lattice, love,
> Listen to me!
> While the moon's in the sky
> And the breeze on the sea!

Jenny watched the tall, dark young man with the rather melancholy smile bow again and again to the crowd.

"Stephen Collins Foster?" she murmured to Christopher.

Christopher nodded enthusiastically. "He was born here in

Pittsburgh only twenty-four years ago and already he's writing songs that tear your heart out. This one, I understand, was written to Miss Susan Pentland, a neighbor's little girl. And you should hear his songs of the South—'Old Folks at Home,' and——"

Jenny saw Stephen Foster come down from the platform and join a smiling brown-haired girl.

"His wife?" she asked.

"And just a bride. She was Jane McDowell. Old Dr. McDowell's daughter."

Jenny stood listening to the strangely haunting serenade. "Songs that tear your heart out." Surely Stephen Foster's gift was a great and beautiful one that enabled him to speak for people in music. Christopher laughed at her absorption in the melody. She was looking at Stephen Foster again. Although he seemed happy there was the same look of melancholy in his eyes that had been in his smile. Was this what gave him the power to compose? Jenny wondered. Was he familiar with tears as well as laughter? And through them both had he learned to speak the universal language of a song?

Meanwhile, she was conscious of the parasol girls beginning to dance with their beaux again. In shimmering satin, velvet and lace, they whirled to the music of the waltz. Rosalie Blakewell swirled past. She was lovely in her cherry-colored velvet dress which enhanced the golden gleam of her curls. She called to them gaily and seemed very happy until her mother approached her during a short intermission. Jenny couldn't hear what Mrs. Blakewell said, but, after she had spoken, Rosalie looked utterly different. She seemed to dance only half-heartedly. When she smiled it was as though her gaiety was a mask.

Christopher seemed aware of this too, "Poor Rosalie," he said sympathetically. "Why doesn't her mother let her alone?"

"I'm sure I don't know," answered Jenny, disturbed.

"She'll spoil things for Rosalie if she isn't careful."

"No mother wants to spoil things for her daughter." Jenny said, startled.

Christopher scowled. "Then Mrs. Blakewell'd better watch out."

"You'd better watch out," Jenny bantered merrily. "Mrs. Blakewell's watching *you!*"

Victoria was standing near the grand staircase, tall, distinguished, and haughtily beautiful in an amber satin gown. She was looking directly at Christopher through a beribboned lorgnette. Jenny could fancy her saying: "So—you've taken up with riffraff. This is a fine situation indeed!"

Suddenly Christopher made an extravagantly elaborate gesture. He drew Jenny's hand through his arm. "Let's really give her something to watch!"

Before she was aware of what he was doing, Christopher led Jenny through the dancing throng toward the staircase. Almost under Mrs. Blakewell's nose he summoned a steward to bring his fur-lined greatcoat. When it was brought he put it around Jenny's shoulders.

"No catching cold," he warned, so Mrs. Blakewell could hear. "We're going up to the top deck."

Again she looked through her lorgnette, her eyes sharp with concern. As Christopher turned to lead Jenny up the staircase, Mrs. Blakewell approached him with hauteur, saying, "Christopher, aren't you forgetting——"

"I beg your pardon?" Christopher's hauteur matched her own.

Mrs. Blakewell looked down her nose at Jenny. It was as if she were evaluating, item by item, Jenny's blue dress, the pink satin ribbon in her hair, the old silver buckles on her none too new slippers. Evaluating them and adding them up to—nothing—absolutely nothing.

"It's just that I regret to see you . . ." she began again.

Christopher interrupted her shortly. "I'm sorry, Mrs. Blakewell." He bowed low and punctiliously. "*I* have no regrets, I'm certain." Turning again to Jenny, he said, "And now, shall we go?"

Jenny felt her cheeks burning with fire. She desperately hoped that she didn't look so scarlet as she felt. She had the good sense to keep her head lifted proudly as she went up the stairs with Christopher's hand on her arm. She was sure that what had happened had been byplay, that no one else in the ballroom had seen or heard or probably cared. If others were wondering why Christopher was hovering around the girl who had come aboard with the minstrels, they probably attributed it to his innate courtesy and little more.

"Christopher! You shouldn't have!"

They were standing at the door of the wheelhouse on the upper deck. Christopher laughed gaily. "It was wonderful, wasn't it? Wonderful!"

"But Victoria Blakewell will never forgive you," worried Jenny.

"And who do you think will care? Now, pretty Jenny," he pattered her hand, "forget all about her and concentrate on beautiful things like the sound of those throbbing violins coming up to us from the ballroom."

Jenny sighed happily. Since he had braved Mrs. Blakewell's displeasure here in what must surely be a stronghold of the parasol girls, he had made her feel as on that first day—one of a piece with him.

"Pretty, isn't it?" He was looking down on the town.

"It isn't Pittsburgh." Jenny laughed. "It's a picture-book town tonight."

"Funny," said Christopher.

"Funny?"

He rubbed his eyes. "I'm used to seeing green grass at Christmas down South."

"I don't think I'd like that. Christmas wouldn't be Christmas without snow to me."

"I think I like snow better too." He looked down at her and smiled. "You're enjoying this, aren't you?"

She spoke so soberly that he laughed aloud. "I'm enjoying this so much that I don't even know where my brood has gone to!"

"They're eating Santa Claus in ice cream. The last I saw of Carlotta she was flirting with Father for all the world like a parasol girl."

"She ought to be spanked."

"No, she shouldn't because Father loves it. And Mady had her arms around his neck."

"That's odd. Usually she's so shy."

Christopher looked at her, bantering. "And you, Jenny, are you shy too?"

She looked away from him. "I—I suppose so," she said, embarrassed.

"You won't be always," teased Christopher.

A church bell in a snow-covered steeple rang out in the night. It was followed by the striking of a clock.

"Twelve o'clock!" Jenny counted in surprise.

He shook her hand gaily. "I never miss a midnight waltz. Come back to the ballroom and dance with me."

"I've never danced a waltz—I know only the country dances we used to do in the barn."

The way he smiled gave her confidence. "Come now, don't worry. I'll lead you easily."

"But I ought to leave the boat with the minstrels," she protested further.

"They won't be leaving, you just see! Father will insist on their staying and having fun."

Christopher hurried her out of the wheelhouse and raced along the deck. Still hand in hand, they went down the long staircase. Jenny's hair was jeweled with snowflakes. Snow stars were melting in her eyes. Christopher took his coat from her shoulders and for a moment she stood all asparkle in the candlelight of the ballroom.

"You're beautiful, Jenny."

"Am I?" She looked incredibly happy.

He led her out on the shining floor. As the measure of the waltz went on she felt enchanted in his arms. Suddenly he drew her aside. He titled her lovely face upward and laid a gay kiss on her lips.

"Christopher!"

He looked down at her innocently. "There's mistletoe above us. You're standing right under it."

It was the first time Jenny had ever been kissed by a boy. Suddenly the room was whirling with the young romance of it. All the stars on the Christmas tree seemed to shine just for her. All the candle flames in the room seemed to burn just to light a pathway to her heart. She went on dancing with Christopher, conscious of a new and bewildering wonder. When at last Jenny lifted her eyes shyly, he was looking away from her, but over his shoulder she saw Victoria. And Mrs. Blakewell's eyes were filled with such rancor that Jenny's were somehow held by them.

She had seen that kiss, that first, sweet kiss of Jenny's!

 *Sixteen*

Trouble in the Clinger

T he Sunday after Christmas Goat Hill was blanketed in snow and wore a hood of fog. Nothing could be seen from the clinger's windows, not even the walk that led to the flight of wooden steps down into the city. Stephen had to take a lantern to find his way to the stable to give King his morning oats and Sandy had to be tied in her stall to keep her from wandering. Even on a day like this, Sandy would be a nomad.

Jenny was clearing the breakfast table. Although time had passed quickly since the party on the *River Queen,* they were still talking about it. They had sat a long time at the table this morning remembering things they had forgotten or hadn't yet had time to tell. Even Stephen had been loquacious. Captain White had talked to him about merchandising glass. He had told him many interesting things about glasshouses he had visited in the Ohio Valley. Stephen had been fascinated.

As for Jenny, the special glow of the party still held her in its spell. The romance of it kept going through her thoughts like the golden notes of a love song. Christopher. That kiss under the mistletoe. His flaunting of Mrs. Blakewell made Jenny feel that he and she were sharing something secret that was denied even to the parasol girls.

"Jenny." Carlotta was standing in the doorway of the other room.

"Yes?"

"I wish you'd come here."

Jenny picked up a pitcher. "I haven't time. I want to get these dishes done."

"But this is important."

"Important?" Jenny turned to look at Carlotta. "I can't see what's so——"

"But it is," Carlotta interrupted. "I don't want Mady to know or Stephen either, and now that they've gone to the stable——"

Jenny smiled tolerantly. "Very well, if you must be so secret."

She went into the other room. Carlotta closed the door. "I want to tell you about Rosalie," she announced.

"Rosalie!"

Carlotta sat down on the edge of her bed. "She's in trouble. I'm sure she's in trouble."

"Why didn't you tell me before?" Jenny was instantly concerned.

"We haven't been alone—and——"

"Well?"

"I've been sort of trying to figure things out."

Jenny looked impatient. "You should have asked me to help you, especially in a case like this. What makes you think Rosalie's unhappy?"

There was a short dramatic pause before Carlotta spoke again. "I saw her crying all alone the night of the Christmas party."

"Rosalie crying!" Jenny was startled.

"She—she cried so hard it scared me," Carlotta added solemnly. "I went into the ladies' lounge and there she was, all in a heap."

"Did she know that you saw her?"

Carlotta shook her head. "I didn't want to meddle until I found you. I hurried back to the ballroom but you weren't there. Neither was Christopher."

Jenny realized that Carlotta must have been looking for her while she and Christopher had been in the wheelhouse.

"We did go up on deck for a little while," she enlightened Carlotta.

Carlotta accepted Jenny's words noncommittally. "Anyhow, when I saw you again, Rosalie was back in the ballroom, all powdered up so no one could tell she had been crying. And she was dancing with Stephen Foster."

"You should have told me then and there," Jenny said soberly. "Maybe I could have helped her."

"But she was laughing by that time," Carlotta explained.

Jenny remembered vividly the happenings that must have led to such a scene as Carlotta described. The fact that Christopher had taken her up to the wheelhouse must have so angered Mrs. Blakewell that she had berated Rosalie even before the midnight waltz. It was easy now for Jenny to understand Victoria Blakewell's look of hostility and open chagrin when she had seen Christopher kiss her under the mistletoe. This was too much—entirely too much to take from riffraff! Yet if Rosalie cared for Christopher a shade beyond the point of friendship, he apparently didn't know it. It was all very puzzling to Jenny.

"What do you think we should do?" Carlotta asked.

"Nothing yet. We'll just have to wait and see what happens."

"Jenny! Jenny!" Stephen was calling her from the kitchen.

"Yes, Stevie?" she opened the door.

He was standing at the kitchen sink, filling a lantern with oil. He spoke without looking up.

"Sandy's gone. We had her tied to a post in the stable and she broke the rope and got out. Mady and I are going to look for her and we'll need a lantern in this fog."

"She's not a goat, she's a gypsy!" Carlotta laughed. "She never stays at home."

"I guess you shouldn't talk," Stephen bantered.

Jenny took Carlotta's coat from a nail on the kitchen door. "It won't be much fun trying to find her in weather like this. You'd better go along and help."

Carlotta shrugged her shoulders. "I guess I can find her if anyone can."

"You coming, Jenny?" asked Stephen.

She looked at the breakfast dishes, still unwashed. "I'll clean up the kitchen first. If you haven't found her by the time I've finished, I'll come and look too."

She helped Carlotta into her coat and made her put a shawl over her head. She reminded Stephen to take his mittens as he picked up the lantern.

"Where's Mady?" she asked.

"She's waiting for me at the stable," said Stephen.

"Be careful now," Jenny warned as they went out into the fog.

A half hour later the dishes were done and the kitchen was tidy. Jenny put more wood on the fire in the fireplace and added coal to the kitchen stove. She looked at the clock a bit anxiously. The brood must be having trouble finding Sandy, she thought, worried. She would put on her coat and join the search.

She was about to go out when somebody knocked at the kitchen door. She opened it to find Christopher standing there smiling. "Hello, Jenny."

"Christopher!"

"May I come in? Or are you going out?" She stood aside to let him enter. "I was," she began. "The children——"

"Yes, I know. They're out there looking for Sandy."

"You saw them?"

He put a package down on the table. "As I understand it—" he grinned—"they've got Sandy cornered. They're coaxing her to come down from a rock."

"They're all right then." Jenny looked relieved. "Sandy's just up to her usual tricks."

"Why don't you let her stay up there? She'll come down when she gets tired."

"Sandy never gets tired. And she supplies our milk, remember? Why, if it weren't for Sandy and King——"

Christopher nodded understandingly as she paused. "This clinger would be running at a loss, I suppose?"

"Decidedly. Sandy saves a milk bill and King takes up the slack. Why, even Timothy Drew says that King's a prize horse."

Christopher stood at the table and began unwrapping his package.

"Stop singing praises to your horse and your goat and pay some attention to me."

Jenny leaned on the back of a chair. "Poor neglected Christopher!"

He continued unwrapping with a plainly injured air. "Why I bring a present," he teased, "I'm sure I don't know."

"A present!"

"And a very nice one too."

"But Christopher, don't you know that Christmas is over?"

He tore off the last bit of paper from a handsomely bound leather book.

"I don't believe it," he said flatly, and gave her the book with a smile.

"Oh, what a beautiful book! *A Christmas Carol,* by Charles Dickens," she read. "Charles Dickens," she repeated vaguely. "Who is he, Christopher?"

Christopher bowed from his waist in a courtly fashion. He drew up a chair to the kitchen table and took Jenny's hand with elaborate courtesy.

"Pray, be seated, my lady," he bantered, "and we'll have a lesson in what you call elegance."

She sat down, laid the book on the table and opened it.

"Now tell me." Jenny puckered her eyebrows seriously.

Christopher smiled.

"Part of being 'elegant' lies in knowing what is thought the best in contemporary literature. Charles Dickens is a writer, Jenny, an English writer of note and great fame. He visited Pittsburgh just a few years ago."

Jenny's eyes grew large with interest. "The man who wrote this," she said, completely fascinated, "came here from England?"

Christopher nodded. "Pittsburghians, as he called them, went to see him by the thousands. He held levees, which is another word for receptions. He was on tour in America and everywhere he went, people loved him." Christopher smiled wryly as he continued. "Charles Dickens didn't like traveling on our steamboats, however. He called them 'ugly, top-heavy tubs,' but that was eight years ago, before we learned to build them with the grace of the *River Queen*. And he praised heaven that the Mississippi, great father of rivers, had no young children like him ... that it is the most hideous river in the world."

Jenny looked up and smiled. While he had been talking her eyes had glanced at the words on the page of the open book.

"But he must have had a sense of humor," she said. "Look at the name of one of his characters—Scrooge."

"He has a charming sense of humor. And he used it delightfully all through the *Christmas Carol*."

Jenny laughed as she read at random: "'Oh, but he was a tight-fisted hand at the grindstone, Scrooge! a squeezing, wrenching, grasping, scraping, clutching, covetous, old sinner!' This is wonderful, Christopher! My whole brood will love it!"

Christopher leafed through the book. "Begin at the beginning. You'll like it even better."

"'Marley was dead, to begin with,'" she read. "Oh, I wonder if Andrew has seen this!"

"Who's Andrew?"

Jenny turned a page as she answered, "A little messenger boy in town. He was the one who told Stevie about Colonel Anderson's free library for working boys."

"Well, if he likes books," said Christopher, "he has read Charles Dickens'. He wrote *Nicholas Nickleby, The Old Curiosity Shop, Oliver Twist* and *Pickwick Papers*."

"Have you read them all?" she asked in astonishment.

Christopher laughed. "I like to read, Jenny, so, of course, I've read them all. Life isn't all music and dancing on the *River Queen*. My cabin is lined with books and I read far into the night."

"I'd love to do that," Jenny smiled wistfully.

"I keep to myself a lot, I guess," Christopher went on. "And I really do study. I read books on history and navigation—" his friendly eyes were alight with enthusiasm—"but let's not get back to steamboats! We're discussing elegance, aren't we?"

Jenny liked this new side of Christopher. It showed a part of him not yet revealed to her, a rather sober, serious part that had probably been more evident in the boy before his father became captain of the *River Queen*.

She smiled and pushed back her chair. "And speaking of elegance, don't you think we should have a cup of tea?"

Christopher got up too and walked across the kitchen. "Charles Dickens and I," he observed, "have one thing in common. I lack his genius, Jenny, but I share his taste for good food. There are so many things to eat in his books—" he chuckled—"honestly, it makes you hungry."

Jenny turned to him impulsively. "I know I shall love his book. Thank you for bringing *A Christmas Carol,* Christopher."

"Don't be so sober about it," he teased.

She tied on her apron as she spoke again. "I'll read it to the brood when they come in. We'll light the candles on the Christmas tree and sit in front of the fire. That's how we got most of our schooling. Mother taught us to write, and read us everything she could lay her hands on."

Christopher looked wistful. "Why can't I join the family circle?"

"The family circle would love it," she answered, smiling.

Jenny was completely happy. It was a lovely thing to be making tea for Christopher, to be drinking it here in the clinger kitchen, cozily protected from the cold white fog haunting the windowpanes. She wished the children would come in and leave Sandy to her fate. Christopher was right. The goat should just be left on the rock until she grew tired enough to come down.

"More tea?" she asked Christopher.

"Umm! It's good."

She was about to fill his cup again when a quick step was heard outside the door. A moment later Stephen entered and Jenny instantly saw that his face was drawn and white as chalk. His voice, habitually low, was shrill.

"It's Mady, Jenny! She fell from the rock and she's hurt!"

"Oh, dear heaven!" Jenny's words were a poignant cry.

She flew past Stephen and out the door, Christopher following in haste. What happened in the next quarter hour remained forever confusing to her. She remembered that some sure instinct had told her which way to go through the fog, remembered, too, that when they had come to the rock, Carlotta was kneeling beside little Mady, rubbing her sister's hands, her big tears falling hotly on them. Jenny remembered also how Christopher had gathered Mady up in his arms and carried her back to the clinger, as still and inert as the rock on which Sandy had perched herself. Meanwhile the goat had *ba-ba-ba*ed mournfully, realizing with animal instinct that something frightful had happened.

Christopher laid Mady on the bed. Still there was no sign of life. Her eyes were closed, blood dripped from an ugly gash in her temple. Her hair, wet with snow and fog, was matted with it.

"You've tea ready, Jenny. Bring some for Mady."

Jenny brought the tea in haste. Christopher succeeded in getting a little of it down Mady's throat, and a faint rose seemed to tinge her cheeks.

"That will help," he said soberly. "Now I'll run for a doctor."

"There's one at the foot of the hill," said Jenny, her voice suddenly breaking. "And, hurry, Christopher, please!"

Carlotta brought a basin of water and gave it to Jenny with trembling hands. She undressed Mady and washed her face and tucked her warmly under the bedcovers.

"Heat a brick in the oven, Stevie," Jenny ordered. "Her feet are still freezing."

The three of them waited anxiously at Mady's bedside. Jenny's troubled eyes never left the child's face. Carlotta was kneeling on the floor, stifling her sobs. Stephen, too, was watching Mady as she lay there, seemingly lost to them all.

"Can't—can't we do something?" he whispered to Jenny desperately.

She looked at him gravely, her eyes beseeching. "Yes, Stevie, darling, we can all pray."

She knelt beside Carlotta. Stephen knelt, too, and they joined hands. Jenny said softly, "Please, God, make little Mady well. In thy dear name, dear Father, Amen."

"Amen," breathed Carlotta, and sobbed.

"Dear God, make her well," repeated Stephen.

So Christopher and the doctor found them, white and stricken, on their knees. Christopher helped Jenny rise.

"Come," he said solicitously. "Let the doctor take care of her now."

He led her and Carlotta into the kitchen. Stephen followed after a long, lingering look at Mady. His fine boyish face was strained. Jenny hovered around the kitchen doorway, watching the doctor. He was a young man and gentle. He asked for a glass of water and towels and Carlotta flew to get them for him. He felt Mady's pulse. He noted the color of her face and size of the pupils in her eyes. Finally he examined her head, tenderly explored the open wound in her temple. And Mady never moved. During his whole examination she lay there inert, scarcely breathing, it seemed to frightened Jenny.

"Please!" she implored involuntarily once as the doctor looked toward her. "Is she—is she—?"

The doctor smiled reassuringly, but somehow Jenny knew he was smiling only to comfort her and not because he personally felt all would be well with Mady. She watched him bandage Mady's head. All the while she was thinking with grief that seemed to turn her heart into stone, It's serious—serious.

When the doctor had done all he could do, he joined the group in the kitchen. Even Christopher faced him with concerned and anxious eyes.

"She's in a coma," the doctor explained. "It may last for days—or for weeks—it's impossible to tell just yet."

"But—but what can we do for her?" pleaded Jenny. "How shall we care—?"

The doctor looked sympathetic. "We can do nothing at all for a while. If she should happen to stir or open her eyes you must call me at once. Meanwhile, I'll come every day and do the best I can to bring her back."

"How—how much danger—?" Jenny asked tremulously.

The doctor patted her hand. "She has a stout little heart—and we'll hope," he said.

When he had gone, the clinger seemed surrounded with sorrow. Jenny and Carlotta and Stephen sat silent, stunned by what had happened to Mady. The kitchen seemed very quiet without her. None of them had realized until now that Mady was really the heart of this room. Always she had been here, as domestic as a little old woman, as unobtrusive and necessary as the ticking of the clock. She was not, however, unobtrusive now. Her very absence brought her to mind. All her piquant eagerness to keep up with what was "going on in the family" haunted the shadowy corners until they seemed to be crying her name.

"I should have been the one to be hurt," moaned Carlotta. "I've never been as useful as Mady. Why, she can cook a lot better than I can——"

As Carlotta paused to wipe the tears from her eyes, Jenny interrupted her honest observations. "No one should have been hurt. And when Mady gets well we'll have to look after her better. We forget she's only eight years old because she's so capable."

Stephen tiptoed toward the bedroom. "I'm not leaving her till she wakes," he vowed in a choked voice.

Christopher moved to the stove. "I'm not Mady," he said very quietly. "But I'll try to substitute. I think we all need a cup of good coffee."

Jenny made no effort to stop him as he worked at the stove. Dully she watched him fill the pot with water and take the coffee tin down from the shelf. Then she too tiptoed into the little bedroom and stood beside Stephen, watching Mady's almost imperceptible breathing with grief-stricken eyes.

Coffee helped revive them a little. As they sat sipping it slowly at the kitchen table, Christopher talked quietly and sensibly. They were not to allow themselves to become ill from worry, he told them. Mady would need their combined strength now. They were to hope and hope hard for the best. If they even thought of defeat in their fight to restore her health, it would hamper their progress. Jenny was not to fret about money, he instructed, or what the doctor's bill might be. Such things had their own way of straightening themselves out. And because he must sail at five o'clock and couldn't stay with them longer, they must not think he was leaving them alone. Everything he could do would be done, and if real tragedy threatened, he would leave the boat at whatever point he happened to be and return to Pittsburgh by land the moment he was notified. Above all, he warned them soberly, they must not hesitate to call on him.

"You're very kind to us, Christopher," Jenny told him gratefully.

He looked at the clock on the shelf and realized that he had to make a hurried departure. He, too, went into the bedroom for a last look at Mady, before he made his farewell to the others.

"I'll blow the whistle on the steamboat as we leave the Point," he promised. "It will mean I am saying to you, 'Take heart. All will be well. Take heart!'"

A little after five o'clock when they actually heard the whistle, they all tried to be as gallant as his message urged. "Take heart." Even as bleak as Jenny felt, the words struck a sudden glow in her being. She felt herself warmed against dark days ahead.

Stephen's vow not to leave Mady until she woke, although fired with loyalty, proved not at all practical. Along with Jenny, he realized that come what might, work must go on. Both had to consider the money they earned. Both were gravely aware that meager though it was, it was all they had to carry them through this emergency. If anyone could be spared to stay at home with Mady, Carlotta was the logical one. And stagestruck as she was, and loath to miss a minute of the work at the theater, she nevertheless wholeheartedly took over the chores in the clinger.

If the situation had any aspect of humor, it also came from Carlotta. She was all for killing the goat. Sandy, she protested, had been the cause of this tragedy. If she hadn't been so stubborn up there on the rock, Mady would not have climbed up to make her come down. And if Mady had not climbed, maintained Carlotta, she wouldn't have slipped on the ice. So, get rid of Sandy, said she.

Jenny, however, was sensible. Sandy, she pointed out, was the best milk goat they had ever had. Aside from that practical matter, she had been Mady's pet. Suppose there came a day when Mady wanted her again and they had to tell her that Sandy was dead?

So Carlotta had to be content with laying up treasure for Mady instead of taking vengeance on Sandy. Mady had a favorite candy store down on Carson Street. Every Saturday Jenny had given her a few pennies to spend there. Invariably Mady had stood with her eyes glued to the big glass candy case, trying to choose among many varieties but always ending up with the same choice. There were tiny tin skillets in that candy case. They were filled with smooth candy cream and each had its own tiny shining tin spoon. Some of the cream was pink, some yellow, some blue. On rare occasions it could be had in pale green. These little tin skillets fascinated domestic Mady. She had a whole collection of them. When the candy cream was gone, she washed and polished the pans until they shone like silver. Then she hung them in a row, each with its tiny tin spoon, on the wall above the kitchen sink. So Carlotta began buying skillets with which to delight Mady on the day she should awake.

Three days passed by and still she slept on. Hour followed hour, and she neither opened her eyes nor turned on her pillow. Her lethargy was so complete that Jenny had to bend down and lay her ear close to Mady's heart to make sure it was beating. Each day the doctor came and administered the necessary nourishment. Each day his verdict was the same: "We shall have to be patient and wait."

All who lived on Goat Hill were drawn to the Bayard's clinger. Seldom did a day pass by that Carlotta did not open the door to Mrs. Weimar or Mrs. Stepnosky, waiting with a pot of broth, a bit of fruit, a crusty brown loaf of bread freshly baked. Timothy Drew and old Franz hovered over the brood like beneficent guardians. Big Dan and Francesca came too, genuinely concerned. Sorrow brought people together, thought Jenny. In every corner of the clinger, there seemed to be a spirit of good will.

Meanwhile, every day, she and Stephen worked at their jobs. Mady's illness seemed to have come at the most inconvenient time. Jenny was overworked at the hotel. The Monongahela House was preparing for a capacity guest list with the coming of Jenny Lind. Stephen too was overworked at the glasshouse, where all were feverishly completing designs to be entered in the great spring glass show. And no matter how hard Jenny tried to be reasonable, it made her uneasy to leave Mady in the full charge of Carlotta. There were so many things she herself wanted to do for the little sister, though there was scarcely anything anyone could do.

The fourth day after the accident, Stephen sent word to Jenny at the hotel that he couldn't get home until late. A rush had developed at the glasshouse and he, with every other employee, would have to work overtime to meet it. Old Franz had given Jenny a bag of freshly made sandwiches. She decided to take them to Stephen in case he should have eaten all his lunch and didn't have time to go out for supper.

Stephen, in the glasshouse that night, was something Jenny would always remember. She knew his work was hard, but she hadn't really realized the actual physical strain of it. She had been dwelling too much, she thought now, on what Stephen would someday become. She had entirely lost sight of how much muscle as well as brain it would take to achieve it in Big Dan's way.

When she entered the glasshouse with Stephen's supper, the place was a roaring inferno. Glass blowers were standing at their posts with balls of fire on their blow pipes. The glory hole was ablaze with flames. A gust of air so hot it stifled her swept out from the pot room where potmakers were treading the clay. A worker was melting a batch in a furnace heated to full intensity.

At last she found Stephen, stripped to the waist. It was his job tonight to help "tease" the furnace. This meant feeding it with fuel to maintain the proper degree of heat. He had not only to see that it was intensely white-hot, but also to be sure that it was distributed uniformly in the furnace pit. The glass material had to come directly under its fusing influence—just so—as Big Dan had instructed.

Stephen's face was broiled. Perspiration poured from his forehead. His arms and legs and chest were dripping. For twelve long hours, without relief, he had been feeding that dragon's mouth, as Jenny thought of it. For twelve long hours he had stood tense and alert, carefully straining to see that all went as it should. Shoveling coal was hard on his back. When Jenny approached she saw him bend wearily over his shovel as if he could no longer stand. He tried to straighten up to his accustomed height but his knees sagged and threatened to buckle.

"Stevie . . ." Jenny's voice was alarmed.

He looked up, none too pleased that she was here to see him bending under the strain.

"What are you doing here?" he asked. "You should be home with Mady."

Jenny produced her bag. "I thought you wouldn't have time for supper so I brought you these. I won't stay," she hastened to add. "I just didn't want you to go hungry."

He leaned on his shovel, a little shamefaced. "I didn't mean to bite your head off."

She silenced him at once. "You're tired. You're overtired. You ought to come home."

Stephen suddenly smiled. In spite of his effort, his smile seemed tired too.

"I will in a couple of hours." He winked at her comically. "Now you get out of here or you know what Jo is liable to say——"

"Promise to eat your sandwiches?" she begged.

"I'll eat," he comforted her by saying. "I'll eat them all."

"And don't forget to drink your milk." Jenny turned to go.

The glaring furnace heat oppressed her. The sight of Stephen, so exhausted, caused a dull ache in her heart. What she did not know as she climbed the hill was that Stephen had no milk to drink. Every day he had been selling the milk she gave him with his lunch. By the time the doctor's bill was presented he'd have quite a few extra pennies saved. And, thought Stephen heroically, water tasted almost as good.

Seventeen

A Cup of Tea for Jenny Lind

When Jenny reached the clinger that evening she found Francesca there with Carlotta. They were talking quietly in the kitchen while Mady slept on.

"Jenny . . ." Francesca rose to greet her as she came wearily through the door.

"Hello, Francesca. How are you?"

Carlotta regarded her sister with keen, appraising eyes. "You look fagged out."

Jenny hung up her shawl. "Guess I am. So's Stevie." Before Carlotta could speak again she was crossing the threshold of the bedroom. "Is Mady—?"

"Mady seems just the same to me." Carlotta followed her into the room. "But the doctor says she's beginning to breathe better."

Jenny stood looking down at the small white face on the pillow. She had never realized before that Mady had such long lashes. They fringed her eyelids now like pale golden threads of silk against white wax. If only she'd open her eyes! thought Jenny desperately.

Carlotta, standing beside her, touched her shoulder. "I've made you a cup of hot chocolate," she whispered. "Come and drink it. Maybe you'll feel better."

Jenny was grateful for the chocolate. She was glad, too, that Francesca was there. Somehow, since Mady's accident, the clinger seemed bleak unless there was company. It was probably because she and Stevie and Carlotta all had more time to think their own gloomy thoughts if there was no one there to cheer them up.

"Listen!" Carlotta was instantly on her feet, almost upsetting her cup. "It's—it's——"

She flew out of the kitchen and into the bedroom, Jenny following fast.

"She's trying to sit up! Mady's honestly trying——" Carlotta cried half-hysterically.

"Quiet!" warned Jenny, as Francesca, too, came into the room. "And, hurry, Carlotta, go for the doctor!"

As Carlotta flew out the door again, Jenny went to Mady's bedside.

"Jen—Jenny . . ."

The little girl had opened her eyes, and was staring at her sister bewilderedly.

"Mady! Mady! Oh, my darling!"

Jenny gently forced the child back down on her pillow. She wouldn't allow her to speak although Mady tried to mumble some words.

"You've been sick, Mady-kins," Jenny explained to her softly. "You mustn't talk and exert yourself."

After a moment it seemed that Mady was glad enough not to talk. By the time the doctor came, both Jenny and Francesca feared that she had sunk again into a coma. The doctor reassured them. Mady was only weak, he affirmed, and would be weak for a long time, but the period of her coma was over and she would now take a decided turn for the better. *Yes, the coma was over and Mady would get well!*

"Thank God, oh, thank God!" Jenny knelt at the bedside and wept.

When Stephen came home and discovered that Mady was conscious, he, too, was overcome with gladness. Jenny saw him wipe tears from his eyes furtively.

Days passed more pleasantly in the clinger as Mady began to mend. Within a week's time she was permitted to sit in Jenny's little rosewood rocker for an hour at a time. From such fussing and spoiling as went on, Mady delightedly said, she could tell they had really missed her! Even Sandy was brought into the house. For one whole evening she lay snuggled up in front of the fire. Mady wanted her there so her pet would know all was forgiven. Sandy made a great fuss and awkwardly put her front hoofs up on Mady's shoulders, *ba-ba*ing a hilarious welcome.

Mady adored the collection of little tin skillets Carlotta had stored up for her, and she was very droll about Carlotta's cooking.

"In no time at all," she promised gaily, "I'll be up and around again, and then I'll bet Carlotta will be scarce!"

In spite of her good intentions, Carlotta was scarce even before Mady was able to be up and around. She did not mean to be, of course, but the sweet lure of the stage proved to be too much one rainy day. Mady always took a nap now, in the afternoons. Since all danger was passed, Carlotta felt reasonably free to leave the clinger for an hour at a time, to follow her own pursuits. On this particular afternoon she had simply gone walking. She liked to walk in the rain, because it seemed romantic. Before she realized it, she was drawn irresistibly to the stage door of the theater. And when Jenny came home hours later, Mady, in her little night robe, was trying to pare potatoes and had already put the kettle on.

"Where's Carlotta?" Jenny was shocked.

"You needn't get so mad about it," Mady retorted, eager to shield her wandering sister. "She just forgot to come home, I guess."

"Forgot!" exploded Jenny, now thoroughly angry. "And you about to catch your very death of cold paddling about in that thin little robe and slippers!"

"But she hasn't been out for such a long time," Mady protested. "And you know Carlotta likes——"

"I don't care what she likes," stormed Jenny. "Now you get back into bed and I'll see that she comes home!"

Mady scrambled into bed. She could count on one hand the times she had seen Jenny as upset as she was now. She sat docilely back against her pillow and allowed Jenny to put a hot brick at her feet which, come to think of it, were cold. She sipped, without protest, the cup of broth Jenny brought her from the kitchen. Then Jenny put her shawl over her head.

"Where are you going?" Mady asked meekly.

Jenny made a disgusted grimace. "To the the theater, Madykins! To the theater!"

A half hour later she stood, just as angry, at the stage door. She had made up her mind that Carlotta would have to get over this theater business—Francesca or no Francesca. There were too many practical problems to be met in the clinger to allow Carlotta the luxury of being stage-struck. From remarks dropped by Francesca herself, it was a precarious career at best, not at all substantial as Stephen's was surely destined to be.

"How do you do, miss." An old man with a pipe in his mouth was blocking the stage door entrance.

"How do you do." Jenny's voice was unusually crisp. "I am Jenny Bayard and I want my sister Carlotta."

"Carlotta!" The old man's face lighted up. "Now don't tell me you're sisters!"

"We're sisters all right," said Jenny grimly. "And I want her to come home."

The old man smiled companionably. "Well, now, maybe you'd better go in and get her. She hasn't been here for so long I think they're keepin' her pretty busy."

Jenny whisked past him impatiently. Busy or not, Carlotta should have been busier at home! She was probably Fanny Kemble-ing herself again, Jenny thought, disgruntled.

"Wait, miss, you're going the wrong way. I'll take you backstage."

The old man was following her affably, evidently pleased to usher in the magnetic little Carlotta's sister. Jenny followed him through a dim corridor. Suddenly a new thought occurred to her. Wouldn't it be wiser, she was thinking, not to let Carlotta know she was here for the time being? Shouldn't she, perhaps, catch a glimpse of this new world of the theater—even Carlotta at her work—and draw her own conclusions? Jenny turned to the old man and surprised him with a smile.

"I've just been thinking," she said slowly, "that I shouldn't disturb my sister if she's as busy as you say."

He took off his cap, scratched his forehead and smiled. "I think she's on stage, miss."

"On stage!"

"She's in the interlude," he added, "and she's pleased as Punch about it." The old man went on loquaciously, "'Pop', she came and told me just about an hour ago, and she looked as sparklin' as a Christmas tree, 'I'm playing Athenee.'"

"Who's Athenee?"

"It's the ballet scene."

Jenny considered all this for a moment. "Backstage." "On stage." "Athenee." The unfamiliar jargon of the theater now made her less angry than curious. Yes, if she were wise, she thought again, she'd make this trip a golden opportunity. Mady would probably be asleep by now, and Stephen should soon be home.

Jenny smiled again at Pop. "All this is new to me," she told him engagingly. "Perhaps I'd better not interfere with Carlotta if she's on stage. She might get embarrassed and not do so well." She paused for a moment, then went on eagerly, "Could you, I wonder, put me where I could see and hear everything without being seen by anyone?"

Pop's face lighted up again. "Sure thing, Miss——"

"My name's Jenny," she supplied.

He took her hand as though they shared a conspiracy. "Well, Miss Jenny," he said with enthusiasm, "I know just the place."

During the next half hour a whole new world was opened to Jenny's wondering eyes. From her vantage point behind the draperies of an empty box, she looked down on the stage with its row of footlights. Men were moving what they referred to as "props" here and there on the boards. There was a French cheval glass, a red plush couch, an armchair done in gold brocade. "Drawing-room props," she heard them called. Open folding doors led into a conservatory upstage. It had glass windows down to the ground on either side. Back in "the wings" Jenny could see other props in the making. Stage-hands were moving table and ottomans on stage, carrying pictures in gilded frames. Scene shifters moved whole card-board walls of the splendid drawing-room set.

There was a busy, practical, yet make-believe air about everything. The busyness was revealed in the actual setting of the stage, the make-believe in its odd assortment of characters. Francesca was down there moving about regally in the extravagant costume of a wealthy society woman. As far as costume was concerned, she might have been Victoria Blakewell, thought Jenny, interested. She was playing the part of a "Mrs. Tiffany," and playing it, indeed, with great dash and aplomb.

"Now, Mrs. Tiffany," Jenny heard the stage director shout, "let's have those lines again."

Francesca spread her pale green taffeta skirts on the red plush couch. She made a royal gesture with her yellow feather fan. Jenny could see she was not really Francesca now. She was, as Carlotta so often said now, "in character." She was speaking to her guest—a fastidiously attired young man who wore elaborate clothes and a great profusion of jewelry. Jenny heard the director call him "Count Jolimaître."

Francesca, as Mrs. Tiffany, was saying: "Count, I am so much ashamed—pray, excuse me! Although a lady of large fortune, and one, Count, who can boast of the highest connections, I blush to confess that I have never traveled—while you, Count, I presume are at home in all the courts of Europe."

And as Francesca paused impressively, the Count replied: "Courts? Eh? Oh, yes, Madam, very true. I believe I am pretty well known in some of the courts of Europe—*police courts*. (The last two words were said "aside.") In a word, Madam, I had seen enough of civilized life—wanted to refresh myself by a sight of barbarous countries and customs—had my choice between the Sandwich Islands and New York—chose New York!"

Francesca smiled a "society" smile. "How very complimentary to our country!" said she.

"That's all," shouted the director as Francesca was about to go on. "Curtain, please. Let's have the interlude!"

As the curtain came down Jenny caught sight of Carlotta hovering like a butterfly among a group of players in the wings. She was wearing a dancer's costume as diaphanous as gossamer and as blue as a summer night. Little minx, thought Jenny, exasperated as she noted the loveliness with which Carlotta wore it. Unconsciously, she and the dress were a single embodiment of rhythm, grace and color.

Again Jenny heard the director's voice. "Ballet scene, please. Ready—on stage!"

In the next few moments Jenny gathered that the "Ballet Interlude" as this scene was called, was to be presented between the acts of *Fashion* which was, of course, the play of the evening. The interlude was adapted from Moliére's "Le Mariage Forcé" which had been originally danced by His Majesty Louis XIV and his court on the twenty-ninth day of January, 1664. Jenny wondered what Carlotta could do in a ballet without having had dancer's training, but she was soon to discover that the director was wise in handling Carlotta and had given her a part that would reveal her potentialities and yet not tax her meager experience.

The curtain went up to reveal a square in Paris in 1661. It was early evening and the square was dimly lighted. There was soft silvery music while a character named Sganarelle spoke his lines and finally slept, leaning against an ancient wall. Presently he seemed to dream and the stage was pervaded with a fairy-blue light such as the stuff that dreams are made of. Again the director's voice: "On stage, Athenee!"

"Athenee," Jenny immediately saw, was Carlotta—little firebrand Carlotta of the sea-green eyes and the red-gold curls, and the airy grace of a leaf on a willow. To a shower of music as light as the notes from a shepherd's pipe, she glided out of the wings alone—not a ballet dancer at all—but more like a sprite from some fairy woodland. She glided toward the sleeping Sganarelle, pantomimed delicately, and even in her gestures, somehow created a fantasy that led even practical Jenny into the Springtime in Paris long, long ago.

Finally Carlotta spoke and her lovely voice held a haunting beauty.

> Sleep, Sganarelle, and dream, for dreams will throng.
> Your dreams you may forget, but not my song!

Very softly, Carlotta half-talked, half-sang:

> The golden years are passing,
> How fast they fly away! Away!
> But care not how the years may go
> If only love will stay.
> In hearts alone too cold for love
> The knell of Youth is rung;
> So take the kiss that waits for you
> For Love is always young,
> Is always, always young!
> So take the kiss that waits for you,

> For Love is always young,
> Is always, always young!

As the song neared its end, she glided away from the sleeping figure like a phantom child bent on capturing a dream. Jenny became aware that everyone in the theater was completely held in thrall by her. Even the director's voice was sober as he ordered quietly: "Once more, Athenee," and Carlotta began her scene again.

This brief part—excepting a line or two at the end of the interlude—was all that Carlotta would do in her first appearance on the stage. Yet, as she repeated the scene, Jenny realized again that the very quality of her acting had captured the imagination of everyone in the house. All were watching Carlotta as if she were a breath-taking flash of flame. Everyone was listening, too, and as Jenny heard Carlotta's musical voice and watched her pretty gesturings, she had the feeling that all present had. Carlotta was lost, irrevocably lost in her part. Jenny didn't call it "theater presence" but she realized that her capricious little sister was actually creating springtime in Paris for them all—that even the veteran actors and actresses were being made aware of it. Imagination. Make-believe. Magic. All these Carlotta was summoning to her aid with a wisdom beyond her years. It was as though the artistry of another actress from another age was welling up inside of her, giving amazing credence to her performance.

And Jenny heard the director say: "Bravo, Carlotta!" He took off his hat and bowed low. Carlotta looked at him, bewildered, as if it were difficult to come back to a workaday world.

"Bravo! Bravo!" Others in the wings took up the cry. A moment later Carlotta, on stage, was surrounded.

Jenny watched the scene for a moment, then as if she had suddenly learned all she had come to discover, she quietly turned and left the theater box. She was glad to leave the building unnoticed. Even Pop was not at the stage door. He, too, had stayed to watch and listen to Carlotta.

As she walked slowly home, Jenny grappled with her problem. Carlotta's performance, however praised, could not really have been perfect. It was probably as short of perfection as Stephen's little star window had been, but the important thing to remember was that it had been inspired. All that was creative in Stephen and took form in glass was also creative in Carlotta, feeding her hunger to be a great actress. Francesca had been quick to detect the inner flame of her, quicker by far than Jenny, who frankly admitted now that she had simply thought Carlotta liked to put on airs.

But—*an actress in the family!* What was she to do about it? And what, for instance, would Christopher say? His only mention of the stage had been to speak of Jenny Lind, and hers was a great name in music.

Again Jenny's thoughts went around in circles. Again she wondered what had gone into the making of the famous singer's career. As on the night she had first met Francesca, she determined to find out. If Carlotta were to begin a lifelong career in the theater at such an early age, it was strictly up to Jenny to see that she was started out on the right foot. Francesca would be in the Pittsburgh theater only for the present season. And what should be done for Carlotta then?

Eager as Jenny was, however, to do what was right for Carlotta, she was soon to learn that, whatever her personal interest in seeing Jenny Lind might be, every attempt to meet her would be barred. The staff at the Monongahela House was warned that the singer desired the utmost privacy. Mrs. Houston told Jenny that it was part of the management's policy to shield celebrities from all public contact they wished to avoid. Jenny was not too dense to see the wisdom of this. Jenny Lind, heaven knew, must long ago have had her fill of people rushing to see her. Naturally anyone of great fame was surrounded morning, noon and night.

So on the day the young Swedish nightingale arrived in Pittsburgh, Jenny almost gave up her desire to catch even a glimpse of her. But not old Franz. He had bought himself a ticket for her concert and was going to hear her sing!

"Ah, Jenny *Liebling*–" he sighed as he stood beside Jenny at their work table, up to his elbows in dough–"for once I am extravagant! I shall hear tonight one of the greatest singers in the world!"

Jenny wished she could tell him what her plans had been, but she had not dared confide in anyone. She smiled as he went on dreamily.

"Tonight I'll see the curtain go up and there she'll be–her voice a call from the Old World." Unconsciously he spoke a little lower. "Maybe she'll sing 'The Herdsman's Song' and it will bring us the midnight sun and the cataracts of Sweden. I spent summers there as a boy, Jenny *Liebling*, and often I'd trail the falls for lost sheep. Ah, I know that country, and to-night I'll be a boy there once again."

"They say her voice has magic in it," Jenny said wistfully, wishing that she and the brood might go to the concert too.

Old Franz sighed again. "That is because it speaks to the heart."

Jenny Lind was to dine privately in her suite at the hotel. Mrs. Houston stayed in the kitchen to supervise this room service personally. Light delectable dishes were prepared for the young prima donna, so exquisitely arranged that they were beautiful to see. Jenny had never realized before that a long-stemmed rose and hand-painted china could well transform a dinner tray into a work of art.

About five o'clock in the afternoon a call came down from the singer's suite that Jenny Lind wished a cup of tea. Mrs. Houston had left the kitchen only a few moments before to see to the needs of other special guests who were taxing the service of the entire hotel. Old Franz took the message from Jenny Lind's maid. A tea tray would be sent up at once, he promised.

"Franz, oh, Franz, please!" Jenny's eyes were shining with excitement.

"*Ja,* Jenny *Liebling?*"

She reached for his hand and pressed it hard. "Let me take it up! Please let me take the tea tray up to her room!"

"You want to see the Swedish singer?" he questioned with a twinkle in his eye.

Jenny forgot herself for a moment. Surely this was happening only because she was *destined* to talk with Jenny Lind just as she had planned!

"I—I want to see her about Carlotta," she told Franz involuntarily.

"Carlotta!" Franz echoed, amazed.

Jenny almost clung to him.

"I'll tell you all about it later. Just let me take the tray up!"

In the next few moments, it was made ready. A fragile pink luster teapot adorned it; a single white rose added its fragrance to the aroma of fine Chinese tea. There were tiny heart-shaped cakes on a painted plate.

"Oh, how pretty you've made it!" Jenny eyed it appreciatively.

She took the tray from Franz and started across the kitchen. She was passing Helen Corrado's table when suddenly the girl wheeled around without warning. Even after it was over, Jenny couldn't determine whether Helen had bumped her elbow or deliberately put out her foot. All that she really knew was that the tray slipped from her hands and crashed as it fell to the floor.

Jenny looked down, terrified to see the teapot broken into bits. Quickly, however, her terror gave way to a deep, wild sweep of anger.

"You did that on purpose!" she accused Helen

"What seems to be the trouble here?" Mrs. Houston had just come back.

"She—she——" Jenny faced her, outraged.

Mrs. Houston silenced her with a gesture. Old Franz was about to speak up in Jenny's defense but Mrs. Houston silenced him also.

"I don't think we need discuss this," she said very coldly. "The damage is done to the teapot, and of course it can't be mended. What we can mend, however, is your insubordination, Jenny."

"*My* insubordination!" Jenny repeated.

Again Mrs. Houston silenced her. "Helen has just informed me," she said slowly and with emphasis, "that you were about to approach Jenny Lind about your sister Carlotta. This hotel will simply not allow a visiting celebrity to be bothered with the personal affairs of a domestic."

Mrs. Houston looked poor miserable Jenny directly in the

eye. "I need not tell you, I think, that your services are no longer required."

"But, Mrs. Houston . . . ." It was Franz's voice again, protesting.

She turned to him with finality. "If you don't mind," she said sarcastically, "I consider this incident closed."

Jenny took off her little white apron. She gave it to Mrs. Houston and slowly walked out of the kitchen.

Eighteen

Three Golden Rivers

So Jenny's pretty plot in Carlotta's interests had resulted only in the loss of her job. As Jenny walked home she could see some justice in Mrs. Houston's belief that the great Swedish singer should not be bothered with the personal problems of Jenny Bayard. Yet, on the other hand, Jenny had heard that among the great and near-great there were those who sought out new talent and nurtured it as Francesca was trying to do.

And Mrs. Houston need not have dismissed her so summarily, especially since Helen Corrado had played the role of informer and had deliberately trapped her. The girl had apparently been listening from her work table to the whole conversation between Jenny and Franz. When she had heard that Jenny was to share a glamorous moment with Jenny Lind, the long-smoldering fires of her jealousy had blazed into flame. While Franz was preparing Jenny Lind's tray Helen must have hurried to meet Mrs. Houston, on her way down the back stairs.

So Jenny traced the pattern of that final episode and traced it correctly. Her throat tightened suddenly and tears welled up in her eyes as she realized that the familiar routine of her days was broken. Never again would she be a part of the big warm hotel kitchen. Never again could she share its vitality. She would miss working with old Franz most of all. Somehow he had become for her the personification of Old World kindliness and generosity, and an innate courtliness brought here to industrial Pittsburgh from the music-loving dream world of Vienna.

Wearily Jenny paused on the wooden steps that went up from the city. Wearily she looked down on it, suddenly seeing it now as an enemy, a fiery-mouthed dragon she and her family had to fight. Springtime was haunting Goat Hill. It would soon be Stevie's birthday and in not so many weeks they could turn the pages of the calendar on their first year in Pittsburgh. What had they accomplished, she wondered now, as far as finding their own niche was concerned?

True, Stephen was progressing fast, and that was what they had come for. True, they had found the clinger and managed to keep it by hard, continuous exertion and consistently doing without. Discouraged as Jenny actually was, she had to admit that their efforts had not all been fruitless. They had, she realized, been four against the world, and certainly Stevie, Carlotta and little Mady had accepted the fact valiantly, knowing that Jenny was their only prop to lean on. The thought gave her courage now. What they had put into their first hard year in Pittsburgh would serve them again in the second. Somehow she'd get another job.

The brisk March winds blew down the hill. They seemed to sweep the valley clean. All three rivers were bright with sunlight. Furnaces, too, were belching fire toward the sky, mingling their orange and blue and copper flares with the silver sheen of the sun. The more crowded portion of the city at the Point was clear-cut and distinct. She could see the Blakewell boat yards on the Allegheny shore. John Blakewell was building more boats this year than ever before. As Christopher had said, it was the golden age for steamboats, and boat after boat was being launched for her maiden voyage to St. Louis and all points south. Pittsburgh was speaking for itself in iron and steel and boat building as well as in glass. Yes, thought Jenny, as she stood looking down on the crooked streets, all that went into the making of a great metropolis was going into Pittsburgh now.

As she stood looking down at the rivers today, Jenny thought that Christopher had become an inspiration to her and the brood as well as their gayest, best friend. She smiled to herself, remembering their first serious talk together right here on this hill. She had told him then that she had been accustomed to thinking of the rivers as Pittsburgh's own private streams. She remembered now how he had given her the vision to realize that they were big national arteries that bound the North to the South and the East to the West in steellike bands of trade. But knowing Christopher had given her vision in many, many things. Books as well as steamboats. Elegance as well as expression in good taste. The parasol girls as well as the pampered world they lived in.

Jenny suddenly shivered and it was not from the cold. She had had the sudden frightening thought of what her life and the brood's would be like if it lacked the luster Christopher gave it. Would he continue to be friends with her as well as with the parasol girls? Would there ever come a day, she wondered, when his choice in favor of her would be made? Again she burned with the memory of his gay Christmas kiss. Again she thanked Stevie and heaven for being the means of bringing her to this fiery monster of Pittsburgh!

Thinking of Stephen, Jenny glanced down at the flatboat on the Monongahela shore. Like the mills and furnaces, it was not so dramatic a spectacle by day as it was by night, but it was still impressive. It was the more impressive to Jenny because she could picture Stevie at work there treading the clay, or mixing the batch, or teasing the furnace for fusing glass. Or if he were not busy at such labors, he would be doing, she hoped, what he liked best—sitting high on his apprentice's stool dreaming up new patterns.

Jenny finally turned her back on the city and walked slowly up to the clinger. She would not tell the brood yet, she decided, that she had lost her job. It would only make them worry. If they knew the circumstances, Carlotta would feel that she, and she alone, had brought on this misfortune. Prejudiced as Jenny had been against Carlotta's stage fever her one experience in the theater box had made her see that there was something creative to be developed in Carlotta. Jenny mentally vowed that Carlotta, like Stephen, should have her chance. Just because Jenny's first attempt to help had ended in disaster, Carlotta was not to be blamed. Carlotta had not asked for help. She had no idea Jenny had been planning to approach Jenny Lind. Jenny had done that strictly on her own and she would have to take the consequences.

As she opened the door, Jenny was surprised to see Big Dan sitting at the kitchen table. Opposite him Mady was smilingly pouring coffee from her favorite coffeepot.

"Jenny! You're home early!" Mady put her cup aside.

Big Dan rose from the table. "You didn't expect to find me here, I know, but I had to come and bring the news."

"Good news, I hope?" Jenny smiled. "But sit down and drink your coffee first."

"Coffee can wait." Big Dan laughed. "But this——"

Jenny laid aside her shawl. She looked at him with radiant eyes. "It *is* good news," she assumed. "And it's about Stevie!"

Big Dan placed a chair at the table for her. "It's about Stevie all right, and it's pretty wonderful."

In the next few moments Jenny and Mady learned that the Committee of Awards for the Glassmakers of Pittsburgh had chosen Stephen's pattern to adorn the tableware at their banquet. This affair would herald the opening of their Annual Springtime Exposition. No one was privileged yet to know exactly what the pattern was. The secret would be zealously guarded until the night the glassware appeared on the table. A special group of workers under Big Dan's supervision would be sworn to secrecy and assigned to make the glass. And what meant most of all, a fine scholarship accompanied the award. What it was and how it would serve the winner would not be announced until the night of the banquet, but Big Dan was sure, he told Jenny, that it would be of amazing proportions.

"Heavenly days!" said Mady. "Stevie's a great man already!" She looked at Jenny who was suddenly crying softly into a corner of her apron. "What's that to cry about?"

Jenny's mouth quivered as she wiped her eyes. "Just when things look blackest," she said, "something happens to make them right."

Big Dan's voice was warm as he rose to go. "So plan to look your prettiest, Jenny. You'll be very proud of Stevie at the show."

"Can we all go to the banquet?" Mady questioned, sitting on the edge of her chair.

Big Dan laughed at her eagerness. "What would it mean to Stevie if Jenny and the brood were not there?"

"Who else will be invited?" Mady persisted.

Big Dan attempted a graceful flourish of his big, clumsy hands. "Ah, my dear child, the very flower of Pittsburgh society!"

Mady shut her eyes tight, then she opened them and said gaily, "Good! We'll see the parasol girls—and I just bet they'll be proud to know us!"

"Don't be too sure," Jenny laughed.

They followed Big Dan to the door. He took Jenny's hand in parting.

"You can be very proud of yourself, my dear," he said soberly. "You've accomplished what you set out to do. You've started Stevie on his way——"

"I couldn't have done anything, Big Dan, if it hadn't been for you. Please believe me grateful."

He patted her awkwardly on the shoulder. "There's an old proverb, Jenny, and it's true, I think. It says that 'cream will always rise.'"

Since Stephen's award shed a saving light on their situation, Jenny told the brood that night that she had lost her job. Their anger was not against Mrs. Houston. Carlotta wanted to pull Helen's hair.

"Don't make so much of it," said Jenny. "There'll be another job for me somewhere."

"When I make more money," volunteered Stephen, "I won't allow you to work."

Jenny laughed at him gaily. "Work's good for everyone, Stevie. Do you think I want to sit on *your* laurels?"

Carlotta made a graceful gesture.

"I'm not going to sit on whatever-you-call-it either. I'm

working, too, until I get to be as great as Fanny Kemble!" She turned from the group at the fireside and walked to her bureau. "And now," she said, opening drawers, "we've got to think about clothes!"

"Clothes?" repeated Jenny.

Carlotta stood, poised and beautiful, and delivered what she felt to be a much-needed lecture.

"That's what I said and I mean it, Jenny. We'll be the honored ones at the banquet and we've got to look halfway decent. If you want to stay friends with Christopher, clothes can do a lot more than you think! Even if they aren't as fine as those old parasol girls'!"

Jenny was reminded of Carlotta's lecture the day the *River Queen* sailed into port scarcely a week later. Christopher came immediately to the clinger. He was eager to learn how things had gone with them since the dark day he had left them after Mady's accident.

Jenny hadn't expected him. When she looked up and saw him standing at the kitchen door, she got up from her knees, embarassed. She and Mady had been polishing the kitchen stove. There was one big, black smudge of polish on her face, another on her apron.

"Why, Christopher!" She stood regarding him, surprised.

"Hello, Sam!" he replied merrily.

"Sam!"

He laughed aloud as Mady hurried across the kitchen to embrace him. "She looks all done up for a minstrel, doesn't she, Mady girl? Let's call her the end man!"

Jenny's face was scarlet as she hastened into the bedroom. She wiped the smudge off her face, put on a clean apron, and wound a ribbon through her hair. Carlotta was right, she scolded herself. She should begin to worry about such things as fashions!

Christopher stayed at the clinger for hours. He had to be told about Mady's sickness and how she finally started to mend, about Carlotta's "Bohemian" doings and what Jenny had tried to do for her. And Jenny told him, too, that she had lost her job, ending up with the brighter news of what had happened to Stephen.

Christopher was gay about it all. "This should be called the Up and Down House instead of the clinger," he maintained. "You're either up on the crest of the wave or down at the bottom of the sea!"

"I still wish Jenny could have talked to jenny Lind," Mady said mournfully. "Then she would know what to do for Carlotta."

"Why doesn't Jenny ask me," Christopher questioned.

"You?"

He went to the stove and put on the kettle. "I've had coffee with Jenny Lind—French drip coffee—the sort I'm making now. I know as well as she does herself what went into the making of her, as our pretty Jenny says."

"Did she start to study when she was as young as Carlotta?" Jenny wanted to know.

"She was younger than Carlotta," he claimed, "when she began preparing for the stage. Jenny Lind was a little girl only nine years old who used to sing to her cat."

"Her—her cat!" exclaimed wide-eyed Mady.

Christopher began to sing off-key.

> Pussy-cat, pussy-cat, where have you been?
> I've been to London to look at the Queen.

Jenny laughed at him merrily as she remonstrated, "Please, Christopher, be sensible! Was she really only nine years old when she began to study?"

"I give you my word," he said, suddenly serious. "That was her age when she was discovered by Herr Croellius and taken to Count Puke at the Royal Theatre School in Stockholm." Christopher took the kettle off the fire as he went on: "'How old is she?' asked the Count. 'Nine,' replied Herr Croellius. 'Nine?' thundered the Count. 'But this is not a crèche! It is the King's Theatre!'" Christopher made a sweeping bow. "That, my dears, was told me by Jenny Lind herself! We talked at a reception down in New Orleans."

"And they allowed her to stay at the school?" Jenny asked eagerly.

"She had what she told me were 'nine shining years of study' at the Royal Theatre School's expense."

"I'm glad that I know," Jenny said softly.

"I heard also," said Christopher, "that her teacher heard her sing 'Agatha's Prayer' in a way that actually struck her dumb. She turned to Jenny Lind and said, 'My child, I have nothing more to teach you. Do as nature tells you.'"

"Do as nature tells you," Jenny repeated his words. "Honestly, Christopher, I think that's what Carlotta does."

It seemed only a few days from that afternoon until the day of the glassmaker's banquet. The intervening time had been spent by Jenny in making clothes for herself and the brood, so they could "appear respectably." Timothy Drew had arranged for King to do enough hauling to enable her to spend some money for remnants at Horne's. She had sat long hours, sewing. Stevie, she said, was "a study in brown" with a gold-embroidered waistcoat. She had made Carlotta a white dotted

Swiss that gave her the look of a fragile white princess and made a flaming aureole of her hair. Mady wore a blue-flowered challis, while Jenny herself looked flower-fresh in a sheer rose-colored "picture dress" and a soft white cashmere shawl.

"I wish we had some jewelry to wear," Carlotta said wistfully.

"Jewelry?" asked Mady, wide-eyed.

Carlotta felt her lovely throat, bare of any ornament. "When I'm a great actress," she promised herself, "I'm going down to Robert's and pick out a gold locket. Some beau will be glad to buy it for me. All the parasol girls buy jewelry there."

They were all assigned to the speaker's table at the banquet. Stephen sat at the right of Big Dan, who was to be the speaker of the evening. The beautifully appointed table, sparkling with flowers and silver, was at right angles to the head of the long festive board at which sat one hundred special guests. These represented Pittsburgh's moguls, influential families like the Blakewells, industrialists who talked in terms of iron and steel and ships and glass. The sound of violins came from an orchestra encircled by potted palms at one end of the spacious room. Garlands of yellow roses seemed to be everywhere.

This note of yellow gold reflected the whole theme of the banquet. A golden banner hung as in the halls of knights of old, proclaiming the theme to the guests. With letters formed in yellow roses, Stephen's pattern—*Three Golden Rivers*—was announced for all to see. And at the place of each guest there stood a tall, thin-blown clear crystal goblet, fine as hand-made Venetian glass, on which the rivers had been gilded. It showed them meeting at the Point, golden with the glow of sunset, as the Bayards had seen them that first eventful day. Above the rivers were the high green hills and above the hills glistened a golden cloud bank in a sunset-tinted sky.

Three Golden Rivers. So Stephen had dreamed them. So they served him now.

Proudly Jenny sat beside him, her face as aglow as her heart. Christopher was smiling at her, pride in his eyes, too, from his place on down the table. Carlotta sent Jenny a penciled note scribbled in her hoydenish way, without respect, on a napkin. It read, "There's frozen-faced Victoria. Wonder what she's thinking now?"

Soon the master of ceremonies was introducing Big Dan as the main speaker of the evening. Jenny looked at him affectionately as he rose clumsily from his place at the table and looked quizzically at the guests. His subject, he said whimsically, was *glass.* It shouldn't be any surprise to them that he would tell its story.

So Big Dan plunged in. And the story he unfolded was fascinating to Jenny. She and Stephen sat completely absorbed in his words. Christopher, she noticed, was listening impressed. Even Rosalie and the parasol girls looked quite as captivated as if he were talking about music or books or fashions.

As he warmed to his subject, Big Dan brought romance to his story. The walls of the banquet room seemed to vanish. Jenny imagined that she saw the saffron-colored sails of early Phoenician ships. Slowly they seemed to move in the sunset across the vivid blue of the Mediterranean Sea, five thousand years before the birth of Christ.

"The sailors who sailed these ships were hungry," Big Dan told them. "They landed on a sandy shore and kindled fires with driftwood. They had crude cooking utensils but no place to put them. One of the sailors brought several blocks of soda from the cargo of the ship, and set them around the fire. Soon the big blocks melted and a fusion of sand and soda took place. As if a miracle were happening right in front of the sailors' eyes, there flowed from this ancient fire the first molten glass. They scooped up the glittering stuff," he continued, "and took it to Syria."

As he went on with his story, Jenny fancied she could see people gathering in marketplaces to look at the glass in wonderment. She listened intently as big Dan pointed out that while authorities differed in opinions, Syria became known as the birthplace of glass manufacture. Many centuries before Christ came to Galilee, the Syrians and Egyptians made glass, Big Dan told the assembly. There were even ancient paintings which pictured glass blowers at work in these countries. It was as though big Dan were unrolling a rich piece of tapestry which showed the beginnings of glass history in full, barbaric colorings. He told how workers discovered that glass, when stained by a mineral element, could take on the color of precious jewels.

"Soon," he was saying, "women wore glass ornaments, and the blue of the sapphire, the gold of the topaz, and the red of the ruby flashed in gems on their necks and bracelets on their wrists. They adored glass bottles and filled them with perfume and oils, and balm and honey."

Again Jenny pictured the early merchant ships carrying these lovely bottles from country to country until they became known to the whole world. Big Dan was an ardent storyteller, and she seemed to see the people of Athens going down to public baths actually lined with colored glass. He traced the history of glassmaking from the year 300 B.C. down through the Venetians on the island of Murano where glassblowers worked for their king in three hundred shops.

He told about the artisans who delved into special fields,

about the new experiments for scientific use. Telescopes and cameras, thermometers and microscopes came into his story. It took on the sweep of an epic as he seemed to wander among the glassmakers in Bohemia, Sweden, Silesia and France. Even Victoria Blakewell listened with interest when he spoke of the famous Hall of Mirrors at Versailles and how glass played its part there.

Dessert was being served as he whimsically arrived in America and spoke of Jamestown, Mannheim and Boston. From the quaintness of hobnail glass and Sandwich paper-weights and bottles, Big Dan came to a note of pure prophecy. "And this glassmaking business is just beginning to be of real service to mankind. Think of what remains to be done in glass that will make people see, glass that will be ground into lenses to advance the cause of science, glass that will be used in countless different ways in countless different laboratories. It will be built into ships and lend new aid to transportation. It will make telescopes that will show us the bright field of heaven so clearly that even Galileo and Sir Isaac Newton would look, if they could, in wonder. Glass will discover a universe unknown to us today." He smiled warmly as he finished. "It will not only reflect pretty girls like those in this audience; it will show humanity, through science, a way to climb up to the stars."

Big Dan turned finally to Stephen. "And speaking of stars, we have a young star here tonight who gave us the theme of this occasion. Meet, my friends, young Stephen Bayard, who designed for you *Three Golden Rivers.*"

Jenny saw Stephen rise and bow with grave courtliness. She felt that her heart would burst with pride. She could scarcely believe what Big Dan was saying.

"I am happy to state," he was telling the audience, "that this year's award will carry with it a full year's study in Europe. Young Stephen will accompany me to my old home in Bohemia to look in on the glassmakers there. My mission is to find skilled craftsmen and bring them back to Pittsburgh to work. The golden age of glassmaking is just beginning, as I told you."

"Stevie! Stevie, darling!" Jenny reached for her brother's hand underneath the table.

"From Bohemia," Big Dan went on, "we'll take the cathedral tour through France and Belgium and Italy. We'll see Notre-Dame in Paris, the Strasbourg cathedral in France, and St. Peter's in Rome. We'll see windows in Old World castles, we'll study the French craftsman's methods, and see what the Venetians have to teach us at Murano. Stephen Bayard will be inspired. He'll come back and picture all America in glass as he's done our rivers for us tonight."

A roar of applause greeted Big Dan as he and Stephen sat down.

Big Dan turned to Jenny. "Happy, Jenny *Liebchen?*" he asked.

She smiled at him with her heart in her eyes. "Stevie has climbed the glass mountain," she said. "And he's almost at the top, thanks to you."

"Then you will let him go with me?"

Jenny nodded. "I should be very ungrateful if I refused."

So Jenny stood at Stephen's side as people crossed the room to greet him. All the while he smiled his shy smile that quickly captured their hearts. But it was when John Blakewell brought his party forward that Jenny's triumph, like Carlotta's, became complete.

"Stephen, it's wonderful!" John Blakewell held out his hand.

"Congratulations to you, and to you, too, Jenny. And there's someone else who——" He turned away from them a moment to bring a stately little old lady forward. "This is Rosalie's Grand'mère Marsha and she wants to add her good wishes to mine."

"Grand'mère Marsha!"

Jenny and Stephen both could have hugged this cameolike little lady who was so interested and gracious and not at all like Victoria, now standing aloof from the group.

"I'm very proud of you both," Grand'mère Marsha was saying, "and doubly proud when I think that you are Marie Bayard's children. She had the same grit and courage and determination that will carry you children through. It's a part of your heritage, I'm inclined to think, and a very fine one it is."

"You're very kind," Jenny said gratefully.

Grand'mère Marsha leaned on her ebony walking stick. "Kind! Fiddlesticks!" She pressed Stephen's hand hard. "And when you get to Paris, my boy, see Versailles as well as the churches!" She turned back to Jenny as others crowded around them, and said, "I shall see you again before I go back to New Orleans."

Rosalie, in a dress as yellow-gold as the roses in the banquet room, greeted them radiantly. And only then did Jenny realize that Christopher was hovering around, looking like the charming "beau" Carlotta always dreamed him into being.

"Jenny," he said in a low voice, smiling.

"Yes?"

"Don't go away. Wait for me here. All of you."

"We'll wait. Thank you, Christopher."

As Jenny turned away to greet another group of people, she heard Victoria Blakewell's voice behind her.

"Christopher," she was saying, "why not ride home with us? There'll be music and dancing at the house——"

And Christopher said without hesitation, "No, thank you, Mrs. Blakewell. My carriage is at the door. I'm taking Jenny home."

Carlotta afterward said that Victoria Blakewell had "bristled with anger." Her amethyst pin rose and fell rapidly on her breast. Without another word to Christopher or anyone she turned away with a shrug of her aristocratic shoulders and a regal swish of her velvet cloak.

Jenny was glad when all the handshaking, as Mady put it, was over. Christopher waited patiently to take them all down to his carriage. They were just about to go out the door when Jenny was surprised to see Mrs. Houston. She had been in charge of the arrangements for the banquet and, now that it was over, she was ready to set her staff to work clearing things away. She greeted Stephen first, congratulated him pleasantly, then turned to Jenny without any preliminaries.

"Jenny, I've been thinking perhaps I was hasty that afternoon. If you would like to come back to the hotel——"

"That's nice of you, Mrs. Houston," Jenny said generously.

She paused for a moment to think before she gave her final word, but Christopher interrupted with a cool edge to his voice.

"That's *very* nice of you, Mrs. Houston, but Jenny is not available. She has other plans." Very coolly he touched his hat. "Good night, Mrs. Houston."

"Christopher, you shouldn't have!" Inside the carriage Jenny turned to him, flabbergasted.

"Why shouldn't he?" grumbled Stephen. "She was only fawning."

"But I don't have other plans," Jenny protested.

Christopher smiled at her distress, suddenly laid his hand on hers. "I have," he soothed her, "and I think you will like them."

"Tell us! Tell us!" cried Carlotta, her eyes like twin blue stars.

Christopher gave orders to his driver to proceed up the hill to the clinger before he explained: "My father has a very close friend of many years' standing. She is very fashionable, very genteel, and very rich. She's building a fine house in Allegheny and I've talked to her about you, Jenny."

"But what could I possibly mean to her?" Jenny was astonished.

Christopher smiled again. "You can mean a lot to Mrs. Alexander, so don't underestimate yourself."

"Mrs. Alexander." Mady repeated the name slowly, impressed.

"Well?" Jenny waited for Christopher to continue with his explanation.

"Seriously, Jenny," he went on, "it's the sort of thing you'll fit into like a glove. She says she could make a place for you in a number of different ways."

"For instance?" asked Jenny as he paused.

"Well, she needs a fine seamstress, so I told her how well you sew and design things. She needs a sort of paid companion so I told her about your capabilities and what a grand little person you are."

"My," breathed Carlotta, "you must have told her lots!"

"Quiet, Carlotta," said Jenny. "Let Christopher——"

Christopher interrupted. "And Mrs. Alexander also needs a person to be in general charge of her kitchen staff. When I told her about your hotel experience and that you can make

Viennese pastries, she practically went into rhapsodies!"

"You must have told her everything!" Jenny was as pleased as she was surprised.

"I told her enough," he began but Jenny interrupted.

"But did you tell her about my little brood and how I couldn't leave them?"

Christopher smiled at the eager look on Mady's small face.

"Yes, I told her about your brood and made them sound as remarkable as they really are. Mrs. Alexander said you may work for her and live in your beloved little clinger or perhaps she could make a place for you all in her gate house——"

"Her—her gate house!" Carlotta was delighted.

Stephen looked at her and bantered. "You just want to see all the fine ladies and gentlemen go by!"

"Maybe I do," she confessed.

Christopher commented on that point too.

"Whether you live in the gate house or not, it will be a fine opportunity for you, Jenny. You will like Mrs. Alexander, I know, and working with her will keep you in touch with that world of elegance you're always dreaming about. Carlotta will be able to study modes and manners of use to her on the stage, and you'll earn quite enough money to send little Mady to school."

Jenny sat back and closed her eyes. A moment later she opened them slowly, and even Christopher could see they had a dreamlike light.

"Well?" he prodded impatiently.

Jenny gave a deep sigh. "It sounds simply wonderful." Impulsively she reached for his hand. "Thank you, Christopher, thank you! I'll love meeting Mrs. Alexander!"

Stephen also looked pleased. He too, spoke to Christopher

gratefully. "I want to thank you too," he said. "I feel better now about going away."

"You're not the only one who will travel," Christopher teased him. "Mrs. Alexander practically commutes to New Orleans where she has a Southern home. Before you get back from Europe, I wager, Jenny will have seen the whole United States!"

"Oh!" Mady's exclamation was a single sigh of rapture.

"And," Christopher went on with a merry gleam in his eyes, "I think I'll teach Jenny French!"

"The final touch of elegance!" she murmured, her eyes sparkling with fun.

The carriage stopped at the door of the clinger. As they all entered the little house, it seemed a place of wonderful dreams.

"No matter where I go," said Jenny, "I'll always love this little house."

"It's tumble-down." Mady laughed.

"The roof leaks," said Carlotta.

"And the chimney needs a new flue," Stephen said very cheerfully.

Christopher had brought a package in from the carriage. Carlotta wanted to ask him what it was, but remembered that Jenny had urged her to be more ladylike and not to ask so many questions. She hoped that Mady would ask for her, but Mady was learning to be ladylike too. Christopher laid the parcel on the table and Carlotta kept telling herself she would burst before she would ask what was in it. If she had guessed she was destined not to know until the next morning, she probably would have burst. Christopher actually waited until the brood had gone to bed and he was quite alone with Jenny.

He was standing in the open doorway. Beyond him was

the blue night sky sprinkled with pin points of spring stars. He turned to Jenny gaily.

"You've caught them, Jenny, right in your hands. I can see stardust on your fingers."

Jenny looked down at her hands and laughed. "Maybe you're right. I hope you are."

"Do you want me to prove it?"

"Can you?" she challenged.

He walked back to the kitchen table. She watched him unwrap the mysterious parcel. She gasped with admiration when she saw what it contained. "A parasol! Oh, Christopher!"

He came back to her and put it into her hands. It was made of blue satin, frothy with ruffles of lace and tiny bow-knots of pink ribbon.

"You've earned this, Jenny." He smiled. "You've earned this for the elegance you've already gained in Pittsburgh."

"True elegance?" she half-whispered.

"True elegance, Jenny. You're the prettiest parasol girl of them all!"

She raised the parasol gracefully as she had seen the other girls do. Even Carlotta could not have improved on Jenny's lovely gesture.

"Parasol girl," she repeated softly. "Oh, thank you, Christopher. Thank you!"

Somewhere in the tumble-down clinger, something seemed to stir. Jenny thought of her happiness and that of her little brood's. Suddenly she looked again for stardust on her fingers.

Afterword

The story of these four young people, Jenny, Stephen, Carlotta, and Mady, is enriched by the strong sense of city and the rivers that play such a significant part in their lives. Stephen found his life work in the glassmaking barges on the Monongahela River, just as many others have. The glass-making industry made Pittsburgh a leader in glass produc-tion almost at the same time that the steel mills in the valleys were becoming so strong. Readers of the story of the Bayard family may want to find out more about the glass industry in its 150 years in the Pittsburgh region. Glassmaking was and is a major industry in Pittsburgh. It has been the subject of a major exhibit at the Senator John Heinz History Center, and books and websites alike provide much information about this important industry.

Other pieces of Pittsburgh history abound in this story by Pittsburgh native Olive Price. Price wrote under several pseud-onyms during her career. Her writings include other stories for young people and a number of plays, including ones for radio, collected in anthologies, although *Three Golden Rivers* would seem to be the most popular. Price grew up on Mount

Washington and her love of the city and its hills is evident throughout the story. WQED's documentary *South Side* explores more of this fascinating piece of Pittsburgh's life.

From the hills and rivers to the life of the city to the glassmaking industry, *Three Golden Rivers* offers readers an opportunity to explore many facets of the city at the midpoint of the nineteenth century. One hundred and fifty years have brought many changes, but this history comes glowingly to life in the Bayard family story. The book has been unavailable for years, but the story rings so true that it is time to bring it back to be enjoyed by new readers. The University of Pittsburgh Press has made this effort because young readers are part of the Press's mission to publish books that contribute to our understanding of Pittsburgh and western Pennsylvania and to serve the needs of the whole community. (A few emendations have been made to the text to meet the needs of today's young readers.) Connections to other books, videos, and websites will be available to anyone who wishes to wander farther along the rivers and in the hills surrounding Pittsburgh in a website at the University of Pittsburgh Press. Look at *http://www.pitt.edu/~press/goldentrianglebooks* for *Three Golden Rivers*.